QUICK FIXES
tales of Repairman Jack

by

F. PAUL WILSON

Copyright © 2011 F. Paul Wilson
All rights reserved.

ISBN: 1461190746
ISBN-13: 9781461190745

Cover by Steven G. Spruill

Publishing History

"A Day in the Life" © 1989 by F. Paul Wilson. First published in *Stalkers*, edited by Ed Gorman and Martin H. Greenberg (Dark Harvest, 1989)

"The Last Rakosh" © 1990 by F. Paul Wilson. First published in The World Fantasy Convention 1990 *Program Book* (11/90) (incorporated into *All The Rage*)

"Home Repairs" © 1991 by F. Paul Wilson. First published in *Cold Blood* edited by Richard Chizmar (Ziesing, 6/91) (incorporated into *Conspiracies*)

"The Long Way Home" © 1992 by F. Paul Wilson. First published in *Dark at Heart* edited by Joe and Karen Lansdale (Dark Harvest, 1992)

"The Wringer" © 1996 by F. Paul Wilson. First published in *Night Screams* (NAL/ROC, 1996) (incorporated into *Fatal Error*)

"Interlude at Duane's" © 2006 by F. Paul Wilson. First published in *Thriller* edited by James Patterson (Mira, 2006)

"Do-Gooder" © 2006 by F. Paul Wilson. First published as a broadside from Lavendier Books (2006)

"Recalled" © 2009 by F. Paul Wilson. First published in *He Is Legend* edited by Christopher Conlon (Gauntlet, 2009)

"Piney Power" © 2010 by F. Paul Wilson. First published in *Fear: 13 Stories Of Suspense And Horror* (Dutton, 2010)

Contents

Foreword i

A Day in the Life 1

The Last Rakosh 45

Home Repairs 73

The Long Way Home .97

The Wringer 123

Interlude at Duane's 175

Do-Gooder 193

Recalled 201

Piney Power 227

The Secret History of the World 243

Bibliography 245

Foreword

I compiled this collection at the insistence of Repairman Jack fans, especially the completists. A number of small presses have approached me to do a signed, limited first edition, but I'm not comfortable with charging a premium price for previously published material. Through the years a number of these stories have been incorporated into Repairman Jack novels:

"Home Repairs " into *Conspiracies*

"The Last Rakosh" into *All the Rage*

"The Wringer" into *Fatal Error*

If you've read those three novels, you have, in effect, read versions of those three stories. For those who are newcomers to the character…

Who is Repairman Jack?

He's an urban mercenary in Manhattan, a self-made outcast who lives in the interstices of modern society. A ghost in our machine: no official identity, no social security number, pays no taxes. He has a violent streak he sometimes finds hard to control. He hires out for cash to "fix" situations that have no legal remedy.

The name Repairman Jack comes from his gunrunner pal, Abe. Jack's not crazy about it, but he lives with it. He's not a vigilante, not a do-gooder. He's not out to right wrongs. Nor is he out to change the world or fight crime. (He's a career criminal, after all, as are many of his friends.) He's not Batman. He's just a guy with a devious mind who likes his work best when he can see to it that what goes around come around. If you follow him carefully you'll see he gets a real jolt out of running a scam or setting up someone to be hoisted on his own petard.

He came from a dream. The scene on the roof in *The Tomb* was that dream. I worked backward and forward from there to create a character who could survive that situation. I decided on an anti-Jason Bourne – with no black-ops, SEAL, or Special Forces training, no CIA or police background, no connection to officialdom. In other words, no safety net. No one in officialdom he could call on. He has to rely on his own wits and his own network.

I've been a libertarian forever, so I figured I'd act out my libertarian dreams, you know, make this guy an anarchist with no identity. But as I've continued his adventures, I've learned that it takes a lot of effort to live below the radar, especially since 9/11.

QUICK FIXES

I intended Jack as a one-shot, which is kind of obvious at the end of *The Tomb*. As I finished that novel, I thought, "Well, this character is definitely series material, so I gotta make it look like the guy is dead or they'll want more." I had books planned out and didn't want to get locked into a series.

Then, later on, Jack became a way out of a trap I'd got myself into with a medical thriller contract. I'd become bored with writing them after doing three and I was contracted to do a fourth… but I had this idea for a techy thriller and thought, why don't I rework this and use Jack again? It'd be great for him. I named it *Legacies* and made his client a doctor so I could call it a medical thriller. The publisher was happy I was bringing back a character my fans wanted to see again, and I was happy to revisit Jack. A win-win.

Legacies was fun and sold well, so I had to do another, and then another, and before I knew it, Jack had taken over my writing career.

But before *Legacies*, I brought him back in shorter works.

Introduction to "A Day in the Life"

Sometime in 1988, one of my phone friends, Ed Gorman (with whom I've spent countless hours in conversation but have never met) mentioned that he and Marty Greenberg were co-editing an anthology called *Stalkers* for Dark Harvest / NAL. Would I care to contribute? I said I'd been itching to revive Repairman Jack, the lead character from *The Tomb* – not in a novel (I still didn't want a series at that time), just a short piece. How about a Jack story? Ed, a Repairman Jack fan since the git-go, told me I *had* to do it.

The Tomb had been published four years earlier. It hit the bestseller lists, won the Porgie Award from *The West Coast Review of Books*, and the mail began pouring in. I'd known right then he was a series character but I didn't want to do a series. I'd closed the novel with Jack's life hanging by a thread, and readers wanted to know: What happened to Repairman Jack? When are you going to do another Repairman Jack novel? Never, I thought. But the book kept selling, and the letters kept coming in.

Hollywood entered the picture. *The Tomb* has been optioned numerous times. Everyone loves the idea of Repairman Jack as a franchise character; but the rakoshi, the Bengali temple demons who provide the horror, have sunk all attempts to adapt it to film. How do you make them look real? The line between horror and hilarity is a couple of nanometers thick. A rakosh is scary; a guy in a rubber suit is dumb.

In the late 80s, Roger Corman's New World Pictures had the novel under option. A combination of low-rent antics by Fred Olen Ray with the title, and a lousy screenplay (they moved the action to Pasadena!), had the project dead in the water. I dashed off a spec script in an eleventh-hour attempt to save it, but too late.

The Hollywood connection provided extra incentive to write a new Repairman Jack story. I had created a number of original action sequences for the screenplay I'd sent New World, and I wanted to protect them. The best way to do that was to copyright them in a story. They're all in "A Day in the Life."

Stalkers turned out to be a hugely successful anthology, reprinted in book clubs and multiple foreign editions. The result: "A Day in the Life" gained Jack even more fans.

For those who care, Levinson never appeared again. He was replaced by Ernie the ID guru when I started writing the novels. Tram previously appeared in "Dat-Tay-Vao." As for Hollywood, as I write this, the novel has been in development hell for over 15 years at Beacon Films.

A Day in the Life

When the cockroach made a right turn up the wall, Jack flipped another *shuriken* across the room. The steel points of the throwing star drove into the wallboard just above the bug's long antennae. It backed up and found itself hemmed in on all sides now by four of the stars.

"Did it!" Jack said from where he lay across the still-made hotel bed.

He counted the shuriken protruding from the wall. A dozen of them traveled upward in a gentle arc above and behind the barely functioning TV, ending in a tiny square where the roach was trapped.

Check that. It was free again. Crawled over one of the shuriken and was now continuing on its journey to wherever. Jack let it go and rolled onto his back on the bedspread.

Bored.

And hot. He was dressed in jeans and a loose, heavy sweater under an oversized lightweight jacket, both dark blue; a black-and-orange knitted cap was jammed on the top of his head. He'd turned the thermostat all the way down but the room remained an oven. He didn't want to risk taking anything off because, when the buzzer sounded, he had to hit the ground running.

He glanced over at the dusty end table where the little Walkman-sized box with the antenna sat in silence.

"Come on, already," he mumbled to it. "Let's do it."

Reilly and his sleazos were due to make their move tonight. What was taking them so long to get started? Almost one a.m. already – three hours here in this fleabag. He was starting to itch.

QUICK FIXES

He could handle only so much TV without getting drowsy. Even without the lulling drone of some host interviewing some actor he'd never heard of, the heat was draining him.

Fresh air. Maybe that would help.

Jack got up, stretched, and stepped to the window. A clear almost-Halloween night out there, with a big moon rising over the city. He gripped the handles and pulled. Nothing. The damn thing wouldn't budge. He was checking the edges of the sash when he heard the faint crack of a rifle. The bullet came through the glass two inches to the left of his head, peppering his face with tiny sharp fragments as it whistled past his ear.

Jack dropped to the floor. He waited. No more shots. Keeping his head below the level of the windowsill, he rose to a crouch, then leapt for the lamp on the end table at the far side of the bed, grabbed it, and rolled to the floor with it. Another shot spat through the glass and whistled through the room as his back thudded against the floor. He turned off the lamp.

The other lamp, the one next to the TV, was still on – sixty watts of help for the shooter. And whoever was shooting had to know Jack would be going for it next. He'd be ready.

On his belly, Jack slid along the industrial grade carpet toward the end of the bed until he had an angle where the bulb was visible under the shade. He pulled out his next to last *shuriken* and spun it toward the bulb. With an electric pop it flared blue-white and left the room dark except for the flickering glow from the TV.

Immediately Jack popped his head above the bed and looked out the window. Through the spider-webbed glass he caught sight of a bundled figure turning and darting away across the neighboring rooftop. Moonlight glinted off the long barrel of a high-powered rifle, flashed off the lens of a telescopic sight, then he was gone.

A high-pitched beep made him jump. The red light on the signal box was blinking like mad. Kuropolis wanted help. Which meant Reilly had struck.

"Swell."

A DAY IN THE LIFE

Not a bad night, George Kuropolis thought, wiping down the counter in front of the slim young brunette as she seated herself. Not a great night, but still to have half a dozen customers at this hour was good. And better yet, Reilly and his creeps hadn't shown up.

Maybe they'd bother somebody else tonight.

"What'll it be?" he asked the brunette.

"Tea, please," she said with a smile. A nice smile. She was dressed nice and had decent jewelry on. Not exactly overdressed for the neighborhood, but better than the usual.

George wished he had more customers of her caliber. And he *should* have them. Why the hell not? Didn't the chrome inside and out sparkle? Couldn't you eat off the floor? Wasn't everything he served made right here on the premises?

"Sure. Want some pie?"

"No, thank you."

"It's good. Blueberry. Made it myself."

The smile again. "No, thanks. I'm on a diet."

"Sure," he mumbled as he turned away to get her some hot water. "Everyone's on a goddamn diet. Diets are gettin' hazardous to my health."

Just then the front door burst open and a white-haired man in his mid-twenties leaped in with a sawed-off shotgun in his hands. He pointed it at the ceiling and let loose a round at the fixture over the cash register. The *boom* of the blast was deafening as glass showered everything.

Matt Reilly was here.

Four more of his gang crowded in behind him. George recognized them: Reece was the black with the white fringe leather jacket; Rafe had the blue Mohican, Tony had the white; and Cheeks was the baby-faced skinhead.

"Aw*right!*" Reilly said, grinning fiercely under his bent nose, mean little eyes, dark brows, and bleached crewcut. "It's ass-kickin' time!"

George reached into his pocket and pressed the button on the beeper there, then raised his hands and backed up against the wall.

"Hey, Matt!" he called. "C'mon! What's the problem?"

"You know the problem, George!" Reilly said.

He tossed the shotgun to Reece and stepped around the counter. Smiling, he closed with George. The smile only heightened the sick knot of fear coiling in George's belly. He was so fixed on that empty smile that he didn't see the sucker punch coming. It caught him in the gut. He doubled over in agony. His last cup of coffee heaved but stayed down.

He groaned. "*Christ!*"

"You're late again, George!" Reilly said through his teeth. "I told you last time what would happen if you didn't stick to the schedule!"

George struggled to remember his lines.

"I can't pay two protections! I can't afford it!"

"You can't afford *not* to afford it! And you don't have to pay two. Just pay me!"

"Sure! That's what the other guy says when *he* wants *his!* And where are *you* then?"

"Don't worry about the other guy! I'm taking care of him tonight! But *you!*" Reilly rammed George back against the wall. "I'm gonna hafta make a example outta you, George! People saw what happened to Wolansky when he turned pigeon. Now they're gonna see what happens to a shit who don't pay!"

Just then came a scream from off to George's right. He looked and saw Reece covering the five male customers in booths two and four, making them empty their pockets onto one of the tables. Further down the counter, Cheeks was waving a big knife with a mean looking curved blade at the girl who'd wanted the tea.

"The ring, babe," he was saying. "Let's have it."

"It's my engagement ring!" she said.

"You wanna look nice at your wedding, you better give it quick."

He reached for it and she slapped his hand away.

"No!"

Cheeks straightened up and slipped the knife into a sheath tucked into the small of his back.

A DAY IN THE LIFE

"Ooooh, you shouldna done that, bitch," said Reece in oily tones.

George wished he were a twenty-five year old with a Schwartzenegger build instead of a wheezy fifty with pencil arms. He'd wipe the floor with these creeps.

"Stop him," he said to Reilly. "Please. I'll pay you."

"Couldn't stop him now if I wanted to," Reilly said, grinning. "Cheeks *likes* it when they play rough."

In a single smooth motion, the skinhead's hand snaked out, grabbed the front of the woman's blouse, and ripped. The whole front came away. Her breasts were visible through a semi-transparent bra. She screamed and swatted at him. Cheeks shrugged off the blow and grappled with her, dragging her to the floor.

One of the men in the booth near Reece leapt to his feet and started toward the pair, yelling, "Hey! Whatta y'think you're doin'?"

Reece slammed the shotgun barrel across his face. Blood spurted from the guy's forehead as he dropped back into his seat.

"Tony!" Reilly said to the Mohican standing by the cash register. "Where's Rafe?"

"Inna back."

George suddenly felt his scalp turn to fire as Reilly grabbed him by the hair and shoved him toward Tony.

"Take George in the back. You and Rafe give him some memory lessons so he won't be late again."

George felt his sphincters loosening. Where was Jack?

"I'll pay! I told you I'll pay!"

"It's not the same, George," Reilly said with a slow shake of his head. "If I gotta come here and kick ass every month just to get what's mine, well, I got better things to do, y'know?"

As George watched, Reilly hit the "NO SALE" button on the cash register and started digging into the bills.

Thick, pincer-like fingers closed on the back of George's neck as he was propelled into the rear of the diner. He saw Rafe off to the side, playing with the electric meat grinder where George mixed his homemade sausage.

QUICK FIXES

"Rafe!" said Tony. "Matt wants us to teach Mr. Greasyspoon some manners!"

Rafe didn't look up. He had a raw chicken leg in his hand. He shoved it into the top of the meat grinder. The sickening crunch of bone and cartilage being pulverized rose over the whir of the motor, then ground chicken leg began to extrude through the grate at the bottom.

"Hey, Tone!" Rafe said, looking up and grinning. "I got a great idea!"

Jack pounded along the second floor hallway. He double-timed down the flight of stairs to the lobby, sprinted across the carpet tiles that spelled out "The Lucky Hotel" in bright yellow on dark blue, and pushed through the smudged glass doors of the entrance. One of the letters on the neon sign above the door was out. *The ucky Hotel* flashed fitfully in hot red.

Jack leaped down the three front steps and hit the pavement running. Half a block to the left, then another left down an alley, leaping puddles and dodging garbage cans until he came to the rear of the Highwater Diner. He had his key ready and shoved it into the deadbolt on the delivery door. He paused there long enough to draw his .45 automatic, a Colt Mark IV, and to stretch the knitted cap down over his face. It then became a Halloween decorated ski mask, and he was looking out through a bright orange jack-o-lantern. He pulled the door open and slipped into the storage area at the rear of the kitchen.

Up ahead he heard the sound of a scuffle, and George's terrified voice crying, "No, don't! *Please* don't!"

He rounded the corner of the meat locker and found Tony and Rafe – he'd know those Mohicans anywhere – from Reilly's gang forcing George's hand into a meat grinder and George struggling like all hell to keep it out. But he was losing the battle. His fingers would soon be sausage meat.

Jack was just reaching for the slide on his automatic when he spotted a meat-tenderizing hammer on a nearby counter. He picked it up and hefted it. Heavy – a good three pounds, most of it in the steel head. Pocketing the pistol, he stepped over to the trio and began a sidearm swing toward Tony's skull.

"Tony! Trick or treat!"

Tony looked up just in time to stop the full weight of the waffle-faced hammer head with the center of his face. It made a noise like *smoonch!* as it buried itself in his nose. He was halfway to the floor before Rafe even noticed.

"Tone?"

Jack didn't wait for him to look up. He used the hammer to crunch a wide part in the center of Rafe's blue Mohican. Rafe joined Tony on the floor.

"God, am I glad to see you!" George said, gasping and fondling his fingers as if to reassure himself that they were all there. "What took you so long?"

"Can't've been more than two minutes," Jack said, slipping the handle of the hammer through his belt and pulling the automatic again.

"Seemed like a *year!*"

"The rest of them out front?"

"Just three – Reilly, the skinhead, and Reece."

Jack paused. "Where's the rest of them?"

"Don't know."

Jack thought he knew. The other three had probably been on that rooftop trying to plug him in his hotel room. But how had they found him? He hadn't even told George about staying at the Lucky.

One way to find out...

"Okay. You lock the back door and stay here. I'll take care of the rest."

"There's a girl out there–" George said.

Jack nodded. "I'm on my way."

He turned and almost bumped into Reilly coming through the swinging doors from the front. He was counting the fistful of cash in his hands.

"How we doin' back–?" Reilly said and then froze when the muzzle of Jack's automatic jammed up under his chin.

"Happy Halloween," Jack said.

"Shit! You again!"

"Right, Matt, old boy. Me again. And I see you've made my collection for me. How thoughtful. You can shove it in my left pocket."

Reilly's face was white with rage as he glanced over to where Tony writhed on the floor next to the unconscious Rafe.

"You're a dead man, pal. Worse than dead!"

Jack smiled through the ski mask and increased the pressure of the barrel on Reilly's throat.

"Just do as you're told."

"What's with you and these masks, anyway?" he said as he stuffed the money into Jack's pocket. "You that ugly? Or do you think you're Spiderman or something?"

"No, I'm Pumpkinman. And this way I know you but you don't know me. You see, Matt, I've been keeping close tabs on you. I know all your haunts. I stand in plain view and watch you. I've watched you play pool at Gus's. I've walked up behind you in a crowd and bumped you as I passed. I could have slipped an ice pick between your ribs a dozen times by now. But don't try to spot me. You won't. While you're trying to hard to look like Billy Idol, I'm trying even harder to look like nobody."

"You *are* nobody, man!" His voice was as tough as ever, but a haunted look had crept into his eyes.

Jack laughed. "Surprised to see me?"

"Not really," Reilly said, recovering. "I figured you'd show up."

"Yeah? What's the matter? No faith in your hit squad?"

"Hit squad?" There was genuine bafflement in his eyes. "What the fuck you talkin' about?"

Jack sensed that Reilly wasn't faking it. He was as baffled as Jack.

He let his mind wander an instant. *If not Reilly's bunch, then who?*

No time for that now. Especially with the muffled screams coming from the front. He turned Reilly around and shoved him back through the swinging doors to the front of the diner. Once there, he bellied Reilly up against the counter and put the .45 to his temple. He saw Reece covering half a dozen customers with a sawed off shotgun. But where was that psycho, Cheeks?

A DAY IN THE LIFE

"Okay, turkeys!" Jack yelled. "Fun's over! Drop the hardware!"

Reece spun and faced them. His eyes widened and he raised the scattergun in their direction. Jack felt Reilly cringe back against him.

"Go ahead," Jack said, placing himself almost completely behind Reilly. "You can't make him any uglier."

"Don't, man!" Reilly said in a low voice.

Reece didn't move. He didn't seem to know what to do. So Jack told him.

"Put the piece on the counter or I'll blow his head off."

"No way," Reece said.

"Don't try me, pal. I'll do it just for fun."

Jack hoped Reece didn't think he was bluffing, because he wasn't. He'd already been shot at twice tonight and he was in a foul mood.

"Do what he says, man," Reilly told him.

"No *way!*" Reece said. "I'll get outta here, but no way I'm givin' that suckuh my piece!"

Jack wasn't going to allow that. As soon as Reece got outside he'd start peppering the big windows with shot. He was about to move Reilly out from behind the counter to block the aisle when one of the customers Reece had been covering stood up behind him and grabbed the pump handle of the scattergun. A second man leapt to his side to help. One round blasted into the ceiling, and then the gun was useless – with all those hands on it, Reece couldn't pump another round into the chamber. Two more customers jumped up and overpowered him. The shotgun came free as a fifth man with a deep cut in his forehead shoved Reece back onto the seat of the booth and began pounding at his face. More fists began to fly. These were *very* angry men.

Jack guided Reilly toward the group. He saw two pairs of legs – male and female, struggling on the floor around the far end of the counter. He shoved Reilly toward the cluster of male customers.

"Here's another one for you. Have fun. Just don't do anything to them they wouldn't do to you."

QUICK FIXES

Two of the men smiled and slammed Reilly down face first on the booth's table. They began pummeling his kidneys as Jack hurried down to where Cheeks was doing his dirty work.

He looked over the edge of the counter and saw that the skinhead held the woman's arms pinned between them with his left hand and had his right thrust up under her bra, twisting her nipple, oblivious to everything else. Her right eye was bruised and swollen. She was crying and writhing under him, even snapping at him with her teeth. A real fighter. She must have put up quite a struggle. Cheeks' face was bleeding from several scratches.

Jack was tempted to put a slug into the base of Cheeks' spine so he'd not only never walk again, he'd never get it up again, either. But Cheeks' knife was in the way, and besides, the bullet might pass right through him and into the woman. So he pocketed the .45, grabbed Cheeks' right ear, and ripped upward.

Cheeks came off the floor with a howl. Jack lifted him by the ear and stretched his upper body across the counter. He could barely speak. He really wanted to hurt this son of a bitch.

"Naughty, naughty!" he managed to say. "Didn't you ever go to Catholic school? Didn't the nuns tell you that bad things would happen to you if you ever did that to a girl?"

He stretched the guy's right hand out on the counter, palm down.

"Like you might get warts?"

He pulled the meat hammer from his belt and raised it over his head.

"Or worse?"

He put everything he had into the shot. Bones crunched like breadsticks. Cheeks screamed and slipped off the counter. He rolled on the floor, moaning and crying, cradling his injured hand like a mother with a newborn baby.

"Never hassle a paying customer," Jack said. "George can't pay his protection without them."

He grabbed Reece's scattergun and pulled him and Reilly free from the customers. Both were battered and bloody. He shoved them toward the front door.

A DAY IN THE LIFE

"I told you clowns about trying to cut in on my turf! How many times we have to do this dance?"

Reilly whirled on him, rage in his eyes. He probably would have leapt at Jack's throat if not for the shotgun.

"We was here *first*, asshole!"

"Maybe. But *I'm* here now, so scrape up your two wimps from the back room and get them out of here."

He oversaw the pair as they dragged Rafe and Tony out the front door. Cheeks was on his feet by then. Jack waved him forward.

"C'mon, loverboy. Party's over."

"He's got my ring!" the brunette cried from the far end of the counter. She held her torn dress up over her breasts. There was blood at the corner of her mouth. "My engagement ring."

"Really?" Jack said. "That ought to be worth something! Let's see it."

Cheeks glared at Jack and reached into his back pocket with his good hand.

"You wanna see it?" he said. Suddenly he was swinging a big Gurkha *kukri* knife through the air, slashing at Jack's eyes. "Here! Get a close look!"

Jack blocked the curved blade with the short barrel of the sawed-off, then grabbed Cheeks' wrist and twisted. As Cheeks instinctively brought his broken hand up, Jack dropped the shotgun. He grabbed the injured hand and squeezed. Cheeks screamed and went to his knees.

"Drop the blade," Jack said softly.

It clattered to the counter.

"Good. Now find that ring and put it on the counter."

Cheeks dug into the left front pocket of his jeans and pulled out a tiny diamond on a gold band. Jack's throat tightened when he saw the light in the brunette's eyes at the sight of it. Such a little thing... yet so important.

Still gripping Cheeks' crushed hand, he picked up the ring and pretended to examine it.

"You went to all that trouble for this itty bitty thing?" Jack slid it down the counter. "Here, babe. Compliments of the house."

QUICK FIXES

She had to let the front of her dress drop to grab it. She clutched the tiny ring against her with both hands and began to cry. Jack felt the black fury crowd the edges of his vision. He looked at Cheeks' round baby face, glaring up at him from seat level by the counter top, and picked up the *kukri*. He held it before Cheeks' eyes. The pupils dilated with terror.

Releasing the broken hand, Jack immediately grabbed Cheek's throat and jaw, twisted him up and around, and slammed the back of his head down on the counter, pinning him there. With two quick strokes he carved a crude "X" in the center of Cheeks' forehead. He howled and Jack let go. He grabbed the shotgun again and shoved Cheeks toward the door.

"Don't worry, Cheeks. It's nothing embarrassing – just your signature."

Once he had them all outside, he used the shotgun to prod them into the alley between the diner and the vacant three story Borden building next door. They were a pitiful bunch, what with Tony and Rafe barely able to stand, Cheeks with a bloody forehead and a hand swollen to twice normal size, and Reece and Reilly nursing cracked ribs and swollen jaws.

"This is the last time I want to do this dance with you guys. It's bad for business around here. And besides, sooner or later one of you is really going to get hurt."

Jack was about to turn and leave them there when he heard tires squeal in the street. Headlights lit the alley and rushed toward him. Jack dove to his left to avoid being hit as the nose of a beat-up Chrysler rammed into the mouth of the alley. His foot slipped on some rubble and he went down. By the time he scrambled to his feet, he found himself looking into the business ends of a shotgun, a 9mm automatic, and a Tec-9 assault pistol.

He'd found the missing members of Reilly's gang.

Even though it made his ribs feel like they were breaking, Matt couldn't help laughing.

"Gotcha! *Gotcha*, scumbag!"

A DAY IN THE LIFE

He picked up the fallen scattergun and jabbed the barrel at Ski-mask's gut. The guy deflected the thrust and almost pulled it from his grasp. Fast hands. Better not leave this guy any openings.

"The gun," he said. "Take it out real slow and drop it."

The guy looked at all the guns pointed at him, then reached into his pocket and pulled out his own by the barrel; it fell to the alley floor with a thud.

"Turn around," Matt told him, "lean on the wall, and spread 'em, police style. And remember – one funny move and you're full of holes."

Matt patted down his torso and legs and told him, "You musta thought I was a stupid jerk to hit this place without back-up. These guys've been waiting the whole time for you to show. Never figured you'd come in the back, though. But that's okay. We gotcha now."

The frisk turned up nothing, not even a wallet. The blue jacket had nothing in the pockets except the cash from the register. He'd get that later. Right now, though, it was game time.

"All right. Turn around. Let's see what you look like."

When the guy turned, Matt reached up and pulled off the pumpkin-headed ski mask. He saw an average looking guy about ten years older than he and his boys – mid-thirties, maybe – with dark brown hair. Nothing special. Matt shoved the mask back on the top of the guy's head where it perched at a stupid looking angle.

"What's your name, asshole?"

"Jack."

"Jack what?"

"O'Lantern. It's an old Irish–"

Suddenly Cheeks was at Matt's shoulder, brandishing the Special Forces knife they kept in the car.

"He's *mine!*" he screeched. "Lemme make his face into a *permanent* jack-o-lantern!"

"Cool it, man."

"Look what he did to me! Look at my fuckin' hand! And look at this!" He pointed the knife at the bloody "X" on his forehead. "Look what he did to my face! He's *mine*, man!"

QUICK FIXES

"You get firsts, okay? But not here, man. We're gonna take Mr. Jack here for a ride, and then we're *all* gonna get a turn with him." He held the shotgun out to Cheeks. "Here. Trade ya."

Matt took the heavy, slotted blade and placed the point against one of the guy's lower eyelids. He wanted to see him squirm.

"Some knife, huh? Just like the one Rambo uses. Even cuts through *bone!*"

The guy winced. His tough guy act was gone. He was almost whining now.

"Wha...what are you going to do?"

"Not sure yet, Mr. Jack. But I'm sure Cheeks and me can think up a thousand ways to make you wish you'd never been born."

The guy slid along the wall a little, pressing back like he was trying to seep into it. His right hand crept up and covered his mouth.

"You're not gonna t-torture me, are you?"

Behind him, Cheeks laughed. Matt had to smile. Yeah, this was more like it. This was going to be *fun*.

"Who? Us? Torture? Nah! Just a little sport. 'Creative playtime,' as my teachers used to call it. I've got this *great* imagination. I can think of all sorts of–"

Matt saw the guy twist his arm funny. He heard a *snikt!* and suddenly this tiny pistol was in the guy's hand and the big bore of the stubby barrel was staring into his left eye from about an inch away. And the guy wasn't whining anymore.

"Imagine *this*, Matt!" he said through his teeth. "You do a lousy frisk."

Matt heard his boys crowding in behind him, heard somebody work the slide on an automatic.

"You got no way out of this," he told the guy.

"Neither do you," the guy said. "You want to play Rambo? Fine. You've got your oversized fishing knife? I've got this Semmerling LM-4, the world's smallest .45. It holds five three-hundred-grain hollowpoints. You know about hollowpoints, Matt? Imagine one of those going into your skull. It makes a little hole going in but then it starts to spread as it goes through your brain. When it leaves your head it'll take most of your brain – not a heavy load

A DAY IN THE LIFE

in your case – and the back half of your skull with it, spraying the whole alley behind you."

Without turning, Matt could sense his boys moving away from directly behind him.

He dropped the knife. "Okay. We call this one a draw."

The guy grabbed the front of his shirt and dragged him deeper into the alley, to an empty doorway. Then he shoved Matt back and dove inside.

Matt didn't have to tell the others what to do. They charged up and began blasting away into the doorway. Jerry, one of the new arrivals, stood right in front of the opening and emptied his Tec-9's 36-round clip in one long, wild, jittery burst. He stopped and was grinning at Matt when a single shot came from inside. Jerry flew back like someone had jerked a wire. His assault pistol went flying as he spun and landed on his face. This big wet red hole gaped where the middle of his back used to be.

"Shit!" Matt said. He turned to Cheeks. "Go around the other side and make sure he doesn't sneak out."

Reece nudged him, making climbing motions as he pointed up at the rusty fire escape. Matt nodded and boosted him up. It creaked and groaned as Reece, his scattergun clamped under his arm, headed for the second floor like a ghost in white fringed leather. Matt hoped he got real close to the bastard before firing – close enough to make hamburger out of his head with the first shot.

Everybody waited. Even Rafe and Tony had come around enough to get their pieces out and ready. Tony was in bad shape, though. His nose was all squished in and he made weird noises when he breathed. His face looked *awful*, man.

They waited some more. Reece should have found him by now.

Then a shotgun boomed inside.

"Awright *Reece!*" Rafe shouted.

Matt listened a moment to the quiet inside. "Reece! Y'get him?"

Suddenly someone came flying out the door, dark blue jacket and jack-o-lantern ski mask, stumbling like he was wounded.

"Shit, it's *him!*"

Matt opened up and so did everyone else. They pumped that bastard so full of holes a whole goddamn medical center couldn't patch him up even if they got the chance. And then they kept on blasting as he fell to the rubble-strewn ground and twisted and writhed and jolted with the slugs. Finally he lay still.

Cheeks came running back from the other side of the building.

"Y'get 'im?" he said. "Y'get 'im?"

"Got him, Cheeks!" Rafe said. "Got him *good!*"

Matt pointed the guy's own .45 at him as he approached the body. No way he could be alive, but no sense in taking chances. That was when he noticed that the guy's hands were tied behind his back. Matt suddenly had a sick feeling that he'd been had again. He pulled off the ski mask, knowing he'd see Reece's face.

He was right. And he had a sock shoved in his mouth.

Behind Matt, Cheeks howled with rage.

Abe ran his fingers through the shoulder fringe of the white leather jacket.

"So, Jack. Who's your new tailor? Now that Liberace's gone, you're thinking maybe of filling his sartorial niche? Or is this Elvis you're trying to look like?"

Jack couldn't help smiling. "Could be either. But since I don't play piano, it'll have to be Elvis. You can open for me, seeing as you've got the Jackie Mason patter down perfect. You write for him?"

"What can I say?" Abe said with an elaborate shrug. "He comes to me, I give him material."

Jack pulled off the jacket. He'd known he'd get heat from Abe for it, but it was a little too cold out tonight for just a sweater. But he was glad Abe was still in his store. He kept much the same hours as Jack.

Jack rolled up the right sleeve of his sweater and set the little Semmerling back into the spring holster strapped to his forearm. Not the most comfortable rig, but after tonight he ranked it as one of the best investments he'd ever made.

A DAY IN THE LIFE

"You had to use that tonight?"

"Yeah. Not one of my better nights."

"*Nu?* You're not going to tell me how such a beautiful and stylish leather coat fits in?"

"Sure. I'll tell you downstairs. I need some supplies."

"Ah! So this is a for-buying visit and not just a social call. Good! I'm having a special on Claymores this week."

Abe stepped to the front door of the Isher Sports Shop, locked it, making sure the "SORRY, WE ARE CLOSED" sign faced toward the street. Jack waited as he unlocked the heavy steel door that led to the basement. Below, light from overhead lamps gleamed off the rows and stacks of pistols, rifles, machine guns, bazookas, grenades, knives, mines, and other miscellaneous tools of destruction.

"What'll it be?"

"I lost my forty-five, so I'll need a replacement for that."

"Swishy leather jackets and losing guns. A change of life, maybe? How about a nine millimeter parabellum instead? I can give you something nice in a Tokarev M213, or a TT9, or a Beretta 92F. How about a Glock 17, or a Llama Commander?"

"Nah."

"'*Nah.*' You never want to change."

"I'm loyal."

"To a person you can be loyal. To a country maybe you're loyal. But loyal to a caliber? *Feh!*"

"Just give me another Colt like the last."

"I'm out of the Mark IV. How about a Combat Stallion. Cost you five-fifty."

"Deal. And maybe I should look into one of those Kevlar vests," Jack said, glancing at a rack of them at the far end of the basement.

"For years I've been telling you that. What makes a change of mind now?"

"Somebody tried to kill me tonight."

"So? This is new?"

"I mean a sniper. Right through the hotel room window. Where nobody but me knew I was staying. I didn't even use Jack in the name when I called in the reservation."

"So maybe it wasn't you they were after. Maybe it was meant for anybody who happened to walk by a window."

"Maybe," Jack said, but he couldn't quite buy it. "Lousy shot, too. I spotted a telescopic sight on it and still he managed to miss me."

Abe made a disgusted noise. "They sell guns to anybody these days."

"Maybe I'll take a raincheck on the vest," Jack said, then quickly added, "Oh, and I need another dozen shuriken."

Abe whirled on him. "Don't tell me! Don't *tell* me! You've been spiking cockroaches with my shuriken again, haven't you? Jack, you promised!"

Jack cringed away. "Not exactly spiking them. Hey, Abe, I get bored."

Abe reached into a square crate and pulled out one of the six-pointed models, wrapped in oiled paper. He held it up and spoke to heaven.

"Oy! Precision weapons made of the finest steel! Honed to a razor's edge! But does Mr. *macher* Repairman Jack appreciate? Does he show respect? Reverence? Of course not! For pest control he uses them!"

"Uh, I'll need about a dozen."

Muttering Yiddish curses under his breath, Abe began pulling the shuriken out of the crate and slamming them down on the table one by one.

"Better make that a dozen and a half," Jack said.

First thing the next morning, Jack called George at the diner and told him to meet him at Julio's at ten. Then he went for his morning run. From a booth on the rim of Central Park, he called the answering machine that sat alone in the fourth floor office he rented on Tenth Avenue. He fast-forwarded through a couple of requests for appliance repairs, then came a tentative Asian voice, Chinese maybe:

"Mistah Jack, this is Tram. Please call. Have bad problem. People say you can help." He gave a phone number, a downtown exchange.

A DAY IN THE LIFE

Tram. Jack had never heard of him. He was the last on the tape. Jack reset it, then called this Tram guy. He was hard to understand, but Jack decided to see him. He told him where Julio's was and to be there at 10:30.

After a shave and a shower, he headed to Julio's for some breakfast. He was on the sidewalk, maybe half a block away, when he heard someone shout a warning. He glanced left, saw a man halfway across the street, pointing above him. Something in his expression made Jack dive for the nearest doorway. He was halfway there when something brushed his ankle and thudded against the pavement in an explosion of white.

When the dust finally cleared, Jack was staring at what was left of a fifty-pound bag of cement. The man who had shouted the warning was standing on the other side of the mess.

"That maniac could've killed you!"

"Maniac?" Jack said, brushing the white powder off his coat and jeans.

"Yeah. That didn't fall. Somebody dropped it. Looked like he was aiming for your head!"

Jack spun and raced around the corner to the other side of the building. This was the second time since midnight someone had tried to off him. Or maim him. The cement bag probably wouldn't have killed him, but it easily could have broken his neck or his back.

Maybe he had a chance to catch this guy.

He found the stairs to the upper floors and pounded up a dozen flights, but by the time he reached the roof it was empty. Another bag of cement sat on the black tar surface next to a pile of bricks. Someone was planning to repair a chimney.

Warily, he hurried the rest of the way to Julio's. He didn't like this at all. Because of the nature of his business, he had carefully structured it for anonymity. He did things to people that they didn't like, so it was best that they not know who was doing it to them. He did a cash business and worked hard at being an average looking Joe. No trails. Most of the time he worked behind the scenes. His customers knew his face, but their only contact with him was over the phone or in brief meetings in places like Julio's. And he never called his answering machine from home.

But somebody seemed to know his every move. How?

"Yo, Jack!" said Julio, the muscular little man who ran the tavern. "Long time no see." He began slapping at Jack's jacket, sending white clouds into the air. "What's all this white stuff?"

He told Julio about the two near misses.

"Y'know," Julio said, "I seem to remember hearing about some guy asking aroun' for you a coupla weeks ago. I'll find out who he was."

"Yeah. Give it a shot."

Probably wouldn't pan out to anything, but it was worth a try.

Jack scanned the tavern. It was dustier than usual. The hanging plants in the window were withered and brown.

"Your cleaning man die, Julio?"

"Nah. It's the yuppies. They keep comin' here. So I let the place get run down and dirty, an' they *still* come."

"Déclassé must be in."

"They make me crazy, Jack."

"Yeah, well, we've all got our crosses to bear, Julio."

Jack had finished his roll and was on his second coffee when George Kuropolis came in. He handed George a wad of cash.

"Here's what Reilly's boys took from you last night – minus your portion of the next installment on my fee. Tell the rest of your merchants association to ante in their shares."

George avoided his eyes.

"Some of them are saying you cost as much as Reilly."

Jack felt the beginnings of a surge of anger but it flattened out quickly. He was used to this. It tended to happen with a number of his customers, but more often since *The Neutralizer* hit the air. Before that, people who called him never expected him to work for free. Now because of some damn stupid goody two-shoes TV vigilante, more and more of his customers had the idea it was Jack's civic duty to get them out of jams. He'd been expecting some bitching from the group.

This particular merchants association had had it rough lately. They ran a cluster of shops on the lower west side. With the Westies out of the picture, they'd thought they'd have some peace. Then Reilly's gang came along and began bleeding them dry. Finally one of them, Wolansky, went to the police. Not too long after, a Molotov cocktail came through the front door of his greengrocer, blackening most of his store; and shortly after that his son was crippled in a hit-and-run accident outside their apartment building. As a result, Wolansky developed acute Alzheimer's when the police asked him to identify Reilly.

That was when George and the others got together and called Repairman Jack.

"You going to tell me you don't see the difference?"

"No, of course not," George said hurriedly.

"Well, let me refresh your memory," Jack said. "*You* came to *me*, not the other way round. This isn't television and I'm not *The Neutralizer*. Don't get reality and make-believe confused here. This is my work. I get paid for what I do. I was around before that do-gooder came on the air and I'll be around after he's off. Those knives Reilly and his bunch carry aren't props. Their guns aren't loaded with blanks. This is the real thing. I don't risk my neck for kicks."

"All right, all right," George said. "I'm sorry–"

"And another thing. I may be costing you, but I'm just temporary, George. Like purgatory. Reilly is hell, and hell is forever. He'll bleed you until he's stopped."

"I know. I just wish it was over. I don't know if I can take another night like last night." George began rubbing his right hand. "They were gonna–"

"But they didn't. And as long as they see me as a competitor, they'll save their worst for me."

George shuddered and looked at his fingers. "I sure hope so."

Shortly after George left, an Asian who looked to be on the far side of fifty showed up at the door. His face was bruised and scraped, his left eye was swollen half shut. Julio intercepted him, shook his hand, welcomed him to his place, clapped him on the back, and led him toward the rear of the tavern. Jack noticed that he walked with a limp. A bum right leg. By the time he reached

Jack's table, he had been thoroughly frisked. If Julio found anything, he would lead him right past Jack and out the back door.

"Tram," Julio said, stopping at Jack's table, "this is the man you're looking for. Jack, this is Tram."

They had coffee and made small talk while Tram smoked unfiltered Pall Malls back-to-back. Jack led the conversation around to Tram's background. His fractured English was hard to follow but Jack managed to piece together the story.

Tram was from Vietnam, from Quang Ngai, he said. He had fought in a string of wars for most of his life, from battling the French with the Viet Minh at Dien Bien Phu through the final civil war that had ravaged what was left of his country. It was during the last one that a Cong finger charge finished his right leg. Along with so many others who had fought on the losing side, Tram became a refugee after the war. But things improved after he made it to the States. An American-made prosthesis of metal and plastic took up where his own flesh left off below the knee. And he now ran a tiny laundry just off Canal Street, on the interface between Little Italy and Chinatown.

Finally he got around to the reason he had called Jack.

His laundry had been used for years as a drop between the local mob and some drug runners from Phnom Penh. The set-up was simple. The "importers" left a package of Cambodian brown on a given morning; that afternoon it was picked up by one of the local Italian guys who would leave a package of cash in its place. No one watching would see anything unusual. The laundry's customers ran the ethnic gamut of the area – white, black, yellow, and all the shades between; the bad guys walked in with bundles of dirty clothes and walked out with packages wrapped in brown paper, just like everyone else.

"How'd you get involved in this?" Jack asked.

"Mr. Tony," Tram said, lighting still another cigarette.

Sounded like a hairdresser. "Mr. Tony who?"

"Campisi."

"*Tony Campisi?*" That was no hairdresser.

Tram nodded. "Yes, yes. Knew very good Mister Tony nephew Patsy in Quang Ngai. We call him 'Fatman' there. Was with Patsy when he die. Call medic for him but too late."

A DAY IN THE LIFE

Jack had heard of Tony "the Cannon" Campisi. Who hadn't? A big shot in the dope end of the Gambino family. Tram went on to say that "Fatman" Pasquale had been one of Tony's favorite nephews. Tony learned of Tram's friendship with Patsy and helped Tram get into the States after the U.S. bailed out of Nam. Tony even set him up in the laundry business.

But there was a price to pay. Natch.

"So he put you in business and used your place as a drop."

"Yes. Make promise to do for him."

"Seems like small time for a guy like Campisi."

"Mr. Tony have many place to drop. No put all egg in one basket, he say."

Smart. If the narcs raided a drop, they never got much, and didn't effect the flow through all the other drops around the city. Campisi had a slick rep. Which was probably why he had rarely seen the inside of a Federal courtroom.

"So why the change of heart?"

Tram shrugged. "Mr. Tony dead."

Right. The Gambino family had pretty much fallen apart after old Carlo's death and a deluge of Federal indictments. And Tony "the Cannon" Campisi had succumbed to the Big Casino of the lung last summer.

"You don't like the new man?"

"No like dope. Bad."

"Then why'd you act as middle man for Campisi?"

"Make promise."

Jack's gaze locked with Tram's for an instant. The brown eyes stared back placidly. Not much more needed in way of explanation.

"Right. So what's the present situation?"

The present situation was that the hard guy who had made the drops and pick-ups for Campisi over the years was now running that corner of the operation himself. Tram had tried to tell him that the deal was off – "Mr. Tony dead...promise dead," as Tram put it. But Aldo D'Amico wasn't listening. He'd paid Tram a personal visit the other day. The result was Tram's battered face.

"He belted you around *himself?*"

A nod. "He like that."

Jack knew the type – you could take the guy off the street, but you couldn't take the street out of the guy.

Obviously, Tram couldn't go to the police or the DEA about Aldo. He'd had to find some unofficial help.

"So you want me to get him off your back."

Another nod. "Have heard you can do."

"Maybe. Don't you have any Vietnamese friends who can help you?"

"Mr. Aldo will know is me. Will break my store, hurt my family."

And Jack could imagine how. The Reillys and the D'Amicos... bully boys, pure and simple. The only difference between them was the size of their bank accounts. And the size of their organizations.

That last part bothered Jack. He did *not* want to get into any rough-and-tumble with the mob. But he didn't like to turn down a customer just because the bad guys were too tough.

Maybe he could find a way.

Central to the Repairman Jack method was shielding himself and the customer by making the target's sudden run of bad luck appear unrelated to the customer. The hardest part was coming up with a way to do that.

"You know my price?"

"Have been saving."

"Good." Jack had a feeling he was going to earn every penny of this one.

The brown eyes lit with hope. "You will help?"

"I'll see. When's the next pick-up?"

"This day. At four."

"Okay. I'll be there."

"It will not be good to shoot him dead. He has many friends."

Jack had to smile at Tram's matter-of-fact manner.

"I know. Besides, that's only a last resort. I'll just be there to do research."

"Good. Want peace. Very tired of fight. Too much fight in my life."

A DAY IN THE LIFE

Jack looked at Tram's battered face, thought of his missing leg below the knee, of the succession of wars he had fought in since age fifteen. The man deserved a little peace.

"I read you."

Tram gave him the address of his laundry and a down payment in twenty dollar bills that were old yet clean and crisp – like he had washed, starched, and pressed them. Jack in return gave him his customary promise to deduct from his fee the worth of any currency or valuables he happened to recover from D'Amico & Co. during the course of the job.

After bowing three times, Tram left him alone at the table. Julio took his place.

"The name 'Cirlot' mean anything to you?" he asked.

Jack thought a moment. "Sure. Ed Cirlot. The blackmailer."

A customer named Levinson – Tom Levinson – had come to Jack a few years ago asking to get Cirlot off his back. Levinson was a high end dealer in identities. *Primo* quality. Jack had used him twice in the past himself. So Levinson had called him when Cirlot had found a screw and begun turning it.

Cirlot, it seemed, had learned of a few high-placed foreign mobsters who had availed themselves of Levinson's services. He threatened to tip the Feds to their ersatz I-D the next time they came Stateside. Levinson knew that if that ever happened, their boys would come looking for him.

Cirlot had made a career out of blackmail, it seemed. He was always looking for new pigeons. So Jack set himself up as a mark – supposedly a crooked coin dealer running a nationwide scam from a local boiler room. Cirlot wanted ten large down and one a month to keep quiet. If he didn't get it, the FTC would come a-knockin' and not only close Jack down, but take him to court.

Jack had paid him – in bogus twenties. Cirlot had been caught with the counterfeit – enough of it to make a charge of conspiracy to distribute stick. When he'd named Jack's coin operation as his source, no such operation could be found. He got ten years soft Fed time.

"Don't tell me he's out already."

"*Si*. Good behavior. And he was asking around about you."

QUICK FIXES

Jack didn't like that. Cirlot wasn't supposed to know anything about Repairman Jack. The coin dealer who had stiffed the blackmailer with bogus was gone like he had never existed. Because he hadn't.

So why was Cirlot looking for Repairman Jack? There was no connection.

Except for Tom Levinson.

"I think I'll go visit a certain I-D dealer."

Jack spotted Levinson up on East 92nd Street, approaching his apartment house from the other side. Levinson spotted him at the same time. Instead of waving, he turned and started to run. But he couldn't move too fast because his foot was all bandaged up. He did a quick hop-skip-limp combination that made him look like a fleeing Walter Brennan. Jack caught up to him easily.

"What's the story, Tom?" he said, grabbing Levinson's shoulder.

He looked frightened, and his spiked black hair only heightened the effect. He was a thin, weasely man trying to look younger than his forty-something years. He was panting and his eyes were darting left and right like a cornered animal.

"I couldn't help it, Jack! I had to tell him!"

"Tell him what?"

"About you!" His mouth began running at breakneck speed. "Somehow he connected me and that coin dealer you played. Maybe he had lots of time to think while he was inside. Maybe he remembered that he first heard about a certain coin dealer from me. Anyway, the first thing he does when he gets out is come to me. I was scared shitless, but he doesn't want me. He wants you. Said you set him up for a fall and made him look like a jerk."

Jack turned away from Levinson and walked in a small circle. He was angry at Levinson, and disappointed as well. He had thought the forger was a stand-up guy.

"We had a deal," Jack said. "When I took you on, you were to keep quiet about it. You don't know Repairman Jack – never heard of him. That's part of the deal. Why didn't you play dumb?"

"I did, but he wasn't having any."

"So tell him to go squat."

"I did." Levinson sighed. "Jack...he started cutting off my toes."

The words stunned Jack. "He *what?*"

"My toes!" Levinson pointed to his bandaged left foot. "He tied me up and cut off my fucking little toe! And he was going to cut off another and another and keep on cutting until I told him how to find you!"

Jack felt his jaw muscles tighten. "Jesus!"

"So I told him all I knew, Jack. Which ain't much. I gave him the White Pages number and told him we met at Julio's. I don't know any more so I couldn't tell him any more. He didn't believe me, so he cut off the next one."

"He cut off *two* toes?" Jack felt his gut knot.

"With a big shiny meat cleaver. You want to see?"

"Hell no." He shook off the revulsion. "I took Cirlot for the white collar type. He never seemed the kind to mix it up."

"Maybe he used to be, but he ain't that way now. He's *crazed*, Jack. And he wants to bring you down real bad. Says he's gonna make you look like shit, then he's gonna ice you. And I guess he's already tried, otherwise you wouldn't be here."

Jack thought of the shot through the hotel window and the falling cement bag.

"Yeah. Twice."

"I'm sorry, Jack, but he really *hurt* me."

"Christ, Tom. Don't give it another thought. I mean, your toes...*damn!*"

He told Levinson he'd take care of things and left him there. As he walked away, he wondered how many toes he'd have given up for Levinson.

He decided he could muddle through life without ever knowing the answer to that one.

———

As soon as the car pulled to a stop in front of the laundry, Aldo reached for the door handle. He felt Joey grab his arm.

"Mr. D. Let me go in. You stay out here."

Aldo shrugged off the hand. "I know where you're comin' from, Joey, but don't keep buggin' my ass about this."

QUICK FIXES

Joey spread his hands and shrugged. "Ay. You're the boss. But I still don't think it's right, know what I mean?"

Joey was okay. Aldo knew how he felt: He was Aldo D'Amico's driver and bodyguard, so *he* should be doing all the rough stuff. And as far as Aldo was concerned, Joey could have most of it. But not all of it. Aldo wasn't going to hide in the background all the time like Tony C. Hell, in his day Tony could walk through areas like this and hardly anyone would know him. He was just another *paisan* to these people. Well, that wasn't going to be Aldo's way. *Everybody* was going to know who he was. And when he walked through it was going to be, "Good morning, Mr. D'Amico!" "Would you like a nice apple, Mr. D'Amico?" "Have some coffee, Mr. D'Amico!" "Right this way, Mr. D'Amico!" People were going to know him, were going to treat him with respect. He deserved a little goddamn respect by now. He'd be forty-five next month. He'd done Tony the Cannon's scut work forever. Knew all the ins and outs of the operation. Now it was *his*. And everybody was going to know that.

"I'll handle this like I did yesterday," he told Joey. "Like I told you: I believe in giving certain matters the *personal* touch."

What he didn't tell Joey was that he *liked* the rough stuff. That was the only bad thing about moving up in the organization – you never got a chance for hands-on communication with jerks like the gook who owned this laundry. Never a peep out of the little yellow bastard all the years Tony C. was running things, but as soon as he's gone, the gook thinks he's gonna get independent with the new guy. Not here, babe. Not when the new guy's Aldo D'Amico.

He was hoping the gook gave him some more bullshit about not using his place for a drop anymore. Any excuse to work him over again like the other day.

"Awright," Joey said, shaking his head with frustration, "but I'm comin' in to back you up. Just in case."

"Sure, Joey. You can carry the laundry."

Aldo laughed, and Joey laughed with him.

―――

Jack had arrived at Tram's with a couple of dirty shirts at about 3:30. Dressed in jeans, an Army fatigue jacket, and a baseball cap

A DAY IN THE LIFE

pulled low on his forehead, he now sat in one of the three chairs and read the *Post* while Tram ran the shirts through the machine. It was a tiny hole-in-the-wall shop that probably cost the little man most of his good leg in rent. A one-man operation except for some after-school counter help which Tram always sent on an errand when a pick-up or delivery was due.

Jack watched the customers, a motley group of mostly lower middle class downtowners, flow in and out. Aldo D'Amico and his bodyguard were instantly identifiable by their expensive top coats when they arrived at 4:00 on the button. Aldo's was dark gray with a black felt collar, a style Jack hadn't seen since the Beatles' heyday. He was mid-forties with a winter tan and wavy blow-dried hair receding on both sides. Jack knew he had to be Aldo because the other guy was a side of beef and was carrying a wad of dirty laundry.

Jack noticed the second guy giving him a close inspection. He might as well have had BODYGUARD stenciled on his back. Jack glanced up, gave the two of them a disinterested up-and-down, then went back to the sports page.

"Got something for me, gook?" Aldo said, grinning like a shark as he slapped the knuckles of his right fist into his left palm.

Jack sighed. He knew the type. Most tough guys he knew wouldn't hesitate to hurt somebody, even ice them if necessary, but to them it was like driving a car through downtown traffic in the rain: You didn't particularly like it but you did it because you had to get someplace; and if you had the means, you preferred to have somebody else do it for you.

Not this Aldo. Jack could tell that mixing it up was some kind of fix for him.

Maybe that could be turned around. Jack didn't have a real plan here. His car was parked outside. He intended to pick up Aldo and follow him around, follow him home if he could. He'd do that for a couple of days. Eventually, he'd get an idea of how to stick him. Then he'd have to find a way to work that idea to Tram's benefit. This was going to be long, drawn-out, and touchy.

At the counter, Tram sullenly placed a brown paper wrapped bundle on the counter. The bodyguard picked it up and plopped the dirty laundry down in its place. Tram ignored it.

"Please, Mr. Aldo," he said. "Will not do this any more."

"Boy, you're one stupid gook, y'know that?" He turned to his bodyguard. "Joey, take the customer for a walk while I discuss business with our Vietnamese friend here."

Jack felt a tap on his shoulder and looked up from his paper into Joey's surprisingly mild eyes.

"C'mon. I'll buy you a cup of coffee."

"I got shirts coming," Jack said.

"They'll wait. My friend wants a little private talk with the owner."

Jack wasn't sure how to play this. He wasn't prepared for any rough and tumble here, but he didn't want to leave Tram to Aldo's tender mercies again.

"Then let him talk in the back. I ain't goin' nowhere."

Joey grabbed him under the arm and pulled him out of the chair. "Yeah. You are."

Jack came out of the chair quickly and knocked Joe's arm away.

"Hands off, man!"

He decided that the only way to get out of this scene on his terms was to pull a psycho number. He looked at Joey's beefy frame and heavy overcoat and knew attacking his body would be a waste of time. That left his face.

"Just stay away!" Jack shouted. "I don't like people touching me. Makes me mad! *Real* mad!"

Joey dropped the brown paper bundle onto a chair. "All right. Enough of this shit." He stepped in close, gripped Jack's shoulders, and tried to turn him around.

Jack reached up between Joey's arms, grabbed his ears, and yanked the bodyguard's head forward. As he lowered his head and butted, he had a fleeting glimpse of the sick look on Joey's startled face. He hadn't been expecting anything like this, but he knew what was coming.

When Jack heard Joey's nose crunch against the top of his skull, he pushed him away and kicked him hard in the balls. Joey dropped to his knees and groaned. His bloody face was slack with pain and nausea.

A DAY IN THE LIFE

Jack next leapt on Aldo who was gaping at him with a stunned expression.

"You want some of me, too?" he shouted.

Aldo's overcoat was unbuttoned and he was leaner than Joey. Jack went for the breadbasket: right-left combination jabs to the solar plexus, then a knee to the face when he doubled over. Aldo went down in a heap.

But it wasn't over. Joey was reaching a hand into his overcoat pocket. Jack jumped on him and wrestled a short barreled Cobra .357 revolver away from him.

"A gun? You pulled a fucking *gun* on me, man?" He slammed the barrel and trigger guard across the side of Joey's head. "*Shit, that makes me mad!*"

Then he spun and pointed the pistol at the tip of Aldo's swelling nose.

"You!" he screamed. "You started this! You didn't want me to get my shirts! Well, you can have them! They're old anyway! I'll take *yours!* All of them!"

He grabbed the bundle of dirty shirts from the counter and then went for the brown paper package on the chair.

"Jesus, no!" Aldo said. "No! You don't know what—"

Jack leapt on him and began pistol whipping him, screaming, "Don't tell me what I don't know!"

As Aldo covered his head with his arms, Jack glanced at Tram motioned him over. Tram got the idea. He came out from behind the counter and shoved Jack away, but not before Jack had managed to open Aldo's scalp in a couple of places.

"You get out!" Tram cried. "Get out or I call police!"

"Yeah, I'll get out, but not before I put a couple of holes in this rich pig here!"

Tram stood between him and Aldo. "No! You go! You cause enough trouble!"

Jack made a disgusted noise and ran out with both bundles. Outside he found an empty Mercedes 350 SEL idling at the curb by a fire hydrant. *Why not?*

As he gunned the heavy car toward Canal Street, he wondered at his screaming psycho performance. Pretty convincing. And easy, too. He'd hardly stretched at all to get into the part.

That bothered him a little.

"Fifty thousand in small bills," Abe said after he'd finished counting the money that had been wrapped inside the dirty laundry. He had it spread out in neat piles on a crate in the basement of his store. "If I were you, I shouldn't complain. Not so bad for an afternoon's work."

"Yeah. But it's the ten keys of cocaine and the thirty of Cambodian brown." The wrapped package had housed some of the heroin. The cocaine and the rest of the heroin had been in a duffel bag in the trunk. "What am I going to do with *that?*"

"There's a storm drain outside. Next time it rains..."

Jack thought about that. The heroin would definitely go down the drain. Any alligators or crocs living down in the sewers would be stoned for life. But the cocaine...that might come in handy in the future, just like the bogus twenties had come in handy against Cirlot.

Cirlot. Something about him was perking in the back of Jack's mind.

"I've always wanted a Mercedes," Abe said.

"What for? You haven't been further east than Queens and further west than Columbus Avenue in a quarter century."

"Someday I might like maybe to travel. See New Jersey."

"Yeah. Well, that's not a bad idea. No doubt about it, the best way to see New Jersey is from the inside of a Mercedes. But it's too late. I gave the car to Julio to dispose of."

Abe sagged. "Chop shop?"

Jack nodded. "He's going to shop it around for quick cash. Figures another ten grand, minimum, maybe twenty."

A take of sixty-seventy K so far from one visit to Tram's laundry. Which meant that Jack would be returning Tram's down payment and giving him a free ride on this job. Which was fine for Tram's bank account, but Jack didn't know what his next step was. He'd shaken things up down there. Now maybe it would be best to sit back and watch what fell out of the trees.

He headed for Gia's. He kept to the windy shadows as he walked along, kept looking over his shoulder. Cirlot had seemed to know where he was going, and when he'd be there. Was he watching him now?

Jack didn't like being on this end of the game.

But how did Cirlot know? That was what ate at him. Jack knew his apartment wasn't bugged – the place was like a fortress. Besides, Cirlot didn't know where he lived. And even if he did, he couldn't get inside to place a bug. Yet he seemed to know Jack's moves. How, dammit?

Jack made a full circuit of Gia's block and cut through an alley before he felt it was safe to enter her apartment house.

Two fish-eye peepholes nippled Gia's door. Jack had installed them himself. One was the usual height, and one was Vicky-height. He knocked and stood there, pressing his thumb over the lower peephole as he waited.

"Jack, is that you?" said a child's voice from the other side.

He pulled his thumb away and grinned into the convex glass. "Ta-daaa!"

The deadbolt slid back, the door swung inward, and suddenly he was holding a skinny little girl in his arms. She had long dark hair, blue eyes, and a blinding smile.

"Jack! Whatcha bring me?"

He pointed to the breast pocket of his fatigue jacket. Vicky reached inside and pulled out a packet of bubblegum cards.

"Football cards! Neat! You think there's any Jets in this one?"

"Only one way to find out."

He carried her inside and put her down. He locked the door behind them as she fumbled with the wrapper.

"Jack!" she said, her voiced hushed with wonder. "They're all Jets! *All* Jets! Oh, this is *so* neat!"

Gia stepped into the living room. "The only eight-year old in New York who says 'neat.' Wonder where she got that from?"

She kissed him lightly and he slid an arm around her waist, pulling her close to him. She shared her daughter's blue eyes and bright smile, but her hair was blonde. She brightened up the whole room for Jack.

"I don't know about you," he said, "but I think it's pretty neat to get five – *five* – members of your favorite team in a single pack of bubblegum. I don't know anybody else who's got that kind of luck."

Jack had gone through a dozen packs of cards before coming up with those five Jets, then he had slipped them into a single wrapper and glued the flaps back in place. Vicky had developed a thing for the Jets, simply because she liked their green and white jerseys – which was as good a reason as any to be a Jets fan.

"Start dinner yet?" he asked.

Gia shook her head. "Just getting ready to. Why?"

"Have to take a raincheck. I've got a few things I've got to do tonight."

She frowned. "Nothing dangerous, I hope."

"Nah."

"That's what you always say."

"Well, sure. I mean, after surviving the blue meanies on that ship, everything else is a piece of cake."

"Don't mention those things!" Gia shuddered and hugged him. "Promise you'll call me when you're back home?"

"Yes, mother."

"I'm serious. I worry about you."

"You just made my day."

She broke away and picked up a slim cardboard box from the couch. "Land's End" was written across one end.

"Your order arrived today."

"Neat." He pulled out a bright red jacket with navy blue lining. He pulled off the fatigue jacket and tried it on. "Perfect. How do I look?"

"Like every third person in Manhattan," Gia said.

"Great!"

"All you need is a Hard Rock Cafe sweat shirt and the picture will be complete."

Jack worked at being ordinary, at being indistinguishable from everybody else, just another face in the crowd. To do that, he had to keep up with what the crowd was wearing. Since he didn't have a charge card, Gia had ordered the jacket for him on hers.

"I'd better turn off the oven," Gia said.

"I'll treat tomorrow night. Chinese. For sure."

A DAY IN THE LIFE

"Sure," she said. "I'll believe it when I smell it."

Jack stood there in the tiny living room, watching Vicky spread out her football cards, listening to Gia move about the kitchen over the drone of *Eyewitness News*, drinking in the rustle and bustle and noises and silences of a *home*. The domestic feel of this tiny apartment – he wanted it. But it seemed so out of reach. He could come and visit and warm himself by the fire, but he couldn't stay. As much as he wanted to, he couldn't gather it up and take it with him.

His work was the problem. He had never asked Gia to marry him because he knew the answer would be no. Because of what he did for a living. And he *wouldn't* ask her for the same reason: Because of what he did for a living. Marriage would make him vulnerable. He couldn't expose Gia and Vicky to risk like that. He'd have to retire first. But he wasn't even forty. Besides go crazy, what would he do for the next thirty or forty years?

Become a citizen? Get a day job? How would he do that? How would he explain why there was no record of his existence up till now? No job history, no Social Security hours, no file of 1040's. The IRS would want to know if he was an illegal alien or a Gulag refugee or something. And if he wasn't, they'd ask a lot of questions he wouldn't want to answer.

He wondered if he had started something he couldn't stop.

And then he was looking out through the picture window in Gia's dining room at the roof of the apartment house across the street and remembering the bullets tearing through the hotel room less than twenty-four hours ago. His skin tingled with alarm. He felt vulnerable here. And worse, he was exposing Gia and Vicky to his own danger. Quickly he made his apologies and good-byes, kissed them both, and hurried back to the street.

He stood outside the apartment house, slowly walking back and forth before the front door.

Come on, you son of a bitch! Do you know I'm here? Take a shot! Let me know!

No shot. Nothing fell from the roof.

Jack stretched his cramped fingers out from the tight fists he had made. He imagined some vicious bastard like Cirlot finding

QUICK FIXES

out about Gia and Vicky, threatening them, maybe hurting them... it almost put him over the edge.

He began walking back toward his own apartment. He moved quickly along the pavement, then broke into a run, trying to work off the anger, the mounting frustration.

This had to stop. And it was going to stop. Tonight, if he had anything to say about it.

———

Jack stopped at a pay phone and called Tram. The Vietnamese told him that Aldo and his bodyguard had limped out and found a cab, swearing vengeance on the punk who had busted them up. Tram was worried that Aldo might take his wrath out on him if he couldn't find Jack. That worried Jack, too. He called his answering machine but found nothing of interest on it

As he hung up he remembered something: Cirlot and phones. *Yes.* That was how the blackmailer had got his hooks into his victims. The guy was an ace wiretapper.

Jack trotted back to his brownstone. But instead of going up to his apartment, he slipped down to the utility closet. He pulled open the phone box and spotted the tap immediately: jumper wires attached to a tiny high frequency transmitter. Cirlot probably had a voice-activated recorder stashed not too far from here.

Now things were starting to make sense. Cirlot had learned from Levinson that Jack met customers at Julio's. He'd hung around outside until he spotted Jack, then tailed him home.

Jack clucked to himself. He was getting careless in his old age.

Soon after that, Cirlot had shown up, probably as a phone man, inserted the tap, and sat back and listened. Jack had used his apartment phone to reserve the room at the Lucky Hotel...and he had called Julio this morning to tell him he'd be over by ten thirty. It all fit.

Jack closed the phone box, leaving the tap in place.

Two could play this game.

———

Jack sprawled amid the clutter of Victorian oak and bric-a-brac that filled the front room of his apartment and called George at the diner. This was his second such call in half an hour, except that the first had been made from a public phone. He had told George to expect this call, and had told him what to say.

"Hello, George," he said when the Greek picked up the other end. "You got the next payment together from your merchants association?"

"Yeah. We got it. In cash like usual."

"Good deal. I'll be by around midnight to pick it up."

"I'll be here," George said.

Jack hung up and sat there, thinking. The bait was out. If Cirlot was listening, chances were good he'd set up another ambush somewhere in the neighborhood of the Highwater Diner at around midnight. But Jack planned to be there first to see if he could catch Cirlot setting up. And then they would settle things. For good. Jack wasn't going to have anybody dogging his steps back to Gia and Vicky, especially someone who had chopped a couple of toes off a former customer.

On his way downtown an hour later, Jack called his answering machine again. He heard a message from George asking him to call right away. When he did, he heard a strange story.

"I asked you to *what?*" Jack said.

"Meet you in the old Borden building next door. You said there'd been a change of plans and it was probably safer if you didn't show up at the diner. So I was to meet you next door at ten thirty and hand over the money."

Jack had to smile. This Cirlot was slicker than he'd thought.

"Did it sound like me?"

"Hard to say. The connection was bad."

"What did you say?"

"I agreed, but I thought it was fishy because it wasn't the way we had set it up before. And because you said you'd be wearing a ski mask like last night. That sounded fishy, too."

"Good man. I appreciate the call. Call me again if you hear from anyone who says he's me."

"Will do."

Jack hung up. Instead of hailing a cab to go downtown, he ducked into a nearby tavern and ordered a draft of Amsterdam.

QUICK FIXES

Curiouser and curiouser.

Cirlot seemed more interested in ripping him off than knocking him off – at least tonight. Tom Levinson's words came back: *Gonna make you look like shit, then he's gonna ice you.*

So that was it. Another piece fell into place. The bag of cement had missed him. Okay – no one could expect much accuracy against a moving target with a heavy, cumbersome object like that. But the shooter outside the Lucky Hotel had had a telescopic sight. Jack had been a sitting duck. The guy shouldn't have missed.

Unless he'd wanted to. That had to be it. Cirlot was playing head games with him, getting him off balance until he had a chance to humiliate him, expose him, make him look like a jerk. He wanted to payback in kind before he killed Jack.

Ripping off one of his fees would be a good start.

Jack's anger was tinged with amusement.

He's playing my own game against me.

But not for long. Jack was the old hand here. It was his game. He'd invented it, and he'd be damned if he'd let Cirlot outplay him. The simplest thing to do was to confront Cirlot in that old wreck of a building and have a showdown.

Simple, direct, effective, but lacking in style. He needed to come up with something very neat here. A masterstroke, even.

And then, as he lifted his glass to drain the final ounces of his draft, he had it.

―――

Reilly was waiting his turn at the pool table. He didn't feel like shooting much. With Reece and Jerry dead, everybody was down and pissed. All they'd talked about since last night was finding that jack-o-lantern guy. The only laugh they'd had all day was when they learned that Reece's real name was *Mau*rice.

Just then Gus called over from the bar. He was holding the phone receiver in the air.

"Yo! Reilly! You're wanted!"

"Yeah? Who?"

"Said to tell you it's Pumpkinhead."

Reilly nearly tripped over his stick getting to the phone. Cheeks and the others were right behind him.

A DAY IN THE LIFE

"Gonna find you, fucker!" he said as soon as he got the receiver to his head.

"I know you are," said the voice on the other end. "Because I'm gonna tell you where I am. We need a meet. Tonight. You lost two men and I almost got killed last time we tangled. What do you say to a truce? We can find some way to divide things up so we both come out ahead."

Reilly was silent while he controlled himself. Was this fucker crazy? A *truce*? After what he did last night?

"Sure," he managed to say. "We can talk."

"Good. Just you and me."

"Okay." *Riiiiight.* "Where?"

"The old place we were in last night – next to the Highwater. Ten-thirty okay?"

Reilly looked at his watch. That gave him an hour and a half. Plenty of time.

"Sure."

"Good. And remember, Reilly: Come alone or the truce is off."

"Yeah."

He hung up and turned to his battered boys. They didn't look like much, what with Rafe, Tony, and Cheeks all bandaged up, and Cheeks' hand in a cast. Hard to believe only one guy had done all this. But that one guy was a mean dude, full of tricks. So they weren't going to take any chances this time. No talk. No deals. No hesitation. No reprieve. They were going to throw everything they had at him tonight.

"That really him?" Cheeks asked.

"Yeah," said Reilly, smiling. "And tonight we're gonna have us some punkin pie!"

"Aldo, this man insists on speaking to you!"

Aldo D'Amico glared at his wife and removed the ice pack from his face. He had a brutal headache from the bruises and stitches in his scalp. His nose was killing him. Broken in two places. The swelling made him sound like he had a bad cold.

He wondered for the hundredth time about that punk in the laundry. Had the gook set them up? Aldo wanted to believe it, but it just didn't wash. If he'd been laying for Aldo, he'd have had his store filled with some sort of gook army, not one white guy. But Christ the way that one guy moved! *Fast.* Like liquid lightning. A butt and a kick and Joey was down and then he'd been on Aldo, his face crazy. No. It hadn't been a set-up. Just some *stunad* punk. But that didn't make it any easier to take.

"I told you, Maria, no calls!"

Bad enough he'd be laughed at all over town for being such a *gavone* to allow some nobody to bust him up and steal his car, and even worse that his balls were on the line for the missing money and shit, so why couldn't Maria follow a simple order? He never should have come home tonight. He'd have been better off at Franny's loft on Greene Street. Franny did what she was told. She damn well better. He paid her rent.

"But he says he has information on your car."

Aldo's hand shot out. "Gimme that! Hello!"

"Mr. D'Amico, sir," said a very deferential voice on the other end. "I'm very sorry about what happened today at that laundry. If I'da known it was someone like you, I wouldn'a caused no trouble. But I didn't know, y'see, an I got this real bad temper, so like I'm sorry–"

"Where's the car?" Aldo said in a low voice.

"I got it safe and I wanna return it to you along with the money I took and the, uh, other laundry and the, uh, stuff in the trunk, if you know what I mean and I think you do."

The little shit was scared. Good. Scared enough to want to give everything back. Even better. Aldo sighed with relief.

"Where is it?"

"I'm in it now. Like I'm talkin' on you car phone. But I'm gonna leave it somewhere and tell you where you can find it."

"Don't do that!" Aldo said quickly.

His mind raced. Getting the car back was number one priority, but he wanted to get this punk, too. If he didn't even the score, it would be a damn long time before he could hold his head up on the street.

"Don't leave it *anywhere!* Someone might rip it off before I get there, and that'll be on your head! We'll meet–"

"Oh, no! I'm not getting plugged full of holes!"

Yes, you are, Aldo thought, remembering the punk pointing Joey's magnum in his face.

"Hey, don't worry about that," Aldo said softly. "You've apologized and you're returning the car. It was an accident. We'll call it even. As a matter of fact, I like the way you move. You made Joey look like he was in slow motion. Actually, you did me a favor. Made me see how bad my security is."

"Really?"

"Yeah. I could use a guy like you. How'd you like to replace Joey?"

"Y'mean be your bodyguard? I don't know, Mr. D'Amico."

"Think about it. We'll talk about it when I see you tonight. Where we gonna meet?"

"Uuuuh, how about by the Highwater Diner? It's down on–"

"I know where it is."

"Yeah, well there's an old abandoned building right next door. How about if I meet you there?"

"Great. When?"

"Ten-thirty."

"That's kinda soon–"

"I know. But I'll feel safer."

"Hey, don't worry! When Aldo D'Amico gives his word, you can take it to the bank!"

And I promise you, punk, you're a dead man!

"Yeah, well, just in case we don't hit it off, I'll be wearing a ski mask. I figure you didn't get a real good look at me in that laundry and I don't want you getting a better one."

"Have it your way. See you at ten-thirty."

He hung up and called to his wife. "Maria! Get Joey on the phone. Tell him to get over here now!"

Aldo went to his desk drawer and pulled out his little Jennings .22 automatic. He hefted it. Small, light, and loaded with high velocity longs. It did the job at close range. And Aldo intended to be real close when he used this.

———

A little before ten, Jack climbed up to the roof of the Highwater Diner and sat facing the old Borden building. He watched Reilly and five of his boys – the whole crew – arrive shortly afterwards. They entered the building from the rear. Two of them carried large duffel bags. They appeared to have come loaded for bear. Not too long after them came Aldo and three wiseguys. They took up positions outside in the alley below and out of sight on the far side.

No one, it seemed, wanted to be fashionably late.

At 10:30 sharp, a lone figure in a dark coat, jeans, and what looked like a knit watch cap strolled along the sidewalk in front of the Highwater. He paused a moment to stare in through the front window. Jack hoped George was out of sight like he had told him to be. The dark figure continued on. When he reached the front of the Borden building, he glanced around, then started toward it. As he approached the gaping front entry, he stretched the cap down over his face. Jack couldn't see the design clearly but it appeared to be a crude copy of the one he'd worn last night. All it took was some orange paint...

Do you really want to play Repairman Jack tonight, pal?

For an instant he flirted with the idea of shouting out a warning and aborting the set-up. But he called up thoughts of life in a wheelchair due to a falling cement bag, of Levinson's missing toes, of bullets screaming through Gia and Vicky's apartment.

He kept silent.

He watched the figure push in through the remains of the front door and disappear inside. In the alley, Aldo and Joey rose from their hiding places and shrugged to each other in the moonlight. Jack knew what Aldo was thinking: *Where's my car?*

But they leapt for cover when the gunfire began. It was a brief roar, but very loud and concentrated. Jack picked out the sound of single rounds, bursts from a pair of assault pistols, and at least two, maybe three shotguns, all blasting away simultaneously. Barely more than a single prolonged flash from within. Then silence.

Slowly, cautiously, Aldo and his boys came out of hiding, whispering, making baffled gestures. One of them was carrying an Uzi, another held a sawed-off. Jack watched them slip inside, heard shouts, even picked out the word "car."

Then all hell broke loose.

A DAY IN THE LIFE

It looked as if a very small, very violent thunderstorm had got itself trapped on the first floor of the old Borden building. The racket was deafening, the flashes through the glassless windows like half a dozen strobe lights going at once. It went on full force for what seemed like twenty minutes but ticked out to slightly less than five on Jack's watch. Then it tapered and died. Finally... quiet. Nothing moved.

No. Check that. Someone was crawling out a side window and falling into the alley. Jack went down to see.

Reilly. He was bleeding from his mouth, his nose, and his gut. And he was hurting.

"Get me a ambulance, man!" he grunted as Jack crouched over him. His voice was barely audible.

"Right away, Matt," Jack said.

Reilly looked up at him. His eyes widened. "Am I dead? I mean...we offed you but good in there."

"You offed the wrong man, Reilly."

"Who cares...you can have this turf...I'm out of it...just get me a fucking ambulance! Please?"

Jack stared at him a moment. "Sure," he said.

Jack got his hands under Reilly's arms and lifted him. The wounded man nearly passed out with the pain of being moved. But he was aware enough to notice that Jack wasn't dragging him toward the street.

"Hey...where y'takin' me?"

"Around back."

Jack could hear the sirens approaching. He quickened his pace toward the rear.

"Need a doc...need a ambulance."

"Don't worry," Jack said. "There's one coming now."

He dumped Reilly in the rearmost section of the Borden building's back alley and left him there.

"Wait here for your ambulance," he told him. "It's the same one you called for Wolansky's kid when you ran him down last month."

Then Jack headed for the Highwater Diner to call Tram and tell George that they didn't need him anymore.

Introduction to "The Last Rakosh"

In 1990 I was slated to be guest of honor at the World Fantasy Convention along with Susan Allison, Robert Bloch, L. Sprague de Camp, Raymond Feist, David Mattingly, and Julius Schwartz. (What a lineup!) It's traditional for the guests to contribute a story to the convention program. The chairman that year was Bob Weinberg and his wife, Phyllis, was a major Repairman Jack fan. She begged me for a Repairman Jack story. How could I say no?

I began with the premise that not *all* the rakoshi had died when Jack blew up Kusum's ship, and then I used some of the new characters from *Freak Show*, the anthology I'd started putting together for HWA. And that eventually led to "The Peabody-Ozymandias Traveling Circus & Oddity Emporium."

The Last Rakosh

1

Vicky's scream pierced them, froze them.

Gia turned to Jack and he saw the panic in her eyes. It came again, Vicky's voice, high-pitched, quavering with terror. But where was she? She'd wandered ahead of them down the midway only a moment ago.

Jack took off toward the sound, moving as fast as the crowd would permit, bumping and pushing those he couldn't slide past. She couldn't have gone far in just a couple of minutes.

Then he spotted her skinny eight-year-old form darting toward him through the press, her face a strained mask of white, her blue eyes wide with fear. When she spotted him, she burst into tears and held out her arms as she stumbled forward, her voice a shriek.

"Jack! Jack! It's back! It's gonna get me again!"

She leaped and he caught her in his arms, holding her tight. She was quaking with fear.

"What is it, Vicks? What's the matter?"

"The monster! The monster that took me to the boat! It's here! Don't let it get me!"

"It's okay, it's okay," he said soothingly in her ear. "No one can hurt you when I'm around."

Out of the corner of his eye he saw Gia hurrying toward them. He gently peeled Vicky off himself and transferred the child to her mother's arms. Vicky immediately wrapped her arms and legs around Gia.

"My God, what happened?" Gia said, her expression fluctuating between fear and anger.

"She thinks she saw a rakosh."

Gia's eyes widened. "But that's—"

"Impossible. Right. But maybe she saw something that looks like one."

"No!" said Vicky from where her face was buried against her mother's neck. "It's one of them! I *know* it is!"

"Okay, Vicks," Jack said, gently rubbing her trembling back. "I'll check it out." He nodded to Gia. "Why don't you take her outside."

"We're on our way. After what I've seen here, I wouldn't be half surprised if she really had seen one."

"I know what you mean."

Jack watched Gia slip through the crowd, carrying Vicky. When she was out of sight he turned and headed in the direction Vicky had come.

Wouldn't be half surprised myself, he thought.

Not that there was a single chance in hell of one of Kusum's rakoshi being alive. They'd all died last summer on the water between Governor's Island and the Battery. He'd seen to that. His incendiary bombs had burned them all to a crisp in the hold of the ship that housed them. Of course there had been that one that had come ashore, the one he'd dubbed Scar-lip, but it had swum back out into the burning water and had never returned. The rakoshi were dead, all of them. The species was extinct.

But if by some miracle one had survived, it might well be part of Ozymandias Oddities. Julio had given Jack the tickets last week, saying it was the weirdest show he'd ever seen. He hadn't been kidding. Jack had never seen freaks like these. By definition freaks were supposed to be strange, but these folk went beyond strange into the positively alien. Jack hadn't realized what the "oddities" would be. And the more he'd seen, the less comfortable he'd felt. The very idea of deformed people putting themselves on display repulsed him; it was demeaning; and those who paid to gawk seemed as demeaned as the freaks on display; maybe more so.

THE LAST RAKOSH

But there was nothing sad or pathetic about these freaks. They were bizarre, frightening, and many seemed belligerently proud of their deformities, as if the people strolling the midway were the freaks.

And maybe we are.

Jack moved slowly, steadily through the press, glancing left and right at the little stages on which each freak was exhibited. There were animals – a two-headed cow, a five-legged goat – and human giants, dwarves, pinheads, and...others, less easily described. Next to a guy with tentacles for arms who called himself "Octoman" was an old circus cart with iron bars on its open side, one of the old cages on wheels once used to transport and display lions and tigers and such. The sign above it said "Man-Shark." Jack noticed people leaning across the rope border; they'd peer into the cage, then back off with uneasy shrugs.

This deserved a look.

Jack pushed to the front of the crowd and squinted into the dimly lit cage. Something was there, slumped in the left rear corner, head down, chin on chest, immobile. Something huge, a seven-footer at least. Dark-skinned, manlike and yet... undeniably alien.

Jack felt the skin along the back of his neck tighten as ripples of warning shot down his spine. He knew that shape. But that was all it was. A shape. So immobile. It had to be a dummy of some sort, or a guy in a rubber suit. A damn good suit. No wonder Vicky had been terrified.

But it couldn't be the real thing. Couldn't be...

Jack ducked under the rope and took a few tentative steps closer to the cage, sniffing the air. No stench. The one thing he remembered about the rakoshi was their stench, like rotting meat. Nothing like that here. He got close enough to touch the bars but didn't. The thing was a damn good dummy. He could almost swear it was breathing. He whistled and whispered, "Hey you in there!" The thing didn't budge. He rapped his ring on one of the iron bars. "Hey–!"

Suddenly it moved, the eyes snapping open as the head came up, deep yellow eyes that almost seemed to glow. Imagine the offspring from a pairing of a giant gorilla with a mako shark. Hairless cobalt skin, hugely muscled, no neck worth mentioning, no external ears, narrow slits for a nose. Huge talons, curved for tearing, extended from the tips of the three huge fingers on each hand as the yellow eyes fixed on Jack. The lower half of its huge shark-like head seemed to split as the jaw opened to reveal rows of razor-sharp teeth. It uncoiled its legs and slithered toward the front of the cage.

Along with the instinctive revulsion, the memories surged back: the cargo hold full of their dark shapes and glowing eyes, the unearthly chant, the disappearances, the deaths...

Jack backed up a step. Two. Behind him he heard the crowd *Oooh* and *Aaah* as it pressed forward for a better look. He took still another step back until he could feel their excited breaths on his neck. They didn't know what one of these things could do, didn't know their power, their near indestructibility. Otherwise they'd be pressing the other way.

Jack felt his heart kick up its already rising tempo when he noticed how the creature's lower lip was distorted by a wide scar. He knew this creature, this particular rakosh. Scar-lip. The one that had kidnapped Vicky, the one that had escaped Kusum's ship and had almost got to Vicky on the shore. The one that had almost killed Jack. He ran a hand across his chest. Even through the fabric of his shirt he could feel the three long ridges that ran across his chest, souvenir scars from the creature's talons.

Scar-lip was alive.

But how? How had it survived the blaze on the water? How had it wound up on Long Island in a traveling freak show?

The creature was on its feet now, its talons encircling the iron bars, its yellow eyes burning into Jack. It knew him too.

One of the workmen came by then, a beefy roustabout with a shaven head, thin lips, and the eyes of a snake. He carried a blunt elephant gaff and rapped it against the bars.

"So you're up, ay?" he said to the rakosh in a harsh voice. "Maybe you've finally learned your lesson." He turned to the crowd. "Here he is ladies and gentleman, the one and only Man-Shark. The only one of his kind. He's exclusively on display here at Ozymandias Oddities. Tell your friends, tell your enemies. You've never seen anything like him and never will anywhere else. Guaranteed." He spotted Jack. "Here, you. Get behind the rope. This thing's dangerous! See those claws? One swipe and you'd be sliced up like a tomato by a Ginsu knife! We don't want to see our customers get sliced up." His eyes said otherwise as he none too gently prodded Jack with the pole. "Back now."

Jack slipped back under the rope, never taking his eyes off Scar-lip. Now that it was up front in the light, he saw that the rakosh didn't look well. Its skin was dull, and relatively pale, nothing like the shiny deep cobalt he remembered. It looked thin, almost wasted. It stared at Jack a moment longer, then it looked down. Its talons retracted, slipping back inside the fingertips, the arms dropped to its sides, the shoulders drooped, then it turned and shuffled back to the rear of the cage where it slumped again in the corner and hung its head.

Drugged. That had to be the answer. They had to keep the rakosh tranquilized to keep it manageable. Even so, it didn't look too healthy.

But drugged or not, healthy or not, it had remembered Jack, recognized him. Which meant it could remember Vicky. And if it ever got free, it might come after Vicky again, to complete the task its dead master had set for it last summer.

The roustabout had begun banging on the rakoshi's cage in a fury, screaming at it to get up and face the crowd. Jack turned and headed for the exit. He knew what had to be done.

Scar-lip had to die.

2

Jack parked his car at the edge of the Monroe meadows at around midnight and waited in the front seat for the circus to bed down for the night. Chilly. An autumn mist had formed, hugging the ground. No moon above, but plenty of stars. Enough light to get him where he wanted to go without a flashlight.

At least Vicky wasn't frightened anymore. Jack had hated lying to her, but seeing the relief he her eyes when he'd told her the rakosh she'd seen had really been a man in a rubber costume had made it seem like the right thing to do. He'd told her every last rakosh was dead. A lie, but only a temporary lie, just for a couple of hours. By morning it would be true.

Things quieted down by one a.m. Jack waited until two, then went around to the Vic's rear and removed a pair of gallon cans from the huge trunk. The gasoline sloshed heavily within as he strode across the uneven ground toward the hulking silhouette of the freak show tent. The performers' and hands' trailers stood off to the north by the big eighteen-wheel truck.

No guards in sight. If any were about, they were probably concentrated around the menagerie area. Jack slipped under the canvas sidewall and listened. Quiet. A couple of incandescent bulbs had been left on, one hanging from the ceiling every thirty feet or so. Keeping to the shadows along the sidewall, Jack made his way toward Scar-lip's cage.

His plan was simple: flood the floor of the rakosh's cage and douse the thing itself with the gas, strike a match, then head for the trailers shouting "Fire!" at the top of his lungs. He knew from experience that once a rakosh started to burn, it would be quickly consumed. He just hoped the performers and roustabouts would arrive with their extinguishers in time to keep the whole tent from going up. He didn't like the plan, didn't like endangering the tent or anybody nearby, but it was the most efficient and direct plan he could come up with on such short notice. He had to protect Vicky at any cost, and this was the only sure way he knew of killing a rakosh.

He approached the cage warily from the blind end, then made a wide circle around to the front. Scar-lip was stretched out on the cage floor, sleeping, its right arm dangling through the bars. It opened its eyes as he neared. Their yellow was even duller than this afternoon. Its talons extended only part way as it made a half-hearted, almost perfunctory swipe in Jack's direction. Then it closed its eyes and let the arm dangle again. It didn't seem to have strength for anything more.

Jack stopped and stared at the creature. And somehow he knew.

It's dying.

He stood there a long time and watched Scar-lip doze in its cage. Was it sick or had it simply reached the end of its days? What was the life-span of a rakosh, anyway? He shifted the gas cans in his hands and realized he couldn't do it. He could torch a vital, aggressive, healthy rakosh without a qualm, because he knew if positions were reversed it would tear off his head in a second and devour his remains. But there didn't seem to be any question that Scar-lip would be history before too long. So what was the use? Why endanger the carny folk unnecessarily with a fire?

Suddenly he heard voices down the midway. He ducked in the other direction, into the shadows.

"I tell you, Hank," said a voice that sounded familiar, "you should've seen the big wimp this afternoon. Something got it riled. It had the crowd six deep around its cage while it was up."

Jack peeked out and recognized the bald-headed roustabout who'd prodded him back behind the rope this afternoon. He had another man with him, taller, younger, but just as beefy, with a full head of sandy hair. He carried a bottle of what looked like bourbon while the bald one carried a six-foot iron bar, sharpened at one end. Neither of them was walking too steadily.

"Maybe we taught it a good lesson last night, huh, Bondy?" said Hank.

"Just lesson number one. The first of many. The first of many."

They stopped before the cage. Bondy took a swig from the bottle and handed it back to Hank.

"Look at it," Bondy said. "The blue wimp. Thinks it can just sit around all day and sleep all night. No way, babe! You got to earn your keep, wimp!" He took the sharp end of the iron bar and jabbed it at the rakosh. "*Earn* it!"

The point pierced Scar-lip's shoulder. The creature, moaned like a cow with laryngitis and rolled away. The bald guy kept jabbing at it, stabbing its back again and again while Hank stood by, grinning.

Jack turned and crept off through the shadows. The two roustabouts had found the only other thing that could harm a rakosh – iron. Fire and iron. The creatures were impervious to everything else. As Jack moved away, he heard Hank's voice rise over the tortured cries of the dying rakosh.

"When's it gonna be my turn, Bondy? Huh? When's my turn?"

The hoarse moans followed Jack out into the night. He stowed the cans back in the trunk, and got as far as opening the door car door. And then he knew he couldn't leave.

"Shit!" he said and pounded the roof of the Vic. "Shit! Shit! *Shit!*"

He slammed the door closed and ran back to the freak show tent, repeating the word all the way.

No stealth this time. He ran directly to the section he'd just left, pulled up the sidewall, and charged inside. Bondy still had the iron pike – or maybe he had it back again. Jack stepped up beside him just as he was preparing for another jab at the trapped, huddled creature. He snatched the pike from his grasp.

"That's enough, asshole."

Bondy looked at him with a wide-eyed, shocked expression, his forehead wrinkling up to and beyond where his hairline should have been. Probably no one had talked to him that way in a long, long time.

"Who the fuck are you?"

"Nobody you want to know right now. Maybe you should call it a night."

Bondy took a swing at Jack's face. He telegraphed it by baring his teeth. Jack raised the rod between his face and the fist. Bondy screamed as his knuckles smashed against the metal, then did a knock-kneed walk in a circle with the hand jammed between his thighs, groaning in pain.

Suddenly a pair of arms wrapped around Jack's torso, trapping him in a fleshy vise.

"I got him, Bondy!" Hank's voice shouted from behind Jack's left ear. "I got him!"

Bondy stopped his dance, looked up, and grinned. As he charged, Jack rammed his head backward, smashing the back of his skull into Hank's nose. Abruptly, he was free. He still held the iron bar, so he angled the blunt end toward Bondy and drove it hard into his solar plexus. The air *whooshed* out of him and he dropped to his knees with a groan, his face gray-green. Even his scalp looked sick.

Jack glanced up and saw Scar-lip crouched at the front of the cage, gripping the bars, its yellow gaze flicking between him and the groaning Bondy, but lingering on Jack, as if it was trying to comprehend what he was doing, and why. Tiny rivulets of dark, almost black blood trailed down its skin.

Jack flipped the pike a hundred and eighty degrees and pressed the point against Bondy's chest.

"What kind of noise am I going to hear when I poke you with *this* end?"

Behind him Hank's voice, very nasal now, started shouting.

"Hey, Rube! Hey, Rube!"

As Jack was trying to figure out just what that meant, he gave Bondy a poke with the pointed end – not enough to break the skin, but enough to scare him. He howled and fell back on the sawdust, screaming.

"Don't! Don't!"

Meanwhile, Hank had kept up his "Hey, Rube!" shouts. As Jack turned to shut him up, he found out what it meant.

The tent was filling with carny folk. Lots of them, all running his way. In seconds he was surrounded. The workers he could handle, but the freaks, gathered in a crowd like this, in the murky light, in various states of dress, were almost terrifying. Jack was struck by the degree and diversity of their deformities. And none of them looked too friendly.

Hank was holding his bloody nose, wagging his finger at Jack.

"Now you're gonna get it! Now you're gonna get it!"

Bondy seemed to have a sudden infusion of courage. He hauled himself to his feet and started toward Jack.

"You goddam sonova–"

Jack rapped the end of the iron bar across the side of his bald head, staggering him. With an angry murmur, the circle of carny folk abruptly tightened. Jack whirled, spinning the pike around him.

"Right," he said. "Who's next?"

QUICK FIXES

He hoped it was a convincing show. He didn't know what else to do at the moment. The circle tightened further, slowly closing in on him like a noose. Jack searched for a weak spot, preparing to make a run for it. As a last resort, there was always the .45 caliber Semmerling strapped to his forearm.

Suddenly a deep voice rose above the angry noise of the crowd.

"Here, here! What's going on now?"

The carny folk quieted immediately, but not before Jack heard a few voices whisper about "the boss" and "Oz." They parted ranks to make way for a tall, ungainly man, six three at least, lank dark hair, sallow complexioned, his pear-shaped body swathed in a huge silk robe embroidered with oriental designs. Although he looked doughy about the middle, the hands that protruded from his sleeves were thin and bony at the wrist. He stopped at the edge of the circle and took in the scene. His expression was slack but his eyes were bright, dark, cold, more alive than the rest of him. Those eyes finally settled on Jack.

"Who are you and what are you doing here?"

"Protecting your property," Jack said, gambling.

"Oh, really?" The smile was sour, almost cruel. "How magnanimous of you." Abruptly his expression darkened. "Do not insult my intelligence, sir! I can call the police or we can deal with this in our own way."

"Fine," Jack said. He threw the pike at the newcomer's feet. "Maybe I had it wrong. Maybe you pay baldy here to poke holes in your attractions."

"Hey, boss–" Bondy began, but the tall man silenced him with a flick of his hand. He looked down at the pike where sawdust clung the dark fluid coating its point, then up at the rakosh with its dozens of oozing wounds. Color began to darken his cheeks as his head turned slowly toward Bondy.

"You harmed this creature, Mr. Bond?"

The bald man quailed under the scrutiny. "We was only trying to get it to put on more of a show for the customers."

"And you feel you can get more out of it by mistreating it?"

"We thought–"

"I know what you thought, Mr. Bond. And many of us know how the Man-Shark felt. We've all known mistreatment during the course of our lives. We don't look kindly upon it. You will retire to your quarters immediately and wait for me there." He gestured to a couple of the freaks – one who looked like an alligator and another who looked like a walking lump of muscle. "See that he gets there and stays there." Then he returned his attention to Jack. "And what is your interest in this matter?"

"I don't like bullies," Jack said. He didn't have to fake any sincerity for that statement.

"No one does. But why should you be interested in this particular creature? Why should you be here at all?"

"Even a rakosh has a right to die in peace."

When he saw the boss freeze, Jack knew immediately that he'd made a mistake. The glittering eyes fixed on him.

"What did you say? What did you call it?"

"Nothing," Jack said.

"No, I heard you. You called it a rakosh." Oz – Jack assumed it was short for Ozymandias – stepped over to the cage and stared into Scar-lip's yellow eyes. "So that's what you are...a rakosh. How fascinating!" He turned to the rest of his employees. "It's all right. You can all go back to bed. I wish to speak to this gentleman before he goes."

"You didn't know what it is?" Jack said as the crowd dispersed.

"Not until this moment," said Oz, continuing to stare at the rakosh. "I thought they were a myth. I found it drifting off Governor's Island last summer. I'd gone out with a group of souvenir-hunters to look for wreckage from the ship that had exploded and burned the night before. I thought the creature was dead, but when I found it was alive, I had it brought ashore. It looked rather vicious so I put it into a spare cage."

"Lucky for you."

The boss smiled. "I should say so. It almost tore the cage apart before it exhausted itself. But since then its health has followed a steady downhill course. We've fed it fish, foul, beef, horse meat, even vegetables – although one look at those teeth and there's no question that it's a carnivore – but no matter what we've tried, it's health continues to fail."

Jack now understood why Scar-lip was dying. Rakoshi required a very specific species of flesh to thrive. And this one wasn't getting it. Jack had no intention of telling the boss what it was.

"You're sure it's a rakosh?"

"Well..." Jack said, trying to sound tentative. "I saw a picture of one in a book once. I...I *think* it looked like this. But I'm not sure. I could be wrong."

"But you're not," the boss said, turning and staring hard into his eyes. "I'm certain you're not." He laughed. "A rakosh! Wonderful! And it's mine!"

Jack glanced at Scar-lip's slouched, wasted form.

Yeah, but not for long.

"You must allow me to reward you for succoring the poor creature, and for identifying it."

"Not necessary. Just let it die in peace, okay?"

"No one will torment it again, I assure you. I *guarantee* it."

"Good enough," Jack said and turned to leave.

"By the way," the boss said. "How can I get in touch with you if I wish?"

"You can't," Jack called back over his shoulder. And then he ducked under the sidewall and was out in the fresh air again.

3

A quiet, rainy day. Too quiet. After finishing the Sunday *Times* and the comics from the *News,* Jack wandered around his apartment, looking for something to do. Business was a little slow this week, so he had no fix-it work to attend to. He'd called Gia but there was nothing happening there. Vicky had a sore throat and Gia wasn't feeling so hot herself.

Swell.

But maybe that was for the best. It had been a day and a half since he'd last seen Scar-lip. He wondered if the rakosh was still alive.

Only one way to find out.

THE LAST RAKOSH

The crowd was thin. Driving through a downpour to the north shore of Long Island and tramping across a muddy field to see a collection of nature's mistakes and missteps was not most folks' idea of a fun Sunday. Not Jack's either. The air trapped in the sideshow midway was rank, redolent of wet hay and sweaty bodies. Most of those bodies seemed to be clustered around the Man-Shark cage.

Watching the rakosh die?

Jack hurried toward the crowd, thinking how some people would stand around and watch anything, but stopped short when he saw what was in the cage.

It was Scar-lip, all right, but the creature he'd seen thirty-six hours ago had been a pale reflection of this monster. The rakosh rearing up in the cage and rattling the bars was full of vitality and ferocity, had unmarred, glistening blue-black skin, and bright yellow eyes that glowed with a fierce inner light. Jack stood mute and numb on the edge of the crowd. This was a nightmare, one that was beginning to repeat itself. The moribund rakosh was now fiercely alive, and it wanted *out!*

Suddenly it froze and Jack saw that it was looking his way, its cold yellow eyes fixed on him.

He turned and hurried from the tent. Outside in the rain he asked everyone he met where he could find the boss. Eventually he wound up outside a sleek, medium-sized Airstream. A plate on the aluminum door read *O. Prather*. He pounded on it.

"Ah!" said Oz as he opened the door and looked down at Jack. "Our friend from the other night. Come in! Have you seen the rakosh? Isn't it magnificent?"

Jack stepped up and inside, just far enough to get out of the rain that drummed on the trailer's roof.

"What did you do to it?"

Oz stared at him, genuinely puzzled.

"Why, my good man, I've cared for it. I looked up the proper care and feeding of rakoshi in one of my books on Bengali mythology, and acted appropriately."

Jack felt a chill. He was sure it wasn't entirely from his soaked clothing.

"What...just *what* did you feed it?"

The boss's large brown eyes were completely guileless, utterly remorseless.

"Oh, this and that. Whatever the text recommended. You don't really believe for an instant that I was going to allow that magnificent creature to languish and die of malnutrition, do you? I assume you're familiar with–"

"I *know* what a rakosh needs to live!"

"Do you now? Do you know everything about rakoshi?"

"No, of course–"

"Then let's assume I know more than you. And I tell you now that there is more than one way to keep them healthy. I see no need to discuss it beyond that. Let's just say that it got exactly what it needed." He stepped closer to Jack and edged him outside. "Good day, sir." He closed the door.

Yeah, Jack knew exactly what it needed. He just wondered who'd supplied the meal.

Jack stood there a moment, realizing that a worst-case scenario had come true. But he still had those two cans of gasoline in his trunk. It was time to go back to plan A.

As he turned, he found Hank standing behind him. His nose was fat and discolored; a couple of dark crescents had formed under each eye. The rain darkened his sandy hair, plastering it to his scalp and running down his face. He stared at Jack, his face a mask of rage.

"It's all your fault!" Hank said.

"You're probably right," Jack said and began walking in the direction of his car. He had no time for this dolt.

"Bondy was my only friend. He got fired because of you."

Jack stopped, turned.

"Really? When did you see him last?"

"Friday morning – when you got him in trouble."

A tiny worm began nibbling at Jack's stomach lining.

"And you never saw him once after that? Not even to say good-bye?"

Hank shook his head. "Uh-uh. The boss kicked him right out. By sun-up he was gone with all his stuff." Hank's expression was miserable. "He was the only one around here who liked me. All the freaks and geeks keep to theirselves."

Jack sighed as he stared at Hank. Well, at least now he knew the source of Scar-lip's dietary supplement.

No big loss to civilization.

"You don't need friends like that, kid," he said and turned away again.

"You'll pay for it!" Hank screamed into the downpour. "Bondy'll be back and when he gets here we'll get even with you. You just wait!"

Don't hold your breath waiting for him.

He wondered if it would do any good to tell him that Bondy hadn't been fired; that, in a way, he was still very much with the freak show. But that would only endanger the big dumb kid.

Hank ranted on. "And if he don't come back, I'll getcha myself. And that Man-Shark too!"

No you won't. Because I'm going to get it first.

Jack kept walking, wondering what he could do to kill the time between now and the early hours of the morning.

4

Jack returned to the Monroe meadows at around 1:30 a.m. He drove across the grass, intending to pull right up to the tent, duck under the flap, splash Scar-lip with gas, light a match, and send it back to hell.

Jack slewed the big Crown Vic to a halt on the muddy meadow and stared in disbelief at the empty space before his headlights. The tent was gone. Only a single trailer remained behind. Jack got out and pounded on the door until an old geezer in over-sized boxer shorts answered.

"What the hell you want?"

"What happened? Where'd they go?"

"You're a little old to be wantin' to run off with the circus, ain't you?"

"Cut the comedy, pal. Where are they?"

"On the road. Makin' the jump to Jersey. They open in Cape May tomorrow night."

QUICK FIXES

Jack ran back to his car. Jersey. A couple of possible routes: south to the Verrazano and across Staten Island, or straight back across Manhattan and the GW Bridge into Jersey. Either way, they'd have to wind up southbound on the Garden State Parkway. Jack chose the latter route. It would place him near the top of the state. If he headed south, sooner or later he'd catch up to them.

The Parkway ground to a halt a few miles north of Atlantic City. Jack glanced at his watch: almost 3:30. No such thing as a traffic jam at this hour. Had to be an accident. A State Trooper roaring by with all lights flashing confirmed it. Jack had a bad feeling about the cause of that accident.

Fighting the crawling in his gut, he turned onto the right shoulder and followed the trooper. The cop stopped behind a train of trucks and trailers arrayed along the side of the road. Jack stopped behind him and ran up as he got out of his cruiser.

"Officer, I'm Dr. Jackson, the vet for the show. Were any of the animals hurt?"

"Right now I don't know anymore than you do, Doc. Let's go see what's going on."

Jack's trooper ran into a fellow fuzz along the way and Jack gleaned from their conversation that one of the trucks carrying the animal cages had gone out of control and skidded off the road. The driver was hurt but all the animals seemed okay.

"I'll just go on ahead and check on them," Jack said. The troopers waved him on.

But Jack didn't get that far. He came upon the boss's Airstream first. He recognized the man's tall, ungainly frame in the glow of the headlights.

"It got loose, didn't it?" Jack said, coming up beside him.

The taller man rotated the upper half of his body and looked at Jack.

"Oh, it's you. You do get around, don't you."

It took most of Jack's dwindling self-control to keep from decking him right then and there.

"You had to feed it, didn't you? Had to bring it up to strength. God damn you, you knew the risk you were taking!"

THE LAST RAKOSH

"It was caged with iron bars. You should know that they're proof against a rakosh. No, there's a human culprit here. The cage was unlocked. The creature got loose and tried to break through the front wall of the truck into the cab. The driver's lucky he's alive."

"Where's the rakosh?"

For the first time Jack detected a trace of fear in Oz's eyes. "I don't know."

"Damn! Where's Hank?"

"Hank? What would you want with that imbecile?" His eyes narrowed. "Unless–"

"You got it."

The boss slammed a bony fist into a palm.

"I thought he'd learned his lesson before. Well, he'll learn it now." He turned and called into the night. "Everyone – find Hank! Find him and bring him to me at once!"

But no one brought Hank. Hank was nowhere to be found.

"He must have run off when the rakosh got free," the boss said.

"Or got carried off."

"There was no blood found anywhere near the truck, so it's quite likely that the young idiot is still alive."

It occurred to Jack that Hank might be stupid enough to chase after the rakosh. If he had, he wouldn't be alive for long.

"We've got to find it," Jack said.

"Nothing I'd like better," said the boss, "although I have a feeling you'd prefer to see it dead."

"You've got that right." Jack looked around in the darkness. "Where are we anyway?"

"Southeast New Jersey, on the edge of the Pine Barrens."

Jack cursed under his breath. The Barrens. Swell. A million or so acres of unsettled land. If the rakosh was loose in there they'd never find it.

"We're not too far from Leeds Point, you know," Oz said, pointing east across the road. "The birthplace of the Jersey Devil."

"Save the history lesson for later," Jack said. "Are you sending out a search party?"

"No. I can't risk the men. Besides, we've got to be set up in Cape May for a show tonight. But maybe tomorrow—"

"Tomorrow will be too late." Jack said, turning away.

"Well, you certainly can't go after a rakosh in the dark."

"I know," Jack said through his teeth.

He headed back toward his car, afraid that if he stayed a minute longer he'd break the man's neck. The traffic was starting to move now, so he drove to Exit 44 and followed the winding back roads through the area. The Parkway seemed to act as a time warp down here. Traveling east he found a nuclear power plant and typically quaint but unquestionably twentieth century towns like Smithville and Leeds Point. West of the Parkway was wilderness — 2,000 square miles of pines, scrub brush, vanished towns, hills, bogs, creeks, all pretty much unchanged in population and level of civilization from the time the Indians had the Americas to themselves. From the Revolutionary days on, it had served as a haven for people who didn't want to be found. Hessians, Tories, smugglers, Lenape Indians, heretical Amish, escaped cons — at one time or another, they'd all sought shelter in the Pine Barrens.

Now a rakosh was loose in the pines. And if Scar-lip got too much of a head start, it would be lost forever.

Jack drove around until he found an all-night 7-11. He bought half a dozen bottles of Snapple, drank one, then emptied the rest onto the side of the road. He put all the empties into a duffel bag in his trunk. When dawn began to lighten the low overhang of clouds that lidded the area, he took 9 north until it intersected the Parkway, then got back on southbound until he came to the site of the accident. He pulled off the shoulder onto the grass just past the truck tire ruts. He took one of the gallon cans of gas and placed it in the duffel bag along with some old rags in the trunk. The bottles clinked within as he headed for the trees. It seemed logical Scar-lip would have traveled directly down the slope and into the trees rather than cross the highway.

Jack looked for a break in the brush — a deer path or the like — and found it. The sand was wet. He saw what looked like deer tracks, and more: the deep imprints of big, alien, three-toed feet, and work-boot prints coming after. Scar-lip, with Hank following

THE LAST RAKOSH

– obviously behind because the boot prints occasionally stepped on the rakosh tracks.

As soon as he was out of sight of the road Jack filled the Snapple bottles with gas and stuffed their mouths with pieces of rag. Then he began following the tracks.

The trail wound this way and that; the scrawny pines closed in around him as he followed the tracks. He'd gone maybe half a mile when the trail changed.

The otherwise smooth sand was kicked up ferociously for a space of about a dozen feet, ending with two large, oblong gouts of blood, drying thick and brown on the sand, with little droplets of the same speckled around them. A cloud of flies hovered over the spot. A twelve-gauge Mossberg pump action lay in the sand. Jack lifted it and sniffed the barrel. Unfired. Not that firing it would have changed the outcome here.

Only one set of prints led away along the trail – the three-toed kind.

Jack crouched, staring around, listening, looking for signs of movement. Nothing. He glanced at the flies partying on Hank's blood, then started again down the trail. His foot slipped on something a few feet further on. The sharpened steel rod Bondy had used to torment the rakosh lay half buried in the sand. He switched the duffel bag to his left hand, picked up the rod, and carried it in his right like a spear. He had two weapons now. He felt like an Indian hunter, armed with an iron spear and a container of magic burning liquid.

Half an hour later, as he was stepping over a fallen log in the center of a small clearing, his foot handed on something soft and yielding. Jack glanced down and saw a very dead Hank staring up at him. He let out an involuntary yelp, then whirled and scanned the area for signs of the rakosh. Nothing stirred. He dropped the iron spear and pulled one of his Molatov cocktails from the bag. He held his butane lighter ready before he chanced a closer look at Hank. Dead blue eyes fixed on the overcast sky; the pallor of his bloodless face accentuated the dark rims of his shiners and blended almost perfectly with the sand under his head; his right arm was missing at the shoulder; flies taxied around the stump.

A noise behind him. Jack whirled. Scar-lip stood at the edge of the clearing, Hank's arm dangling from its three-fingered right hand. The rakosh held it casually, like a lollipop. The upper half of the arm had been stripped of its flesh; pink bone dragged in the sand.

Jack lit the tail on the cocktail and moved to where he could straddle the duffel bag. He pulled out a second bottle and lit it from the first. His heart was turning in overdrive, his lungs pumping to keep up. He knew from past encounters how powerful these creatures were, how quick and agile in spite of their mass. But he also knew that all he had to do was hit it with one of these flaming babies and it would all be over.

With as little warning and as little wind-up as he dared, he tossed the one in his right hand, saw the rakosh duck left, threw the other left-handed to try to catch it on the run. Both missed. The first landed in an explosion of flame, but the second skidded on the sand and lay there intact, its fuse dead, smothered. As the rakosh shied away from the flames, Jack pulled out a third cocktail. He had just lit the fuse when he sensed something hurtling toward him through the air, close. Too close. He ducked but not soon enough. The twirling remnant of Hank's arm hit him square in the face. As he sprawled back, he felt the third cocktail slip from his fingers. He turned and dove and rolled. He was clear when it exploded, but he kept rolling because it had landed on his duffel bag. He was back by Hank's body when the other three went up.

As soon as the initial explosion of flame subsided, Scar-lip charged across the clearing. Jack was still on his back in the sand. Instinct prompted his hand toward the Semmerling but he knew bullets were useless. Instead he reached for the iron spear, swung it around so the butt was in the dirt and the point aimed toward the onrushing rakosh. Jack's mind flashed back to his apartment rooftop last summer when Scar-lip's mother was trying to kill him, when he had run her through. That had only slowed her then, but this was iron. Maybe this time....

He steadied the point and braced for the impact.

The impact came, but not the one he'd expected. In one fluid motion, Scar-lip swerved and batted the spear aside, grabbed the shaft and tossed it into the pines. Jack was left flat on his back with a slavering, three-hundred pound inhuman killing machine towering over him. He tried to roll to his feet but the rakosh caught him with its foot and pinned him to the sand. Jack struggled to slip free but Scar-lip increased the pressure until Jack thought his ribs would cave in. He popped the Semmerling into is hand – useless, but all he had left. And no way was he going out with a fully loaded pistol. As he stopped struggling and readied to fire, the pressure from the foot eased. He lay still and it let up completely, although the foot remained on his chest.

Jack looked up at Scar-lip and met the creature's yellow eyes. It gave one more thrust against his chest with its foot, then backed off a couple of steps.

Slowly, hesitantly, Jack sat up. Was this some sort of game?

But rakoshi didn't play games. They killed and ate and killed again.

Scar-lip backed off another step and pointed down the trail Jack had come.

No. This couldn't be. It was letting him go. Why? Because Jack had stopped Bondy from tormenting it? Not possible. Rakoshi knew nothing about fair play, about debts or gratitude. Those were human emotions and –

Then Jack remembered that Scar-lip was part human. Kusum had been its father. It carried some of Kusum in it.

Jack got to his feet and edged toward the trail, always keeping his face toward the rakosh, unable to quite believe this, afraid that if he turned his back on the creature it would strike. Much as he hated to leave the rakosh alive and free here in the wild, he didn't see that he had much choice. He'd been beaten. The foot on the chest had signaled that. He had no weapons left, and he was certainly no match one on one.

So it was time to go. He took to the trail. One last look over his shoulder before the pines and brush obscured the clearing showed the rakosh standing alone on the sand, surveying its new domain.

Jack got lost on the way out. The trail forked here and there and he couldn't be sure of the sun's position through the cloud cover. His release by Scar-lip had left him bewildered and a little dazed, neither of which had helped his concentration. But the extra hour of walking gave him time to think about his next move. He felt an obligation to let people know that there was something very dangerous prowling the Pine Barrens. He couldn't go public with the story, and who'd believe him anyway?

He heard voices up ahead and hurried toward them. The brush opened up and he found himself facing a worn two-lane blacktop. A couple of Jeep Cherokees were parked on the shoulder. Four men, thirty to forty in age, were busily loading their shotguns, slipping into their day-glo orange vests. Their equipment was expensive, top of the line. Their weapons were Remingtons and Berettas. Gentlemen sportsmen, out for the kill.

Jack asked which way to the Parkway and they pointed off to the left. A guy with a dainty goatee gave him a disdainful up-and-down.

"You could get killed walking through the woods like that, my friend," he said. "It's deer season. Someone might pop you if you aren't wearing colors."

"I'll be sticking to the road from here on," Jack said. He hesitated. He felt he owed these guys a warning. "Maybe you fellows ought to think twice about going in there today."

"Shit," said a skinny one with glasses. "You're not one of those animal rights creeps are you?"

The air suddenly bristled with hostility.

"I'm not any kind of creep, *pal*," Jack said through his teeth and took faint satisfaction in seeing the skinny guy step back and tighten his grip on his shotgun. "I'm just telling you that there's something real mean in there."

"Like what?" said the goatee, grinning. "The Jersey Devil?"

"No. But it's not some defenseless herbivore that's going to lay down and die when you empty a couple of shells at it. You're not the top of the food chain in there, guys."

"We can handle it," said the skinny one.

"Really?" Jack said. "When did you ever hunt something that posed the slightest threat to you? I'm warning you, there's something in there that fights back and I doubt any of your type can handle that."

"What's this?" said the third hunter. "A new tactic? Scare us off with spook stories? It won't work."

The fourth hunter hefted a shiny new Remington over-under.

"The Jersey Devil! I want one! Wouldn't that be some head to hang over the fireplace?"

As they laughed and slapped each other high fives, Jack shrugged and walked away. He'd tried.

Hunting season. He had to smile. Scar-lip's presence in the Pine Barrens gave the term a new twist. He wondered how these mighty hunters would react when they learned that the season was open on *them.*

And he wondered if there was any truth to those old tales of the Jersey Devil. Probably hadn't been a real Jersey Devil before. But there was now.

<Dedicated to Jack's good friend, Phyllis Weinberg>

Introduction to "Home Repairs"

Richard Chizmar had asked me for a crime story for an anthology he was editing called *Cold Blood*. So in May of 1990, a few weeks after finishing "The Last Rakosh," I began work on a Jack story with the working title of "Domestic Problem." I ended up calling it...

Home Repairs

The developer didn't look like Donald Trump.

He was older, for one thing – mid-fifties, at least – and fat and balding to boot. And nowhere near as rich. One of the biggest land developers on Long Island, as he was overly fond of saying. Rich, but not Trump-rich.

And he was sweating. Jack wondered if Donald Trump sweated. The Donald might perspire, but Jack couldn't imagine him sweating.

This guy's name was Oscar Schaffer and he was upset about the meeting place.

"I expected we'd hold this conversation in a more private venue," he said.

Jack watched him pull a white handkerchief from his pocket and blot the moisture from a forehead that went on almost forever. Supposedly Schaffer had started out as a construction worker who'd got into contracting and then had gone on to make a mint in custom homes. Despite occasional words like venue, his speech still carried echoes of the streets. He carried a handkerchief too. Jack couldn't think of anyone he knew who carried a handkerchief – who *owned* a handkerchief.

"This is private," Jack said, glancing at the empty booths and tables around them. "Julio's isn't a breakfast place." Voices drifted over from the bar area on the far side of the six-foot divider topped with dead plants. "Unless you drink your breakfast."

Julio came strutting around the partition carrying a coffee pot. His short, forty-year-old frame was grotesquely muscled under his tight, sleeveless shirt. He was freshly shaven, his mustache trimmed to a line, drafting-pencil thin, his wavy hair was slicked back. He reeked of some new brand of cologne, more cloying than usual.

Jack coughed as the little man refilled his cup and poured one for Schaffer without asking.

"God, Julio. What *is* that?"

"The smell? It's brand new. Called *Midnight*."

"Maybe that's when you're supposed to wear it."

He grinned. "Naw. Chicks love it, man."

Only if they've spent the day in a chicken coop, Jack thought but kept it to himself.

"Is that decaf?" Schaffer asked. "I only drink decaf."

"Don't have any," Julio said as he finished pouring. He strutted back to the bar.

"I can see why the place is deserted," Schaffer said, glancing at Julio's retreating form. "That guy's downright rude."

"It doesn't come naturally to him. He's been practicing lately."

"Yeah? Well somebody ought to see that the owner gets wise to him."

"He is the owner."

"Really?" Schaffer mopped his brow again. "I tell you, if I owned this place, I'd–"

"But you don't. And we're not here to talk about the tavern business. Or are we?"

"No." Schaffer suddenly became fidgety. "I'm not so sure about this anymore."

"It's okay. You can change your mind. No hard feelings."

A certain small percentage of customers who got this far developed cold feet when the moment came to tell Repairman Jack exactly what they wanted him to fix for them. Jack didn't think Schaffer would back out now. He wasn't the type. But he'd probably want to dance a little first.

"You're not exactly what I expected," Schaffer said.

"I never am."

Usually they expected either a glowering Charles Bronson-type character or a real sleazo. And usually someone bigger. No one

HOME REPAIRS

found Jack's wiry medium frame, longish brown hair, and mild brown eyes particularly threatening. It used to depress him.

"But you look like a...yuppie."

Jack glanced down at his dark blue Izod sports shirt, beige slacks, brown loafers, sockless feet.

"We're on the Upper West Side, Mr. Schaffer. Yuppie Rome. And when in Rome..." Schaffer nodded grimly.

"It's my brother-in-law. He's beating up on my sister."

"Seems like there's a lot of that going around."

People rarely sought out Jack for domestic problems, but this wouldn't be the first wife-beater he'd been asked to handle. He thought of Julio's sister. Her husband had been pounding on her. That was how Jack had met Julio. They'd been friends ever since.

"Maybe so. But I never thought it would happen to Ceilia. She's so..."

His voice trailed off.

Jack said nothing. This was the time to keep quiet and listen. This was when he got a real feel for the customer.

"I just don't understand it. Gus seemed like such a good guy when they were dating and engaged. I liked him. An accountant, white collar, good job, clean hands, everything I wanted for Ceil. I helped him get his job. He's done well. But he beats her." Schaffer's lips thinned as they drew back over his teeth. "Dammit, he beats the shit out of her. And you know what's worse? She takes it! She's put up with it for ten years!"

"There are laws," Jack said.

"Right. Sure there are. But you've got to sign a complaint. Ceil won't do that. She defends him, says he's under a lot of pressure and sometimes he just loses control. She says most of the time it's her fault because she gets him mad, and she shouldn't get him mad. Can you *believe* that shit? She came over my place one night, two black eyes, a swollen jaw, red marks around her throat from where he was choking her. I lost it. I charged over their place ready to kill him with my bare hands. He's a big guy, but I'm tough. And I'm sure he's never been in a fight with someone who punches back. When I arrived screaming like a madman, he was ready for me. He had a couple of neighbors there and he was standing inside his front door with a baseball bat. Told me if I tried anything he'd defend himself, then call the cops and press charges for assault and battery. I told him if he came anywhere near my sister again, he wouldn't have an unbroken bone left in his body to dial the phone with!"

"Sounds like he knew you were coming."

"He did! That's the really crazy part! He knew because Ceil had called from my place to warn him! And the next day he sends her roses, says how much he loves her, swears it'll never happen again, and she rushes back to him like he's done her a big favor. Can you beat that?"

"Nothing to keep you from getting a bat of your own and waiting in an alley or a parking lot."

"Don't think I haven't thought of it. But I've already threatened him – in front of witnesses. Anything happens to him, I'll be number one suspect. And I can't get involved in anything like that, in a felony. I mean I've got my own family to consider, my business. I want to leave something for my kids. I do Gus, I'll end up in jail, Gus'll sue me for everything I'm worth, and my wife and kids will wind up in a shelter somewhere while Gus moves into my house. Some legal system!"

Jack waited through a long pause. It was a familiar Catch-22 – one that kept him in business.

Schaffer finally said, "I guess that's where you come in."

Jack took a sip of his coffee"I don't know how I can help you. Busting him up isn't going to change things. It sounds like your sister's got as big a problem as he does."

"She does. I've talked to a couple of doctors about it. It's called co-dependency or something like that. I don't pretend to understand it. I guess the best thing that could happen to Ceil is Gus meeting with some sort of fatal accident."

"You're probably right," Jack said.

Schaffer stared at him. "You mean you'll...?"

Jack shook his head. "No."

"But I thought–"

"Look. Sometimes I make a mistake. If that happens, I like to be able to go back and fix it."

HOME REPAIRS

Schaffer's expression flickered between disappointment and relief, finally settling on relief.

"You know," he said with a small smile, "as much as I'd like Gus dead, I'm glad you said that. I mean, if you'd said okay, I think I'd have set you to it." He shook his head and looked away. "Kind of scary what you can come to."

"She's your sister. Someone's hurting her. You want him stopped but you can't do it yourself. Not hard to understand how you feel."

"Can you help?"

Jack drained his coffee and leaned back. Past the pots of dead brown plants hanging in the smudged front window he could see smartly dressed women wheeling their children, or white-uniformed nannies wheeling other people's children in the bright morning sunlight.

"I don't think so. Domestic stuff is too complicated to begin with, and this situation sounds like it's gone way past complicated into the twilight zone. Not my thing. Not the situation my kind of services can help."

"I know what you're saying. I know they need shrinks – at least Ceil does. Gus...I don't know. I think he's beyond therapy. I got the feeling Gus *likes* beating up on Ceil. Likes it too much to quit, no matter what. But I want to give it a try."

"Doesn't strike me as the type who'll go see a shrink because you or anyone else says so."

"Yeah. But if he was hospitalized..." Schaffer raised his eyebrows, inviting Jack to finish the thought.

Jack was thinking it was a pretty dumb thought as Julio returned with the coffee pot. He refilled Jack's but Schaffer held a hand over his.

"Say," Schaffer said, pointing to all the dead vegetation around the room, "did you ever think of watering your plants?"

"Wha' for?" Julio said. "They're all dead."

The developer's eyes widened. "Oh. Right. Of course." As Julio left, he leaned over the table toward Jack. "Is there some significance to all these dead plants?"

"Nothing religious. It's just that Julio isn't happy with the caliber of his clientele lately."

"Well he's not going to raise it with these dead plants."

"No. You don't understand. He wants to lower it. The yuppies have discovered this place and they've been swarming here. He's been trying to get rid of them. This has always been a working man's bar and eatery. The Beamer crowd is scaring off the old regulars. Julio and his help are rude as hell to them but they just lap it up. He let all the window plants die, and they think it's great. It's driving the poor guy nuts."

"He doesn't seem to mind you."

"We go back a long way."

"Really? How–?"

"Let's get back to your brother-in-law. You really think if he was laid up in a hospital bed for a while, a victim of violence himself, he'd have a burst of insight and ask for help?"

"It's worth a try."

"No, it isn't. Save your money."

"Well, then, if he doesn't see the light, I could clue his doctor in and maybe arrange to have one of the hospital shrinks see him while he's in traction."

"You really think that'll change anything?"

"I don't know. I've got to try something short of killing him."

"And what if those somethings don't work?"

His face went slack, his eyes bleak.

"Then I'll have to find a way to take him out of the picture. Permanently. Even if I have to do it myself."

"I thought you were worried about your family and your business."

"She's my sister, dammit!"

Jack thought about his own sister, the pediatrician. He couldn't imagine anyone beating up on her. At least not more than once. She had a brown belt in karate and didn't take guff from anyone. She'd either kick the crap out of you herself or call their brother, the judge, and submerge you to your lower lip in an endless stream of legal hot water. Or both.

But if she were a different sort, and somebody was beating up on her, repeatedly...

HOME REPAIRS

"All right," Jack said. "I know I'll regret this, but I'll look into it. I'm not promising anything, but I'll see if there's anything I can do."

"Hey, thanks. Thanks a–"

"It's half down and half when I've done the job."

Schaffer paused, his expression troubled.

"But you haven't agreed to take the job yet."

"It might take me weeks to learn what I need to know to make that decision."

"What do you need to know? How about–?"

"We're not practicing the Art of the Deal here. Those are the terms. Take it or leave it."

Jack was hoping he'd leave it. And for a moment it looked as if he might.

"You're asking me to bet on a crapshoot – blindfolded. You hold all the aces."

"You're mixing metaphors, but you've got the picture."

Schaffer sighed. "What the hell." He reached into his breast pocket, then slapped an envelope down on the table. "Okay! Here it is."

Without hiding his reluctance, Jack tucked the envelope inside his shirt without opening it. He removed a notepad and pencil from his hip pocket.

"All right. Let's get down to the who and where."

Jack rubbed his eyes as he sat on the lawn chair and waited for the Castlemans to come home. His third night here and so far he hadn't seen a hint of anything even remotely violent. Or remotely interesting. These were not exciting people. On the plus side, they had no kids, no dog, and their yard was rimmed with trees and high shrubs. Perfect for surveillance.

On Monday, Ceil had come home from teaching fifth grade at the local suburban Long Island elementary school. She entered their two-story, center-hall colonial, turned the TV on, and poured herself a stiff vodka. A thin, mousy, brittle-looking woman whose hair was a few shades too blonde to be anyone's natural color. She watched a soap for an hour, during which she smoked three cigarettes and downed another vodka. Then she started slicing and dicing for dinner. Around five-thirty, Gus Castleman came in from a hard day of accounting at Borland Industries. A big guy, easily six-four, two-fifty; crew-cut red hair, round face, and narrow blue eyes. A bulging gut rode side-saddle on his belt buckle. He peeled off his suit coat and grunted hello to Ceil as he went straight to the fridge. He pulled out two Bud Lights and sat down before Eyewitness News. When dinner was ready he came to the kitchen table and they ate watching the TV. After dinner there was more TV. Gus fell asleep around ten. Ceil woke him up after the 11:00 news and they both went to bed.

Tuesday was the same.

On Wednesday, Ceil came home and had her vodkas in front of *Santa Barbara* but didn't slice and dice. Instead she changed into a dress and drove off. When Gus didn't show up, Jack assumed she was meeting him for dinner. Almost eleven o'clock now and they weren't back yet. Jack hung on and waited.

Waiting. That was always the lousy part. But Jack made a point of being sure about anyone before he did a fix. After all, people lied. Jack lied to most people every day. Schaffer could be lying about Gus, might want him laid up for something that had nothing to do with his sister. Or Ceil might be lying to her brother, might be telling him it was Gus who gave her those bruises when all along it was some guy she'd been seeing on the side. Jack needed to be sure Gus was the bad guy before he made a move on him.

So far Gus was just boring. That didn't rate hospital-level injuries.

At the sound of a car in the driveway, Jack slipped out of the lawn chair and eased into the foundation shrubbery around the garage. The car parked on the driveway. He recognized Gus's voice as they got out of the car.

"...just wish you hadn't said that, Ceil. It made me feel real bad in front of Dave and Nancy."

"But no one took it the way you did," Ceil said.

Jack thought he detected a slight quaver in her voice. Too many vodkas? Or fear?

HOME REPAIRS

"Don't be so sure about that. I think they're just too good-mannered to show it, but I saw the shock in Nancy's eyes. Didn't you see the way she looked at me when you said that?"

"No. I didn't see anything of the sort. You're imagining things again."

"Oh, am I?"

"Y-yes. And besides, I've already apologized a dozen times since we left. What more do you want from me?"

Jack heard the front storm door open.

"What I want, Ceil, is that it not keep happening like it does. Is that too much to ask?"

Ceil's reply was cut off as the door closed behind them. Jack returned to the rear of the house where he could get a view of most of the first floor. Their voices leaked out through an open casement window over the kitchen sink as Gus strode into the kitchen.

"...don't know why you keep doing this to me, Ceil. I try to be good, try to keep calm, but you keep testing me, pushing me to the limit again and again."

Ceil's voice came from the hall, overtly anxious now.

"But I told you, Gus. You're the only one who took it that way."

Jack watched Gus pull an insulated pot-holder mitten over his left hand, then wrap a dish towel around his right.

"Fine, Ceil. If that's what you want to believe, I guess you'll go on believing it. But unfortunately, that won't change what happened tonight."

Ceil came into the kitchen.

"But Gus—"

Her voice choked off as he turned toward her and she saw his hands.

"Why'd you do it, Ceil?"

"Oh, Gus, no! Please! I didn't mean it!"

She turned to run but he caught her upper arm and pulled her toward him.

"You should have kept your mouth shut, Ceil. I try so hard and then you go and get me mad."

He saw Gus take Ceil's wrist in his mittened hand and twist her arm behind her back, twist it up hard and high. She cried out in pain.

"Gus, please don't!"

Jack didn't want to see this, but he had to watch. Had to be sure. Gus pressed her flat chest up against the side of the refrigerator. Her face was toward Jack. There was fear there, terror, dread, but overriding it all was a sort of dull acceptance of the inevitable that reached into Jack's center and twisted.

Gus began ramming his padded fist into Ceil's back, right below the bottom ribs, left side and right, pummeling her kidneys. Her eyes squeezed shut and she grunted in pain with each impact.

"I hate you for making me do this," Gus said.

Sure you do, you son of a bitch.

Jack gripped the window sill and closed his eyes. He heard Ceil's repeated grunts and moans and felt her pain. He'd been kidney punched before. He knew her agony. But this had to end soon. Gus would vent his rage and it would all be over. For the next few days Ceil would have stabbing back pains every time she took a deep breath or coughed, and would urinate bright red blood, but there'd be hardly a mark on her, thanks to the mitten and the towel-wrapped fist.

It *had* to end soon.

But it didn't. Jack looked again and saw that Ceil's knees had gone rubbery but Gus was supporting her with the arm lock, still methodically pummeling her.

Jack growled under his breath. All he'd wanted was to witness enough to confirm Schaffer's story. That done, he'd deal with dear sweet Gus outside the home. Maybe in a dark parking lot while Schaffer made sure he had an air-tight alibi. He hadn't counted on a scene like this, but he'd known it was a possibility. The smart thing to do in this case would be to walk away, but he'd been pretty sure he wouldn't be able to do that. So he'd come prepared.

Jack hurried across the back patio and grabbed his duffel bag. As he moved around to the far side of the house, he pulled out a nylon stocking and a pair of rubber surgical gloves; he slipped

HOME REPAIRS

the first over his head and the second over his fingers. Then he removed a .45 automatic, a pair of wire cutters, and a heavy-duty screwdriver. He stuck the pistol in his belt, then used the cutters on the telephone lead, and the screwdriver to pop the latch on one of the living room windows.

As soon as he was in the darkened room, he looked around for something to break. The first thing to catch his eye was the set of brass fire irons by the brick hearth. He kicked the stand over. The clang and clatter echoed through the house.

Gus's voice floated in from the kitchen.

"What the hell was that?"

When Gus arrived and flipped on the lights, Jack was waiting by the window. He almost smiled at the shock on Gus's face.

"Take it easy, man," Jack said. He knew his face couldn't show much anxiety through the stocking mask so he put it all in his voice. "This is all a mistake."

"Who the hell are you? And what're you doing in my house?"

"Listen, man. I didn't think anybody was home. Let's just forget this ever happened."

Gus bent and snatched the poker from the spilled fire irons. He pointed it at Jack's duffel.

"What's in there? What'd you take?"

"Nothing, man. I just got here. And I'm outta here."

"*OhmyGod!*" Ceil's voice, muffled. She stood at the edge of the living room, both hands over her mouth.

"Call the police, Ceil. But tell them not to hurry. I want to teach this punk a lesson before they get here."

As Ceil limped back toward the kitchen, Gus shook off the mitten and the towel and raised the poker in a two-handed grip. His eyes glittered with anticipation. His tight, hard grin told it all. Pounding on his wife had got him up, but he could go only so far with her. Now he had a prowler at his mercy. He could beat the living shit out of this guy with impunity. In fact, he'd be a hero for doing it. His gaze settled on Jack's head like Babe Ruth eyeing a high-outside pitch.

Talking to a psychiatrist was going to turn this guy into a loving husband. Sure.

QUICK FIXES

He took two quick steps toward Jack and swung. No subtlety, not even a feint. Jack ducked and let it whistle over his head. He could have put a wicked chop into Gus's exposed flank then, but he wasn't ready yet. Gus swung the poker back the other way, lower this time. Jack jumped back and resisted planting a foot in the big man's reddening face. Gus's third swing was vertical, from ceiling to floor. Jack was long gone when it arrived.

Gus's teeth were bared now; his breath hissed through them. His eyes were mad with rage and frustration. Jack decided to goose that rage a little. He grinned.

"You swing like a pussy, man."

With a guttural scream, Gus charged, wielding the poker like a scythe. Jack ducked the first swing, then grabbed the poker and rammed his forearm into Gus's face with a satisfying crunch. Gus staggered back, eyes squeezed shut in agony, holding his nose. Blood began to leak between his fingers.

Never failed. No matter how big you were, a broken nose stopped you cold.

Ceil hobbled back to the threshold. Her voice skirted the edge of hysteria.

"The phone's dead!"

"Don't worry, lady," Jack said. "I didn't come here to hurt nobody. And I won't hurt you. But this guy – he's a different story. He tried to kill me."

As Jack dropped the poker and stepped toward him, Gus's eyes bulged with terror. He put out a bloody hand to fend him off. Jack grabbed the wrist and twisted. Gus wailed as he was turned and forced into an arm lock. Jack shoved him against the wall and began a bare-knuckled work-out against his kidneys, wondering if the big man's brain would make a connection between what he'd been dishing out in the kitchen and what he was receiving in the living room. Jack didn't hold back. He put plenty of body behind the punches, and Gus shouted in pain with each one.

How's it feel, tough guy? Like it?

Jack pounded him until he felt some of his own anger dissipate. He was about to let him go and move into the next stage of his plan when he caught a hint of motion behind him. As he turned his head he had a glimpse of Ceil. She had the poker, and she was swinging it toward his head. He started to duck but too late. The room exploded into bright lights, then went dark gray.

An instant of blackness and then Jack found himself on the floor, pain exploding in his gut. He focused above him and saw Gus readying another kick at his midsection. He rolled away toward the corner. Something heavy thunked on the carpet as he moved.

"Christ, he's got a gun!" Gus shouted.

Jack had risen to a crouch by then. He searched for the fallen .45 but Gus was ahead of him, snatching it from the floor before Jack could reach it. Gus stepped back, worked the slide to chamber a round, and pointed the pistol at Jack's face.

"Stay right where you are, you bastard! Don't you move a muscle!"

Jack sat back on the floor in the corner and stared up at the big man.

"All right!" Gus said with a bloody grin. "All *right!*"

"I got him for you, didn't I, Gus?" Ceil said, still holding the poker. She was bent forward in pain. That swing had cost her. "I got him off you. I saved you, didn't I?"

"Shut up, Ceil."

"But he was hurting you. I made him stop. I–"

"I said *shut up!*"

Her lower lip trembled. "I...I thought you'd be glad."

"Why should I be glad? If you hadn't got me so mad tonight I might've noticed he was here when we came in. Then he wouldn't have took me by surprise." He pointed to his swelling nose. "This is your fault, Ceil."

Ceil's shoulders slumped; she stared dully at the floor.

Jack didn't know what to make of Ceil. He'd interrupted a brutal beating at the hands of her husband, yet she'd come to her husband's aid. And valiantly, at that. The gutsy little scrapper who'd wielded that poker seemed miles away from the cowed, beaten creature standing in the middle of the room.

I don't get it.

Which was why he had a policy of refusing home repairs. Except this time.

"I'll go over to the Ferrises'," she said.

"What for?"

"To call the police."

"Hold on a minute."

"Why?"

Jack glanced at Gus and saw how his eyes were flicking back and forth between Ceil and him.

"Because I'm thinking, that's why!"

"Yeah," Jack said. "I can smell the wood burning."

"Hey!" Gus stepped toward Jack and raised the pistol as if to club him. "Another word out of you and–"

"You don't really want to get that close to me, do you?" Jack said softly.

Gus stepped back.

"Gus, I've got to call the police!" Ceil said as she replaced the poker by the fireplace, far out of Jack's reach.

"You're not going anywhere," Gus said. "Get over here."

Ceil meekly moved to his side.

"Not here!" he said, grabbing her shoulder and shoving her toward Jack. "Over there!"

She cried with the pain in her back as she stumbled forward.

"Gus! What are you doing?"

Jack decided to play the game. He grabbed Ceil and turned her around. She struggled but he held her between Gus and himself.

Gus laughed. "You'd better think of something else, fella. That skinny little broad won't protect you from a forty-five."

"Gus!"

"Shut *up!* God, I'm sick of your voice! I'm sick of your face, I'm sick of – God, I'm sick of everything about you!" Under his hands, Jack could feel Ceil jerk with the impact of the words as if they were blows from a fist. A fist probably would have hurt less.

"But – but Gus, I thought you loved me."

He sneered. "Are you kidding? I hate you, Ceil! It drives me up a wall just to be in the same room with you! Why the hell do you think I beat the shit out of you every chance I get? It's all I can do to keep myself from killing you!"

HOME REPAIRS

"But all those times you said—"

"Lies, Ceil. Nothing but lies. And you're such a pathetic wimp you fell for them every time."

"But why?" She was sobbing now. "*Why?*"

"Why not dump you and find a real woman? One who's got tits and can have kids? The answer should be pretty clear: your brother. He got me into Borland 'cause he's one of their biggest customers. And if you and me go kaput, he'll see that I'm out of there before the ink's dry on our divorce papers. I've put too many years into that job to blow it because of a sack of shit like you."

Ceil almost seemed to shrivel under Jack's hands. He glared at Gus.

"Big man."

"Yeah. I'm the big man. I've got the gun. And I want to thank you for it, fella, whoever you are. Because it's going to solve all my problems."

"What? My gun?"

"Yep. I've got a shitload of insurance on my dear wife here. I bought loads of term on her years ago and kept praying she'd have an accident. I was never so stupid as to try and set her up for something fatal – I know what happened to that Marshall guy in Jersey – but I figured, what the hell, with all the road fatalities around here, the odds of collecting on old Ceil were better than Lotto."

"Oh, Gus," she sobbed. An utterly miserable sound.

Her head had sunk until her chin touched her chest. She would have fan-folded to the floor if Jack hadn't been holding her up. He knew this was killing her, but he wanted her to hear it. Maybe it was the alarm she needed to wake her up.

Gus mimicked her. "'Oh, Gus!' Do you have any idea how many rainy nights you got my hopes up when were late coming home from your card group? How I prayed – actually *prayed* – that you'd skidded off the road and wrapped your car around a utility pole, or that a big semi had run a light and plowed you under? Do you have any *idea?* But no. You'd come bouncing in as carefree as you please, and I'd be so disappointed I'd almost cry. That was when I really wanted to wring your scrawny neck!"

"That's about enough, don't you think?" Jack said.

Gus sighed. "Yeah. I guess it is. But at least all those premiums weren't wasted. Tonight I collect."

Ceil's head lifted.

"What?"

"That's right. An armed robber broke in. During the struggle, I managed to get the gun away from him but he pulled you between us as I fired. You took the first bullet – right in the heart. In a berserk rage, I emptied the rest of the clip into his head. Such a tragedy." He raised the pistol and sighted it on Ceil's chest. "Good-bye, my dear sweet wife."

The metallic click of the hammer was barely audible over Ceil's wail of terror.

Her voice cut off as both she and Gus stared at the pistol.

"That could have been a dud," Jack said. "Man, I *hate* when that happens." He pointed to the top of the pistol. "Pull that slide back to chamber a fresh round."

Gus stared at him a second, then worked the slide. An unspent round popped out.

"There you go," Jack said. "Now, give it another shot, if you'll pardon the expression."

He pointed the muzzle at Ceil again, and Jack detected a definite tremor in the barrel now. Gus pulled the trigger but this time there was no scream from Ceil. She only flinched at the sound of the hammer falling on another dud.

"Aw, man!" Jack said, drawing out the word into a whine. "You think you're buying good ammo and someone rips you off! You can't trust anybody these days!"

Gus quickly worked the slide and pulled the trigger again. Jack allowed two more misfires, then he stepped around Ceil and approached Gus.

Frantically Gus worked the slide and pulled the trigger again, aiming for Jack's face. Another impotent click. He began backing away when he saw Jack's smile.

"That's my dummy pistol, Gus. Actually, a genuine government-issue Mark IV, but the bullets are dummy – just like the guy I let get hold of it."

HOME REPAIRS

Jack brought it along when he wanted to see what somebody was really made of. It rarely failed to draw the worst to the surface.

He bent and picked up the ejected rounds. He held one up for Gus to see.

"The slug is real," Jack said, "but there's no powder in the shell. It's an old rule: Never let an asshole near a loaded gun."

Gus charged, swinging the .45 at Jack's head. Jack caught his wrist and twisted the weapon free of his grasp. Then he slammed it hard against the side of Gus's face, opening a gash. Gus tried to turn and run but Jack still had his arm. He hit him again, on the back of the head this time. Gus sagged to his knees and Jack put a lot of upper body behind the pistol as he brought it down once more on the top of his head. Gus stiffened, then toppled face first onto the floor.

Only seconds had passed. Jack spun to check on Ceil's whereabouts. She wasn't going to catch him twice. But no worry. She was right where he'd left her, standing in the corner, eyes closed, tears leaking out between the lids. Poor woman.

Nothing Jack wanted more than to be out of this crazy house. He'd been here too long already, but he had to finish this job now, get it done and over with.

He took Ceil's arm and gently led her from the living room.

"Nothing personal, lady, but I've got to put you in a safe place, okay? Someplace where you can't get near a fire poker. Understand?"

"He didn't love me," she said to no one in particular. "He stayed with me because of his job. He was lying all those times he said he loved me."

"I guess he was."

"Lying..."

He guided her to a closet in the hall and stood her inside among the winter coats.

"I'm just going to leave you here for a few minutes, okay?"

She was staring straight ahead. "All those years... lying..."

Jack closed her in the closet and wedged a ladderback chair between the door and the wall on the other side of the hall. No way she could get out until he removed the chair. Back in the living room, Gus was still out cold. Jack turned him over and tied his wrists to opposite ends of the coffee table. He took two four-by-four wooden blocks from his duffel and placed them under Gus's left lower leg, one just below the knee and the other just above the ankle. Then he removed a short-handled five-pound iron maul from the duffel. He hesitated as he lifted the hammer, then recalled Ceil's eyes as Gus methodically battered her kidneys – the pain, the resignation, the despair. Jack broke Gus's left shin with one sharp blow. Gus groaned and writhed on the floor, but didn't regain consciousness. Jack repeated the process on the right leg. Then he packed up all his gear and returned to the hall.

He pulled the chair from where it was wedged against the closet door. He opened the door a crack.

"I'm leaving now, lady. When I'm gone you can go across the street and call the police. Better call an ambulance too."

A single sob answered him.

Jack left by the back door. It felt good to get the stocking off his head.

―――

When Jack dialed his answering machine the next morning there was only one message. It was from Oscar Schaffer. He sounded out of breath. And upset.

"You bastard! You sick, perverted bastard! I'm dropping the rest of your money off at that bar this morning and then I don't want to see or hear or even think of you again!"

Jack was on his second coffee in Julio's when he spotted Schaffer through the front window. He was moving fast, no doubt as close to a run as his portly frame would allow, clutching a white envelope in his hand. Perspiration gleamed on his pale forehead. His expression was strained. He looked like one frightened man.

Jack had told Julio he was coming so Julio intercepted him at the door as he did all Jack's customers. But instead of leading him back to the Jack's table, Julio returned alone. Jack spotted Schaffer hurrying back the way he had come.

Julio smiled as he handed Jack the envelope.

"What you do to spook him like that?"

HOME REPAIRS

Jack grabbed the envelope and hurried after Schaffer. He caught the developer as he was opening the door to a dark green Jaguar XJ-12.

"What's going on?" Jack said.

Schaffer jumped at the sound of Jack's voice. His already white face went two shades paler.

"Get away from me!"

He jumped into the car but Jack caught the door before he could slam it. He pulled the keys from Schaffer's trembling fingers.

"I think we'd better talk. Unlock the doors."

Jack went around to the other side and slipped into the passenger seat. He tossed the keys back to Schaffer.

"All right. What's going on? The job's done. The guy's fixed. You didn't need an alibi because it was done by a prowler. What's the problem?"

Schaffer stared straight ahead through the windshield.

"How *could* you? I was so impressed with you the other day. The rogue with a code: 'Sometimes I make a mistake. If that happens, I like to be able to go back and fix it.' I really thought you were something else. I actually envied you. I never dreamed you could do what you did. Gus was a rotten son of a bitch, but you didn't have to..." His voice trailed off.

Jack was baffled.

"You were the one who wanted him killed. I only broke his legs."

Schaffer turned to him, the fear in his eyes giving way to fury.

"Don't give me that shit! Who do you think you're dealing with? I practically built that town! I've got connections!" He pulled a sheaf of papers from his pocket and threw it at Jack. "I've read the medical examiner's report!"

"Medical examiner? He's dead?" *Shit!* Jack had heard of people with broken legs throwing a clot to the heart. "How?"

"Aw, don't play cute! Gus was a scumbag and yes I wanted him dead, but I didn't want him tortured! I didn't want him... *mutilated!*"

It was time for Jack's fingers to do a little trembling as he scanned the report. It described a man who'd been pistol-whipped, bound by the hands, and had both tibias broken; then he'd been castrated with a Ginsu knife from his own kitchen and gagged with his testicles in his mouth. After that he'd undergone at least two hours of torture before he died of shock due to blood loss from a severed artery in his neck.

"It'll be in all the afternoon papers," Schaffer was saying. "You can add the clippings to your collection. I'm sure you've got a big one"

"Where was Ceil supposed to be during all this?"

"Locked in the hall closet. She got out after you left. And she had to find Gus like that. No one should have to see something like that. If I could make you pay—"

"When did she phone the cops?"

"Right before calling me – around three a.m."

Jack shook his head. "Wow. Three hours...she spent three hours on him."

"'She'? Who?"

"Ceil."

"What the hell are you talking about?"

"Gus was trussed up and out cold with two broken legs but very much alive on the living room floor when I left. I opened the door to the closet where I'd put your sister, and took off. That was around midnight."

"No. You're lying. You're saying Ceil–" He swallowed. "She wouldn't. She couldn't. Besides, she called me at three, from a neighbor's house, she'd only gotten free–"

"Three hours. Three hours between the time I opened the closet door and the time she called you."

"No! Not Ceil! She..." Schaffer stared at Jack, and Jack met his gaze evenly. Slowly, like a dark stain seeping through heavy fabric, the truth took hold in his eyes. "Oh...my...God!"

He leaned back in the seat and closed his eyes. He looked like he was going to be sick. Jack gave him a few minutes. "The other day you said she needed help. Now she really needs it."

"Poor Ceil!"

"Yeah. I don't pretend to understand it, but I guess she was willing to put up with anything from a man who said he loved her.

HOME REPAIRS

But when she found out he didn't – and believe me, he let her know in no uncertain terms before he pulled the trigger on her."

"Trigger? What–?"

"A long story. Ceil can tell you about it. But I guess when she found out how much he hated her, how he'd wanted her dead all these years, when she saw him ready to murder her, something must have snapped inside. When she came out of the closet and found him helpless on the living room floor, she must have gone a little crazy."

"A *little* crazy? You call what she did a *little* crazy?"

Jack shrugged. He handed back the ME's report and opened the car door.

"Your sister crammed ten years of pay-back into three hours. She's going to need a lot of help to recover from those ten years. *And* those three hours."

Schaffer pounded his mahogany steering wheel.

"Shit! It wasn't supposed to turn out like this!" Then he sighed and turned to Jack. "But I guess things don't always go according to plan in your business."

"Hardly ever."

Jack got out of the car, closed the door, and listened to the Jag roar to life. As it screeched away, he headed back to Julio's. A new customer was due at noon.

Introduction to "The Long Way Home"

Toward the end of May, 1990, Joe Lansdale called, looking for a story for *Dark at Heart*, an anthology he was editing with his wife Karen. He wanted it *dark* but without any supernatural. I suggested a New York mean-streets story starring Jack. He loved the idea. "The Long Way Home" was the result. I started it in late May but due to a crowded plate, didn't finish it until the end of July.

Fifteen years later my agent contacted me about Amazon Shorts, a new feature at Amazon.com that would allow readers to download a short story for a nominal fee. Could I write something for them?

What was on my plate at the time: The tenth Jack novel, an RJ short story for ITW's *Thriller*, scripting five issues of *The Keep* graphic miniseries, adapting four short stories for *Doomed*, revising the text and writing a foreword to the Infrapress edition of *Wheels Within Wheels*, revising *Reprisal* for Borderlands Press, revising *The Tery* and "The Last Rakosh" for Overlook Connection Press.

No, I couldn't do a short story.

But I did have a long-lost Repairman Jack piece called "The Long Way Home" from Joe and Karen's four-hundred-copy anthology that hadn't been seen since 1992. I showed them that.

On the morning of May 11, Amazon, adamant about no previously published material, rejected it. By afternoon they'd reversed themselves. I was told that Jeff Bezos himself had said to screw the technicality in this case.

QUICK FIXES

So I revised the story to bring it into the twenty-first century and sent it in. Amazon Shorts launched in August. "The Long Way Home" became the second most downloaded piece (and the #1 fiction download) during the program's first eighteen months.

The Long Way Home

1

Jack saw the whole thing. Another minute's delay in leaving for home and he'd have been a block away when it went down. And then a different man would have died on the pavement.

But Julio had held him up, detailing his current bitch about all the yuppies chasing out his tavern's regular customers. He was especially irate about one who'd offered to buy the place.

"You believe that?" Julio was saying. "He wanna turn it into a bistro, meng. A *bistro!*"

An incomprehensible stream of Puerto Rican followed. Which meant Julio was royally pissed. He was proud of his command of English and only under extreme provocation did he revert to his native tongue.

"He was only asking. What's wrong with that?"

"Because he offer me a lot of money, meng. I mean a *lot* of money."

"How much?"

Julio whispered it in Jack's ear.

Right: A *lot* of money.

"I repeat: What's wrong with that? You should be proud."

"I don' know 'bout proud, but I was tempted to take it."

"No!" Jack said, genuinely shaken. "Don't say that, Julio. Don't even think it."

"I couldn't help it. But I tol' him to get lost. I mean, I like money much as the next guy, meng, but I only risk so much for it." He jerked a thumb over his shoulder at the motley collection of scruffy locals leaning on the bar behind him. "You know what those guys do to me if I sol' out to a yuppie? Have to run for my life."

"You may still have to if Maria finds out how much you turned down."

"Don' tell her. Don' breathe a word, Jack."

"Your secret's safe with me."

Jack left with his cold six-pack of Rolling Rock long necks and turned the corner onto Amsterdam Avenue, heading downtown. Quiet on the Upper West Side tonight. A lot of the restaurants were closed on Mondays and it was too cold for a casual stroll. Jack had the street pretty much to himself.

Gentrification had slowed in these parts – mainly because everything had been pretty well gentrified – and was seeping into Harlem and even Morningside Heights. This neighborhood, once ethnically and socioeconomically mixed, had homogenized into an all-white, upper-income enclave; neighborhood taverns had metamorphosed into brasseries and bistros, mom-and-pop grocery stores and bodegas into gourmet delis, sidewalk cafés, overpriced boutiques and shoppes – always spelled with the extra "-*pe.*" Rents had taken up residency in *Mir*'s old orbit.

At the next corner Jack spotted a blue-and-white parked by the fire hydrant in front of Costin's. His first instinct was to turn and walk the other way, but that might draw attention.

He checked himself out in his mental mirror: average-length brown hair, NY Jets warm up jacket over a flannel shirt, worn jeans over dirty white sneakers. Just an average Joe. Virtually invisible.

So he stayed on course.

Waiting on the curb for a car to pass, he did a quick scan of the scene. Quiet. Only one cop in the unit, in the passenger seat, looking relaxed. His partner was stepping into Costin's. The light filtering through the open door revealed a very young-looking cop. Baby-faced. Probably picking up some donut-shaped teething biscuits.

Costin's had been there forever – a Paleolithic prototype of the convenience store. Now it was one of the last mom-and-pops in the area. Old Costin had to stay open all hours just to meet the rent. The locals left over from the old days remained loyal, and most of the cops from the Two-oh stopped in regularly to help keep them going.

Jack was halfway across the street when he heard a boom. He knew that sound. Shotgun. Instinctively he ducked behind the nearest parked car on the far side. The sound had been muffled. An indoor shot.

Shit. Costin's.

He set the six-pack down and peeked over the hood. The cop was out of the unit's passenger seat now and on the sidewalk, drawing his pistol. Just then the door to Costin's burst open and a giant leapt onto the top step. He stood six-six at least and looked completely bald under the flat black leather cap squeezed onto the top of his head; the loose sweatsuit he wore only emphasized his massive, bulked-up frame. He was snarling, his shiny black features contorted in rage. He held a sawed-off ten-gauge pump-action against his hip, aimed down at the cop.

In the clear air, lit by the mercury vapor lamps lining the block, the scene had an unreal look, like something out of a movie.

The cop raised his pistol, giving warning, going by the book.

"Drop it or I'll–"

He never got to finish the sentence. The big guy barely blinked as he pulled the trigger.

The left side of the cop's face and neck exploded red. His pistol flew from his hand as he was spun to his left to land face down on the hood of the unit. He left a wet, red smear as he slid across the hood. He rolled over the grille and landed on the asphalt in front of the bumper, flat on his back, twitching.

The big black guy's face changed as soon as the cop went down. The snarl melted into a smile, but the rage remained, hiding behind the teeth he showed. Casually laying the shotgun across his shoulder, he approached the cop like a gardener strolling toward a cabbage patch with his hoe.

"Well, Mr. Man in Blue," he said, standing over the moaning cop. "How's it feel to bleed?"

The cop couldn't speak. Even from down the street Jack could see the blood pumping from his neck. Another sixty seconds and he'd be history.

QUICK FIXES

Jack found himself on the move before he knew it, his sneakers whispering along the pavement as he raced down the sidewalk in a crouch, watching the scene through the windows of the parked cars he kept between himself and the other side of the street.

A voice inside urged him the other way. Cops were the enemy, a threat to his own existence.

This isn't your fight – butt out.

But another, deeper part of him overruled the voice and made him pull the Semmerling from his ankle holster. Still in a crouch, he started across the street.

"You know," the big black was saying, "I could let you bleed some more and make a bigger puddle, and pretty soon you'd be just as dead as if I blowed your head off." He grinned as he worked the pump on the sawed-off. A red-and-brass cartridge arced into the street. "But somehow that wouldn't be the same."

He leveled the truncated barrel into the cop's face.

"Forget it," Jack said as he came up behind him. He had the Semmerling pointed at the back of the guy's head. "You've done enough for one night."

The guy glanced over his shoulder. When his eyes lit on the Semmerling, he smiled.

"Ain't never been threatened with a pop gun before."

"Just drop the hog and take off."

"You mean you ain't gonna arrest me?"

Jack had acted on impulse. At the moment, the best course seemed to be get rid of the shooter and call an ambulance for the cop. Then disappear.

"One more time. Drop it and go."

The guy's voice jumped. "You kiddin' me, man? I could take a couple from that pop gun and sit down for breakfast."

"It's a Semmerling LM-4," Jack said. "World's smallest forty-five."

The gunman paused.

"Oh. Well, in that case–"

The guy ducked to his right as he made a hard swing with the shotgun, trying to bring it to bear on Jack. Jack corrected his aim and pulled the trigger. The Semmerling boomed and bucked in his hand. The gunman's right eye socket became a black hole and his leather cap spun away like a Frisbee. Red mist haloed his head as it jerked back with enough force to yank his feet off the pavement. The sawed-off tumbled from his hand and skittered along the sidewalk as he sprawled back on the sidewalk and flopped around until his body got the message that what little remained of the brain was mush. Then he lay still.

Jack knelt beside the fallen cop. He looked like hell. The mercury light further blanched the deathly pallor of his face. Eyes glazing, going fast. Where the hell was old man Costin? Where was the cop's partner? Why wasn't anyone around to call an ambulance? Jack felt naked and exposed out here on the street, but he couldn't take off now.

He switched the Semmerling to his left hand, located the spot in the fallen cop's throat that was doing the most pumping, and jammed his thumb into it. The flesh was wet and hot and sticky. He'd read novel after novel that mentioned the coppery smell of blood. He didn't get it. He'd never known copper to have an odor worth mentioning, and if it did, it sure as hell didn't smell like this.

Jack was about to look around again for help when he heard footsteps behind him.

"All right! Hold it right there, you fucker!"

Jack turned his head and saw a uniformed cop crouched on his right, taking two-handed aim at his head with a Glock. Another blue-and-white blocked the street behind him.

Jack's gut looped into a knot and pulled tight.

"I'm holding it."

"Drop the gun and put your hands up!"

Jack dropped the Semmerling and raised his left hand.

"C'mon!" The cop said. "Both of them!"

"This guy's already half dead," Jack said. "If I take my hand off this pumper, he'll go the rest of the way in no time."

"Christ!" the cop said, then shouted: "Gerry – you make the call?"

"Ambulance and back-up on the way," said a voice from the unit.

"All right. See who's down."

Another uniform dashed out of the darkness behind the first cop and stopped within half a dozen feet of Jack. He squinted at the ruined face above Jack's hand.

"Oh, Jeez, it's Carella!"

"Shit!" said the first cop. He spoke through clenched teeth as he glared at Jack. "You dirty–"

"Hey-hey!" Jack said. "Let's get something straight here. I didn't shoot your pal."

"Just shut the fuck up! You think I'm stupid?"

Jack bit back an affirmative and jerked his head toward the guy on the sidewalk.

"He did it."

Apparently the cop hadn't seen the other body until now. He jumped to his feet.

"Oh, great. Just great."

The second cop, the one called Gerry, eased around to the sidewalk and checked out the body.

"This one's cooling," he said. "Head wound." He whistled. "Looks like a hot load."

"And I suppose you had nothing to do with that, either?" the first cop said.

"No. Him I did. But there was another cop. He went into Costin's. I heard a shot, and then this guy–"

"Jeez!" Gerry said. "The kid was with Carella!"

"See if he's all right!" the first cop said.

Gerry dashed up the stairs and grabbed the door handle. As he pulled it open, a voice screamed from within.

"Stay back! I got your buddy and the owner in here! Stay back or I'll kill 'em both!"

Gerry scuttled back down the steps.

"We got a hostage situation here, Fred."

"He's got the kid!" Fred said. "God *damn!* Call the hostage team. *Now!*"

As Gerry ran off, an emergency rig howled down the street and screeched to a halt. Jack explained to the EMTs what had happened and why he had his thumb sunk an inch into the wounded man's neck. One of the techs pulled on a rubber glove and substituted his finger for Jack's. He held it there as the wounded cop was lifted onto a stretcher.

Jack watched for a second, then began to edge backward, preparing to slide between two parked cars.

"No, you don't!" Fred the cop said, jerking his pistol up level with Jack's head. "You ain't goin' nowhere! Hands on the car and spread 'em!"

Desperation gnawed on Jack's spine as his eyes hunted for an escape route. The street crawled with uniforms, and they all seemed to be watching him. Slowly he forced his lead-filled limbs to move, slapping his hands against the hood of the patrol car, spreading his feet. He held up okay during the frisk, but he almost lost it when his hands were yanked behind his back and the cuffs squeezed around his wrists.

Cops, arrest, cuffs, interrogation, investigation, fingerprinting, exposure, court, lawyers, judges, jail – a recurrent nightmare for most of his adult life.

Tonight it was real.

2

"You sure you don't want a lawyer?"

Jack looked up at the 20th Precinct's chief of detectives, Lieutenant Thomas Carruthers. Fortyish, wearing a rumpled suit and no tie – a thrown-on set of clothes. Tall, dark, and handsome. Every woman's crystal ball dream. Jack's nightmare.

"Yeah. I'm sure."

"Say it again. I want to make sure I've got it on the tape."

Jack directed his voice toward the tape recorder sitting on the battered oak table between him and Carruthers.

"I'm sure I don't want a lawyer. At least not yet."

Jack did want a lawyer. Very badly. But he didn't know any, at least any he could trust. And the first thing a lawyer would tell him was to keep his mouth shut. He didn't want to do that. These cops thought he'd shot one of their own. Things could get nasty here at the precinct house if he clammed.

A nightmare. Booked, photographed, and worst of all, fingerprinted. He'd wanted to throw an epileptic fit when they'd coated his fingers in ink and began rolling the tips on that white card. But what would that do other than delay the inevitable?

With or without a lawyer he was screwed. If they didn't get him for killing the cop, and if he wasn't prosecuted for killing the guy with the shotgun, he'd still be up for possession of an unregistered firearm. Plus his cover would be permanently blown. Years of hiding in the cracks, of forging an existence in the interstices of society would be wiped away. And then the IRS would get involved, wondering why this man had no Social Security number. They'd begin investigating every nook and cranny of his entire 1040-less life.

And then the shit would really hit the fan.

Jack knew he was facing time. Hard time, soft time, state time, Fed time, it didn't matter. He was going inside, no doubt for a long stretch.

Jack had sworn he'd never do time. And he wouldn't.

"Good." Carruthers spread a selection of Jack's IDs on the table between them. "Maybe now you can tell me what's all this bullshit?"

Jack stared at the contents of his wallet and felt the walls of the interrogation room close in. He said nothing.

"So who the hell are you?"

"The name's Jack."

"I gathered that." He picked up the ID cards and shuffled through them. "Jack Berger, Jack Callahan, Jack Menella, Jack Jones" – Carruthers glanced up at him on that one – "and Jack Schwartz. So yeah, I guess your first name is Jack. But what's the rest?"

"Jack will have to do, I'm afraid."

Carruthers shot forward, leaning over the table, eyes ablaze.

"It won't do at *all*, scumbag! One of our guys is in surgery fighting for his life and another's a hostage and you're up to your neck in it. So Jack ain't gonna cut it!"

Jack didn't flinch; gave back a glare of his own.

"If I hadn't come by, Mr. Detective, your guy in surgery never would've made it *to* surgery. You'd still be scraping his brains off the street. But maybe I should've kept walking. If I had I wouldn't be cuffed up here looking at you. Would you be happier if I'd done that? I know I would."

Carruthers stared at Jack. For an instant, he seemed unsure of himself. As he opened his mouth to reply, another detective, a sergeant named Evans who'd been through a couple of times before, popped into the room again.

Evans had brought Jack into the interrogation room, and had been none too gentle getting him seated. A big guy – his jacket sleeves were tight – and Jack had no doubt that if it had been up to Evans he'd take Jack out in the nearest alley and kick him to death. Slowly.

But the cold light was gone from Evans' eyes as he glanced Jack's way on entering.

Carruthers stiffened at the sight of him.

"What's up, Charlie? Any news?"

Evans shook his head. "Not really. Nothing bad, anyway. No more shots. The hostage team's made phone contact. They're trying to talk the guy down. Sounds really wired. Don't worry, Tom. They'll get him out."

Carruthers nodded absently. "Yeah. How's Carella?"

"Still in surgery as far as I know. Piacentino called from the One-eight. Says if there's anything you need–"

"Tell him we're okay, but thanks for asking." After a pause, Carruthers said, "That it?"

"Nope. Got an ID on the dead guy. A prelim from the M.E. too."

"So who is he?"

"You mean who *was* he. Abdul Khambatta, born Harvey Andrews. Out of Attica two months after a stretch for armed robbery. His sheet's as long as my leg. One bad-news mother."

"What's the M.E. say?"

"No surprises. Single head shot. A pre-frag in the eye."

Carruthers winced. "Ouch."

"Yeah. M.E. said if the guy ever had any brains, you couldn't prove it by him. Matches up with the three rounds left in our mystery man's pop gun."

Carruthers glanced at Jack. "Which isn't registered, of course."

"You got it."

"How do we know the Semmerling belongs to him?"

"His prints are the only ones on it."

"And the sawed-off?"

"Andrews'. 'Scuse me – Khambatta's. Thing's lousy with his prints." He jerked a thumb at Jack. "I think we owe this guy."

"Yeah? Maybe."

Jack watched for some sign of relaxation from Carruthers but saw nothing. The lieutenant stayed wound tight as ever.

Carruthers said, "You ever meet anybody with five IDs who was straight, Charlie? If he's not dirty on this he's dirty on something else."

"So?" Evans did not seem impressed.

"I want to know: Who *is* this guy?"

"Tell you one thing, Tom: His prints aren't on file anywhere. And I mean *anywhere*."

"How come I'm not surprised?"

"I got a better question," Evans said. "How come you're here and not over at Costin's?"

Carruthers walked to the window and stared out at the night, saying nothing.

"I'll take over at this end," Evans said. "You should be there."

Carruthers shook his head, still staring out the window.

"I'll go nuts over there. The hostage team knows what to do. I'll just get in the way, maybe even screw things up."

"No you won't. Why don't–"

"Thanks, Charlie." He turned and flashed him a tight smile. "I appreciate the thought, but let's drop it. Okay?"

Evans shrugged. "Okay. But if you change your mind…"

Carruthers nodded. "Yeah. I know."

When Evans was gone, Carruthers returned to the table, standing as he shifted through Jack's IDs again.

"Prefragmented rounds? What's the matter? You got something against wounding a guy?"

Jack said nothing. Truth was, he'd been loaded for indoor work. And in general, he didn't like to have to shoot someone twice.

Suddenly Carruthers stiffened.

"I'll be damned!" He picked up the IDs and flipped through them again. "Christ! It all fits!"

As Carruthers stared down at him, eyes wide, Jack felt his chest tighten, wondering what he'd found.

"Jesus! I always thought you were make believe. For years I've been catching a word here and there about this urban mercenary who hires out for all sorts of jobs, anything from kinda shady to out and out, down and dirty illegal. But when I ask about it, I get blank stares, dumb grins, and shrugs. So I figure it's one of those urban myths, like the giant alligators in the sewers. But shit! You're him! You're that repairman guy!" He looked at the IDs. "Yeah – all Jacks. You're Repairman Jack."

Jack's throat went dry, giving his voice a croaky sound.

"Who's he?"

"Don't play cute. You're him. Gotta be. Jesus, I don't believe this. I never thought you were real." He looked down at the pile of phony IDs in his hand. "And I guess you aren't. At least not officially, huh?"

"I don't know what you're talking about."

"Yeah. Right. You know, if memory serves, some of the stuff I heard about you was pretty good, some of it wasn't. And what wasn't came from scumbags. But all of it sounded pretty rough. So I take it you're a rough character, Repairman Jack. Speaking of which, why would anyone trust a guy who calls himself Repairman Jack?"

"Maybe it wasn't his idea. Maybe someone called him that and it stuck."

"Yeah, maybe. Sounds to me like a guy with a Robin Hood complex or something."

"And who are you?" Jack said. "The Sheriff of Nottingham?"

While Carruthers mulled that, Jack pulled inside himself and fought the sick dread growing in his gut. This nightmare was deteriorating into a hell ride. He had to get out of here.

Jack considered that. If he could get close enough to Carruthers, even handcuffed, he might be able to do something. Anything. A crazy thought, but he was as good as dead if he stayed in custody, so he didn't see how anything he tried could make matters worse.

"Yeah, well, whatever," Carruthers was saying. He had that worried, distracted look again. "What are we going to do with you, Repairman Jack?"

"How about letting me go?"

Carruthers offered him a small, pursed-lips smile. "Right."

"I did one of yours a favor, so now you do me a favor. Quid pro quo."

Jack knew his request was useless, but he wanted to keep Carruthers talking, get him relaxed, maybe a bit careless.

"Don't bullshit me, pal. The only one who says you helped Carella is you. How do I know you and Andrews and whoever's still holed up in Costin's weren't together on this job?"

"Forget it," Jack said, genuinely insulted. "Boosting a mom-and-pop?"

"Why not? Maybe business is slow. You operate on their level, Mr. Repairman. You're an unknown quantity. You're capable of anything as far as I'm concerned. So maybe Andrews did shoot Carella and maybe you two had a falling out over who was gonna get his service revolver, or who was going to finish him off. So you shot Andrews."

"Sure. And then I tried to finish off your friend by clamping down on that artery in his neck." Jack lifted his cuffed wrists and wiggled the fingers of his right hand. "Here. Take a look. I've still got his blood under my fingernails."

Carruthers stared at Jack's hand but didn't move.

"Come on," Jack said. *Get close... real close.* "See for yourself."

Carruthers shook his head. "Maybe you knew you were about to get caught and were just putting on a show."

Jack dropped his hands. "You're all heart."

Carruthers scowled. "Even if I wanted to let you go – which I don't – it's out of the question."

THE LONG WAY HOME

"We're not just talking about me losing my *way* of life here," Jack said. "We're talking about my *life*. Put me in the spotlight and I'm a dead man. I've made a lot of enemies over the years. I can handle them fine by myself out on the street, but put me in the joint and every slimeball and two-bit wise guy with a grudge who's got a friend inside will be gunning for me. All for helping out a cop."

Evans barged in the door then, grinning.

"Carella's out of surgery! Gonna be okay!"

Carruthers leaned back and closed his eyes. "Thank God!"

"And you know what he says? Some citizen saved his life – blew away the guy who was gonna off him."

The big sergeant looked at Jack and winked.

After a protracted pause, Carruthers opened his eyes, rose from the chair, and went to the window to do his staring routine.

"Our suspect here thinks we should let him go and forget he was ever in custody."

"What suspect?" Evans said, looking around the room. "I don't see no suspect. I don't remember booking anybody tonight. Do you?"

Another long pause, with Jack holding his breath the whole time.

"Check the files," Carruthers said without turning. "See if there's any unaccounted-for paperwork or property out there, and bring it in."

"You got it."

Evans gave Jack a thumbs-up as he left the room.

Jack sat quietly, watching Carruthers' back. He said nothing, fearing to break the spell of unreality that had taken control of the room.

Evans returned in no time with a brown folder and a manila envelope.

"Here it is."

Carruthers joined him at the table. "All of it?"

"Personal property, print cards, booking sheets, photos, and miscellaneous paperwork referring to some suspect I've never heard of."

QUICK FIXES

"Unlock him."

As Evans keyed the cuffs open, Carruthers scooped up Jack's array of ID and dropped it in the envelope. He slid the folder and envelope across the table to Jack.

"Sergeant Evans will take you out the back."

Jack's legs went Wrigley as he stood. He could barely speak.

"I don't–"

"Damn right, you don't," Carruthers said, looking him in the eyes. "You don't know me and I don't know you. And you don't *owe* me and I don't owe you. This is it. We're even. I don't want to see or hear of you again. And if I do see you and you're so much as jaywalking, I'll pull you in. We clear on that?"

"Yeah. And thanks."

"No, thanks, dammit! Just evening up. You didn't have to do what you did but you did; I don't have to do what I'm doing, but I am. Like you said: Quid pro quo. This for that. Now get out of my sight."

Jack got. He followed Evans out to the back of the precinct house.

"Not easy for him to do this," Evans said along the way. "He's a real straight arrow."

"So I gather."

Jack understood what Carruthers was going through in overcoming a career's worth of conditioning, and he appreciated it. He stopped at the back door and faced Evans.

"He thinks we're even but we're not. I owe him. I'll give you a number. If there's ever anything I can do for him–"

"Too bad you can't get his kid brother out of Costin's."

The shock pushed Jack back a step into the alley.

"The hostage cop is Carruthers' brother?"

"Yeah. Patrolman Louis Carruthers. Twenty-two years old. Got any miracles in your pocket?"

Jack remembered something Julio had showed him in the basement of his tavern.

"You never know."

He turned and hurried toward the street.

THE LONG WAY HOME

3

Downstairs, ten feet below the bar, past the cases of booze and kegs of beer, an old hutch stood against the wall. The glass was long gone, and a thick layer of dust hid the scars in the warped mahogany veneer.

Jack coughed and grunted as he and Julio slid it away from the wall.

"See?" Julio said, pointing to the rectangular opening in the brick. "It din go nowhere."

Costin's backed up against Julio's. Years ago Jack had asked if there was an emergency escape route from the tavern – besides the back door. Julio had brought him down here and shown him the old airshaft that ran up from his basement.

"Refresh me on this. Where does it go?"

Julio handed him the flashlight and smiled.

"Up. After that, I don' know. Never wanted to find out. You gonna be the first guy in there since I bought the place."

Jack poked his head and shoulders into the shaft and shone the flash upward. Crumbling brickwork, cobwebs, and an inky blackness that devoured the beam of light. The basement of Costin's was only a few feet away. Maybe the shaft could get him there.

"If this is an airshaft," Jack said, "how come I don't feel any airflow?"

"Because 'bout fifty years ago, somebody covered the buildings with a single roof. Probably a dead end. You wasting you time, meng. 'Sides, it's not like you to get involved in this kinda thing."

"I owe somebody a try."

Jack tied a string around the neck of the flashlight, looped the rest of the length around his neck, and let the light dangle over his sternum where the beam splashed up over his face. A miner's lamp hat would have been better but this would have to do. He pulled on a pair of heavy work gloves.

"Hang around, okay? In case I get stuck."

Julio seated himself on some cases of Yeungling Lager.

"Don' worry. I be right here."

QUICK FIXES

Jack took a deep breath, let it all out, then squeezed through the opening. He hated tight places. Especially *dark* tight places. He straightened inside the rectangular shaft. The crumbling brick surface was rough and craggy. He braced his hands against the wall along the wide axis of the shaft, dug the side of a sneaker into one of the countless little crevices, and began to climb.

A long climb. A three-story struggle, with a long, maiming impact lurking below, hungering for a slip. And above – the very real possibility of finding the upper end of the shaft sealed.

But it wasn't. Jack reached the top and found a two-foot gap between the roof and the last of the bricks. Directly to his right, mated side by side to this one, stood another shaft. Hopefully leading to Costin's.

Jack slid over the top of one and into the other. He had a bad moment when his sneakers began to slip, but he dangled by his hands until his feet found purchase. Then he began the long descent, dragging his denimed butt against the brickwork as an extra brake. The trip down was quicker. He was glad he'd thought of the gloves. Without them his hands would have been raw meat by now.

When he reached bottom he stood perfectly still and let his ears adjust.

Quiet.

He swept the flashlight around and checked out the base of the shaft. The opening was at knee level and blocked with a smooth brown surface. Jack nudged it with his foot and it gave easily. Cardboard.

With the flashlight off, he knelt and inched back the stack of cartons that formed the barrier. He peeked into the basement: empty, cavelike darkness. He listened again. Someone upstairs in the store was talking – shouting – in a high-pitched voice. Even through the floor Jack could feel the hysterical edge on that voice. Only one voice. Probably Khambatta's partner talking on the phone to the hostage team.

Jack squeezed through the opening and stood. From this angle he could make out a faint sliver of light high up and off to his right. Had to be a doorway. He pulled the flashlight free of the string and flicked it on and off, just long enough to find a clear path through the piles of stock. Straight across the floor lay a set of steps. Jack drew the Semmerling and slid through the dark.

As he neared the other end he flicked the flash on and off again. And froze.

Someone on the steps to the door.

Jack waited, listening for movement, for breathing. Nothing. Just an occasional squeak of the floorboards above. And something else. Whoever was up there had stopped talking and was making another sound. Jack cocked an ear toward the ceiling. It sounded almost like... sobbing.

But who was on the stairs?

Jack turned on the flashlight and trained it straight ahead. A man lay sprawled, head down, one arm flung out, the other under him, legs splayed, eyes wide, staring. Very still. And wet. The front of his uniform glistened a deeper blue where a thick, dark fluid had soaked through it. His throat was a ruin and half of his lower jaw had been torn away. But deathly white and upside down though it was, enough of the face was left undamaged for Jack to catch the resemblance to Lieutenant Carruthers.

"The kid." Louis.

"Son of a bitch!"

Another throat shot. Same style as Khambatta's: Aim high in case the cop was wearing a vest.

Jack slipped the Semmerling into his pocket and stretched a hand toward Louis's forehead. No question that he was dead, but Jack needed to touch him. To be absolutely sure.

The skin felt dry and thick and cold. "The kid" was very dead.

Cold black anger surged. Twenty-something years old, stopping by Costin's for a late-night snack, and getting blown away.

"Son of a *bitch!*"

Jack straightened and turned off the flashlight.

What next? He'd come here as a payback, to see if he could get Carruthers' brother out of this jam. But the kid was beyond help. So there was nothing left for him to do.

Except maybe settle a score on the lieutenant's behalf.

But old man Costin was upstairs somewhere. Jack had known Costin since moving to the city. He didn't like to think of the old guy held hostage, maybe face down on the floor, shivering with terror. But he could back away from that. He didn't owe Costin – not enough to risk exposure by making a move on the remaining gunman. Better all around to leave old Costin's fate in the hands of the hostage team.

Time to fade away. Time to head back to the air shaft.

But he didn't move.

Just then the door above slammed open and a wide shaft of fluorescent light pinned him like a frog on a log. A high male voice began screeching at him.

"Hold it, muthafucka! Hold it or I'll blow you away just like I did him!"

Jack turned slowly and saw a wide silhouette in the doorway. He showed his flashlight and his empty right hand.

"I'm not armed."

Jack was glad he'd brought only the tiny Semmerling. It lay flat in his pocket.

"Yeah, right. An' I'm Fiddy Cent. You a cop, fucka. An' you was tryin' to sneak up on me."

"I'm no cop. And I was just leaving."

"The fuck you was. There ain't no door down here. I checked already."

"If you say so." Jack waved his empty hand. "Bye!"

Jack dove into the darkness to his right, rolled to his feet, and ducked behind a stack of canned goods. As a stream of curses erupted from the stairwell, he pulled out the Semmerling and crept toward the rear. Behind him he heard some fumbling against the wall, then a click and the cellar lights lit up – a few dim, widely spaced naked incandescent bulbs set among the ceiling beams. Jack got his first look at the guy as he rushed down the steps, nearly tripping over his feet in his haste.

He had a buzz-cut head and he was fat. No more than five-eight, but at least three-hundred pounds. Baby-faced with huge cheeks and tiny dark eyes barely visible above them. His skin was black as a bible and glistened with sweat. *Fat.* Not brawny fat, not hard fat. Jell-O fat that lurched and rolled around his middle as he moved. The sawed-off shotgun he carried looked like a toy in his pudgy fingers.

"Ain't no use in hiding, fucka. Ain't no way outta here."

Then how'd I get in? Jack thought, wondering when that notion would strike Fatso.

He stayed low, listening as the guy moved through the dimly lit cellar like a bull, knocking over stacks of cans, smashing cases of bottles. The odor of gherkins began to filter through the air. Jack wondered how long it would take Fatso to find the opening.

From the rear of the cellar: "Shee-*it*!"

He'd found it.

And then as Jack crouched and waited, he heard a frantic scratching, scrabbling sound, like Fred Astaire on speed doing a softshoe to Motorhead. Coming from the airshaft entry. Jack crawled over to investigate.

Fatso was there. He had his head and one shoulder rammed into the airshaft opening and was trying to squeeze the rest of his body through. He grunted and groaned as his Pumas scraped madly on the dusty floor in a desperate effort to force his way in. But it wasn't happening. He was a bowling ball trying to drop into a billiard pocket. No way.

Finally, he gave up. Panting, gasping, retching with the exertion, he pulled himself free and slumped to the floor where he cradled his sawed-off shotgun in his lap and began to cry.

Jack was standing over him by now, but for a moment or so he could only stare and listen to the guy sob. Pitiful. He'd wanted to pop the guy. But now...

When he'd heard all he could stand, he raised the Semmerling.

"Okay, Fatso. Cut the blubbering and get up – *without* the shotgun."

Fatso started and looked up at Jack, at the Semmerling, and got to his feet. But the shotgun still hung from his hand.

"I said drop the sawed-off or you're dead."

"Go 'head," he said, sniffling but still clutching the stock grip. "Good as dead already."

"For blowing away a cop – yeah, I guess you are."

"Didn't kill no cop." He was sulky now.

"That's not what you told me a couple of minutes ago. And by the way, how's old man Costin – the owner? He okay?"

Fatso nodded. "Locked him in the crapper."

"At least *somebody's* still alive."

"Ain't never killed nobody! That was Abdul. He done the cop. Didn't have to, neither. Had the drop on the guy but he just pulled the trigger and liked to took his head off."

That jibed with Jack's take on young Carruthers' neck wound. He tasted his saliva turning bitter.

"Swell. He was only twenty-two. A little younger than you, I figure."

"I didn't do it, man!"

"Doesn't matter who pulled the trigger. You're a part of a felony where a killing's gone down. Automatic murder-one for you."

"I knew you was a cop."

"Already told you – not a cop. Don't have to be a cop to know you're heading for a major jolt in the joint."

His fat lips quivered. "Already done that."

He lifted the shotgun and Jack ducked to his right, his finger tightening on the Semmerling's trigger. But the sawed-off barrel kept on rising till the bore was snug against the underside of Fatso's chin.

Jack cringed, waiting for the boom and brain splatter.

It never came. A sob burst through Fatso's lips as he dropped the weapon back to his side and slumped to the floor again.

"I can't *do* it!" he screeched through clenched teeth.

Jack, speechless before this utterly miserable creature, said nothing.

"Can't hack the joint again, man," Fatso moaned. "I *can't!*"

"What'd you go in for?"

"Got a dime for dealin'. Out early."

"What's your name?"

"Henry. Henry Thompson. They call me Fat Henry."

Can't imagine why," Jack thought

"The joint – is that where you met Khambatta?"

Fat Henry nodded again. "He on the back end of three-to-five when I got in. We became... friends."

"You two don't seem to be each other's type."

"He protected me."

Jack nodded. He got the picture.

"I see."

"No, man. You don't see," Fat Henry said, his voice rising. "You don't see *shit!* You don't know what it was like in there! I was *tail* meat! Guys'd be lined up in the shower to get at me! I wanted to *die!*"

"And Khambatta saved you."

Fat Henry let out a tremulous sigh. "Yeah. Sort of. He took me in. Protected me."

"Made you his property so he could have you all to himself."

"I ain't like that, man! I just did what I hadda to get through it! Don't you dump on me if you ain't been there!"

Jack only shook his head. He didn't know how many things were worth dying over, but he was pretty sure that was one of them. And he didn't know what to make of Fat Henry. He was one pathetic son of a bitch, but he wasn't a killer. He was going to be treated as one, though – a cop killer.

"So how come you're still with Khambatta?"

"I ain't. He ain't like that, either – least not outside. We got out about the same time and he call me last week 'bout picking up some quick cheese."

"Swell. What you picked up instead was another trip to Attica."

"No way I'm goin' back inside! I'm getting outta here."

"How?"

"Gettin' a car from the cops."

"You sure about that? What've you told them about their dead pal?"

"Nothin'. Told 'em he's safe and sound but I'll shoot him dead they make a move on me."

"You really think they're going to let you have a car without talking to their man, without making sure he's all right?"

"Yeah. Sure." Fat Henry's voice faltered. "They gotta. Don't they?"

Jack shook his head, slowly, deliberately. "Switch places: Would *you* let you have a car?"

"I ain't goin' back." Tears began to stream down his face. "I'll off myself first!"

"You already tried that."

Fat Henry glared at him. Again he lifted the shotgun. Jack thought he was going to put it under his jaw again; instead he offered it to Jack.

"Here. You do it."

Jack took the weapon and sniffed the bore. It hadn't been fired tonight. He was almost tempted to aim it at Fat Henry's face to see how serious he was about this, but decided against it. Instead, he worked the pump, sending red-and-brass cylinders tumbling through the gloom one after another until they lay scattered on the floor like party favors. He tossed the empty shotgun back to Fat Henry. Hard.

"Do your own dirty work."

"You fucker!"

Thoroughly fed up, Jack stepped over him toward the airshaft opening.

"And I'm not hanging around listening to you blubber."

"I need help, dog." He was whining now.

"No argument there. But there's only one person here who can help you and he's sitting on the floor whining."

"Fuck you!"

Jack had one leg through the opening. He turned and jabbed a finger at Fat Henry.

"You're the one who's fucked, Fatso. Look at your life! What've you ever done with it? You got busted dealing – crack, right? You let yourself be the shower-room bimbo until some tough guy came along and made you his private tool. You went along on this armed robbery bullshit, and now somebody's dead and you're bawling because it's time to pay the piper. You make me sick."

Another whine. "But what can I *do*?"

"First of all, you can get off your ass and onto your feet."

Fat Henry rolled over and struggled to his feet.

THE LONG WAY HOME

"Good," Jack said. "That's a start. Now you've got to go upstairs and face the music."

He stepped back, a caged animal look in his eyes. "Uh-uh."

"Either they take you up there, or they come down those stairs, step over the body of their buddy, and take you here."

"Told you! I can't go back to the joint!"

"You've got to stand up, Henry Thompson. For once in your life you've got to stand up."

"But I *can't!*"

Jack stared him down in the silence that followed.

"Then sit here all night and play with yourself until somebody else makes the choice for you. That seems to be the story of your life, Henry."

Fat Henry looked toward the steps up to the first floor. He stood like a statue, staring.

"I can choose," he said in a soft, far-away voice. "I can choose. I'll show you I can choose."

"Sure you can, Henry."

Jack left him like that.

4

A little while later Jack stood in the street, on the fringe of the crowd around Costin's. He wanted to tell the vultures to go home, that it was going to be a *long* night. He was about to leave for home himself when Fat Henry came out.

Costin's front door slammed open and there he was, all three-hundred pounds of him, brandishing his shotgun and screaming like a wild man. He got off one blast that looked like it was aimed at the moon. All around Jack the crowd screamed and dove for cover, leaving him standing alone as the two-dozen cops out front opened up.

The fusillade slammed Fat Henry back against the doorframe, his sawed-off went spinning, and then he was turning and falling and rolling down the steps. It was over in seconds. No Peckinpah slo-mo. No ballet-like turns. Quick, graceless, ugly, and red. He hit the sidewalk face first and never moved again.

Fat Henry Thompson had finally stood up. And he'd got his wish: He wouldn't be going back to Attica.

Jack turned and walked away, stepping over the prone onlookers as they peeked between their fingers and made horrified noises. As he headed home he tried to put his finger on the feelings massed in his chest like a softball-sized lump of putty – *cold* putty. Not sadness, certainly not glee or satisfaction. More a bleakness. A dark despair for all the hardcore losers in this city, the ones it created and the others it attracted.

He passed a corner litter basket and gave it a hard kick, adding an especially deep dent to its already bruised flanks.

A waste. A damn stupid fruitless futile ass-brained waste.

When he got to his door he realized he didn't have his beer. The six-pack he'd gone out for earlier in the evening was long gone from where he'd left it sitting on the curb. He could really have used a Rock about now. And he could probably find an all-night deli where he could buy some.

Nah.

Jack stepped inside and locked the door behind him.

He couldn't risk it. The way things were going tonight, he might not make it home again.

Introduction to "The Wringer"

In August of 1991, Ed Gorman called requesting a story for the third *Stalkers* anthology. I don't know where I came up with "The Wringer" or its sick villain. The anthology was titled *Night Screams* and wasn't published until 1996(!) The story was never reprinted and I loved its cat-and-mouse dynamic too much to let it molder forever in an out-of-print paperback, so in 2010 I worked it into *Fatal Error*.

The Wringer

1

Munir stood on the curb, unzipped his fly, and tugged his penis free. He felt it shrivel in his hand at the cool caress of the breeze, as if shrinking from the sight of all these passing strangers.

At least he hoped they were strangers.

Please let no one who knows me pass by. Or, Allah forbid, a policeman.

He stretched his flabby, reluctant member and urged his bladder to empty. He'd drunk two quarts of Gatorade in the past two hours to be sure that it would be full to bursting, but he couldn't go. His sphincters were clamped as tightly shut as his jaw.

Off to his left the light at the corner where 45th Street met Broadway turned red and the traffic slowed to a stop. A woman in a cab glanced at him through her window and started when she saw how he was exposing himself to her. Her lips tightened and she shook her head in disgust as she turned away. He could almost read her mind: A guy in a suit exposing himself on a Sunday afternoon in the theater district – New York's going to Hell even faster than they say it is.

But it has *become* hell for me, Munir thought.

He closed his eyes to shut out the bright marquees and the line of cars idling before him, tried to block out the tapping, scuffing footsteps of the pedestrians on the sidewalk behind him as they hurried to the matinees, but a child's voice broke through. "Look, Mommy. What's that man–?"

"Don't look, honey," said a woman's voice. "It's just someone who's sick."

Tears were a pressure behind Munir's sealed eyelids. He bit back a sob of humiliation and tried to imagine himself in a private place, in his own bathroom, standing over the toilet. He forced himself to relax, and soon it came. As the warm liquid streamed out of him, the waiting sob burst free, propelled equally by shame and relief.

He did not have to shut off the flow. When he opened his eyes and saw the glistening puddle before him on the asphalt, saw the drivers and passengers and passers-by staring, the stream dried up on its own.

I hope that is enough, he thought. Please let that be enough.

Averting his eyes, Munir zipped up and fled down the sidewalk, all but tripping over his own feet as he ran.

2

The phone was ringing when Munir got to his apartment. He hit the RECORD button on his answering machine as he snatched up the receiver and jammed it against his ear.

"Yes!"

Pretty disappointing, Mooo-neeer," said the now familiar electronically distorted voice. *"Are all you Ay-rabs such mosquito dicks?"*

"I did as you asked! Just as you asked!"

"That wasn't much of a pee, Mooo-neeer."

"It was all I could do! Please let them go now."

He glanced down at the caller ID. A number had formed in the LCD window. A 212 area code, just like all the previous calls. But the seven digits following were a new combination, unlike any of the others. And when Munir called it back, he was sure it would be a public phone. Just like all the others.

"Are they all right? Let me speak to my wife."

Munir didn't know why he said that. He knew the caller couldn't drag Barbara and Robby to a pay phone.

"She can't come to the phone right now. She's, uh... all tied up at the moment."

Munir ground his teeth as the horse laugh brayed through the phone.

"Please. I must know if she's all right."

THE WRINGER

"*You'll have to take my word for it, Mooo-neeer.*"

"She may be dead." *Allah forbid!* "You may have killed her and Robby already."

"*Hey. Ain't I been sendin' you pichers? Don't you like my pretty pichers?*"

"No!" Munir cried, fighting a wave of nausea. Those pictures — those horrible, sickening photos. "They aren't enough. You could have taken all of them at once and then killed them."

The voice on the other end lowered to a sinister, nasty, growling tone.

"*You callin' me a liar, you lousy, greasy, two-bit Ay-rab? Don't you ever doubt a word I tell you. Don't even think about doubtin' me. Or I'll show you who's alive. I'll prove your white bitch and mongrel brat are alive by sending you a new piece of them every so often. A little bit of each, every day, by Express Mail, so it's nice and fresh. You keep on doubtin' me, Mooo-neeer, and pretty soon you'll get your wife and kid back, all of them. But you'll have to figure out which part goes where. Like the model kits say: Some assembly required.*"

Munir bit back a scream as the caller brayed again.

"No-no. Please don't hurt them anymore. I'll do anything you want. What do you want me to do?"

"*There. That's more like it. I'll let your little faux pas pass this time. A lot more generous than you'd ever be — ain't that right, Mooo-neeer. And sure as shit more generous than your Ay-rab buddies were when they killed my brother.*"

"Yes. Yes, whatever you say. What else do you want me to do? Just tell me."

"*I ain't decided yet, Mooo-neeer. I'm gonna have to think on that one. But in the meantime, I'm gonna look kindly on you and bestow your request. Yessir, I'm gonna send you proof positive that your wife and kid are still alive.*"

Munir's stomach plummeted. "No! Please! I believe you! I believe!"

"*I reckon you do, Mooo-neeer. But believin' just ain't enough sometimes, is it? I mean, you believe in Allah, don't you? Don't you?*"

"Yes. Yes, of course I believe in Allah."

QUICK FIXES

"And look at what you did on Friday. Just think back and meditate on what you did."

Munir hung his head in shame and said nothing.

"So you can see where I'm comin' from when I say believin' ain't enough. Cause if you believe, you can also have doubt. And I don't want you havin' no doubts, Mooo-neeer. I don't want you havin' the slightest twinge *of doubt about how important it is for you to do exactly what I tell you to. 'Cause if you start thinking it really doesn't matter to your bitch and little rat-faced kid, that they're probably dead already and you can tell me to shove it, that's not gonna be good for them. So I'm gonna have to prove to you just how alive and well they are."*

"No!" He was going to be sick. "Please don't!"

"Just remember. You asked for proof."

Munir's voice edged toward a scream. "PLEASE!"

The line clicked and went dead.

Munir dropped the phone and buried his face in his hands. The caller was mad, crazy, brutally insane, and for some reason he hated Munir with a depth and breadth Munir found incomprehensible and profoundly horrifying. Whoever he was, he seemed capable of anything, and he had Munir's wife and child hidden away somewhere in the city.

The helplessness overwhelmed Munir and he began to sob. He had allowed only a few to escape when he heard a pounding on his door.

"Hey. What's going on in there? Munir, you okay?"

Munir stiffened as he recognized his neighbor's voice. He straightened in his chair but said nothing. Charlie lived in the apartment next door. A retired city worker who had taken a shine to Barbara and Robby. A harmless busybody, Barbara called him. He couldn't let Charlie know anything was wrong.

"Hey!" Charlie said, banging on the door again. "I know someone's in there. You don't open up I'm gonna assume something's wrong and call the emergency squad. Don't make a fool out of me."

The last thing Munir needed was a bunch of EMTs swarming around his apartment. The police would be with them and who

THE WRINGER

knew what the crazy man who held Barbara and Robby would do if he saw them. He cleared his throat.

"I'm all right, Charlie."

"The hell you are," Charlie said, rattling the doorknob. "You didn't sound all right a moment ago when you screamed and you don't sound all right now. Just open up so I can–"

The door swung open, revealing Charlie Akers – fat, balding, a cigar butt in his mouth, the Sunday comics in his hand, dressed in wrinkled blue pants, a T-shirt, and suspenders – looking as shocked as Munir felt.

In his haste to answer the phone, Munir had forgotten to latch the door behind him. Quickly, he wiped his eyes and rose to close it.

"Jesus, Munir," Charlie said. "You look like hell. What's the matter?"

"Nothing, Charlie."

"Hey, don't shit me. I heard you. Sounded like someone was stepping on your soul. Anything I can do?"

"I'm okay. Really."

"Yeah, right. You in trouble? You need money? Maybe I can help."

Munir was touched by the offer. He hardly knew Charlie. If only he *could* help. But no one could help him.

"No. Nothing like that."

"Is it Barbara and the kid? I ain't seen them around for a few days. Something happen to–?" Munir realized it must have shown on his face. Charlie stepped inside and closed the door behind him. "Hey, what's going on? Are they all right?"

"Please, Charlie. I can't talk about it. And you mustn't talk about it either. Just let it be. I'm handling it."

"Is it a police thing? I got friends down the precinct house–"

"No! *Not* the police! Please don't say anything to the police. I was warned" – in sickeningly graphic detail–"about going to the police."

Charlie leaned back against the door and stared at him.

"Jesus… is this as bad as I think it is?"

Munir could do no more than nod.

QUICK FIXES

Charlie jabbed a finger at him. "Wait here."

He ducked out the door and was back in less than two minutes with a slip of paper in his hand.

"My brother gave me this a couple of years ago. Said if I was ever in a really bad spot and there was no one left to turn to, I should call this guy."

"No one can help me."

"My brother says this guy's good people, but he said make sure it was my last resort because it was gonna cost me. And he said make sure the cops weren't involved because this guy don't like cops."

No police... Munir reached for the slip of paper. And money? What did money matter where Barbara and Robby were concerned?

A telephone number was written on the slip. And below it, two words: *Repairman Jack*.

3

I'm running out of space, Jack thought as he stood in the front room of his apartment and looked for an empty spot to display his latest treasure.

His Sky King Magni-Glow Writing Ring had just arrived from his connection in southeast Missouri. It contained a Mysterious Glo-signaler (*"Gives a strange green light! You can send blinker signals with it!"*). The plastic ruby unfolded into three sections, revealing a Secret Compartment that contained a Flying Crown Brand (*"For sealing messages!"*); the middle section was a Detecto-Scope Magnifying Glass (*"For detecting fingerprints or decoding messages!"*); and the outermost section was a Secret Stratospheric Pen (*"Writes at any altitude, or under water, in red ink!"*).

Neat. Incredibly neat. The neatest ring in Jack's collection. Far more complex than his Buck Rogers Ring of Saturn, or his Shadow ring, or even his Kix Atomic Bomb Ring. It deserved auspicious display. But where? His front room was already jammed with neat stuff. Radio premiums, cereal give-aways, comic strip tie-ins – crassly commercial junk from a time before he was born.

THE WRINGER

Why did he collect them? After years of accumulating his hoard, Jack still hadn't found the answer. So he kept buying. And buying.

Old goodies and oddities littered every flat surface on the mismatched array of Victorian golden oak furniture crowding the room. Certificates proclaiming him an official member of The Shadow Society, the Doc Savage Club, the Nick Carter Club, Friends of the Phantom, the Green Hornet G-J-M Club, and other august organizations papered the walls.

Jack glanced at the Shmoo clock on the wall above the hutch. He had an appointment with a new customer in twenty minutes or so. No time to find a special spot for the Sky King Magni-Glo Writing Ring, so he placed it next to his Captain Midnight radio decoder. He pulled a worn red windbreaker over his shirt and jeans and headed for the door.

4

Outside in the growing darkness, Jack hurried through the West Seventies, passing trendy boutiques and eateries that catered to the local yuppies and their affluent subgroup, dinks – double income, no kids. They types who were paying $9.50 for a side dish of the Upper West Side's newest culinary rage – mashed potatoes.

The drinkers stood three deep around the bar at Julio's. Two hundred-dollar shirts and three hundred-dollar sweaters were wedged next to grease-monkey overalls. Julio's had somehow managed to hang onto its old clientele despite the invasion of the Giorgio Armani and Donna Karen set. The yups and dinks had discovered Julio's a while back. Thought it had "rugged charm," found the bar food "authentic," and loved its "unpretentious atmosphere."

They drove Julio up the wall.

Julio was behind the bar, under the "Free Beer Tomorrow…" sign. Jack waved to let him know he was here. As Jack wandered the length of the bar he overheard a blond dink in a blue Ralph Lauren blazer, holding a mug of draft beer; he'd been here maybe once or twice before, and was pointing out Julio's famous dead succulents and asparagus ferns hanging in the windows to a couple who were apparently newcomers.

"Aren't they just fabulous?"

"Why doesn't he just get fresh ones?" the woman beside him asked. She was sipping white wine from a smudged tumbler. She grimaced as she swallowed.

Julio made a point of stocking the sourest Chardonnay on the market.

"I think he's making a statement," the guy said.

"About what?"

"I haven't the faintest. But don't you just love them?"

Jack knew what the statement was: Callousless people go home – this is a working man's bar. But they didn't see it. Julio was purposely rude to them, and he'd instructed his help to follow his lead, but it didn't work. The dinks thought it was a put-on, part of the ambiance. They ate it up.

Jack stepped over the length of rope that closed off the back half of the seating area and dropped into his usual booth in the darkened rear. As Julio came out from behind the bar, the blond dink flagged him down.

"Can we get a table back there?"

"No," Julio said.

The muscular little man brushed by him and nodded to Jack on his way to assuming the welcoming-committee post by the front door.

Jack pulled an iPod from his jacket pocket and set up a pair of lightweight headsets while he mentally reviewed the two phone calls that had led to this meet. The first had been on the voice-mail service. He'd called it from a pay booth this morning and heard someone named Munir Habib explaining in a tight, barely accented voice that he needed help. Needed it bad. He explained how he'd got the number. He didn't know what Jack could do for him but he was desperate. He gave his phone number and said he'd be waiting. "Please save my family!" he'd said.

Jack then made a couple of calls on his own. Mr. Habib's provenance checked out so Jack had called him back. From the few details he'd allowed Habib to give over the phone, Jack had determined that the man was indeed a potential customer. He'd set up a meet in Julio's.

THE WRINGER

A short, fortyish man stepped through Julio's front door and looked around uncertainly. His light camel-hair sport coat was badly wrinkled, like he'd slept on it. He had milk-chocolate skin, a square face, and bright eyes as black as the stiff, straight hair on his head. Julio spoke to him, they exchanged a few words, then Julio smiled and shook his hand. He led him back toward Jack, patting him on the back, treating him like a relative. Close up, the guy looked halfway to zombie. Even if he weren't, he wouldn't have a clue that he'd just been expertly frisked. Julio indicated the seat opposite Jack and gave a quick O-K behind his back as the newcomer seated himself.

When Julio got back to the bar, the blond guy in the blazer stopped him again.

"How come they get to sit over there and we don't?"

Julio swung on him and got in his face. He was a good head shorter than the blond guy but he was thickly muscled and had that air of barely restrained violence. It wasn't an act. Julio was feeling mean these days.

"You ask me one more time about those tables, man, and you outta here. You hear me? You *out* and you never come back!"

As Julio strutted away, the blond guy turned to his companions, grinning.

"I just *love* this place."

Jack turned his attention to his own customer. He extended his hand.

"I'm Jack."

"Munir Habib." His palm was cold and sweaty. "Are you the one who...?"

"That's me."

A few beats of silence, then, "I was expecting..."

"You and everybody else." They all arrived expecting someone bigger, someone darker, someone meaner looking. "But this is the guy you get. You've got the down payment on you?"

Munir glanced around furtively. "Yes. It is a lot to carry around in cash."

"It's safe here. Keep it for now. I haven't decided yet whether we'll be doing business. What's the story?"

"As I told you on the phone, my wife and son have been kidnapped and are being held hostage."

A kidnap. One of Jack's rules was to avoid kidnappings. They were the latest crime fad in the city these days, usually over drugs. They attracted feds and Jack had less use for Feds than he had for local cops. But this Munir guy had sworn he hadn't called the cops. Said he was too scared by the kidnapper's threats. Jack didn't know if he could believe him.

"Why call me instead of the cops?"

Munir reached inside his jacket and pulled out some Polaroids. His hand trembled as he passed them over.

"This is why."

The first showed an attractive blond woman, thirty or so, dressed in a white blouse and a dark skirt, gagged and bound to a chair in front of a blank, unpainted wall. A red plastic funnel had been inserted through the gag into her mouth. A can of Drano lay propped in her lap. Her eyes held Jack for a moment – pale blue and utterly terrified. *Caution: Contains lye* was block printed across the bottom of the photo.

Jack grimaced and looked at the second photo. At first he wasn't sure what he was looking at, like one of those pictures you get when the camera accidentally goes off in your hand. A big meat cleaver took up most of the frame, but the rest was –

He repressed a gasp when he recognized the bare lower belly of a little boy, his hairless pubes, his little penis laid out on the chopping block, the cleaver next to it, ominously close.

Okay. He hadn't called the cops.

Jack handed back the photos.

"How much do they want?"

"I don't believe it is a 'they.' I think it is a 'he.' And he does not seem to want money. At least not yet."

"He's a psycho?"

"I think so. He seems to hate Arabs – all Arabs – and has picked on me." Munir's features suddenly constricted into a tight knot as his voice cracked. "Why me?"

Jack realized how close this guy was to tumbling over the edge. He didn't want him to start blubbering here.

THE WRINGER

"Easy, guy," he said softly. "Easy."

Munir rubbed his hands over his face, and when next he looked at Jack, his features were blotchy but composed.

"Yes. I must remain calm. I must not lose control. For Barbara. And Robby."

Jack had a nightmare flash of Gia and Vicky in the hands of some of the psychos he'd had to deal with and knew at that moment he was going to be working with Munir. The guy was okay.

"An Arab hater. One of Kahane's old crew, maybe?"

"No. Not a Jew. At least not that I can tell. He keeps referring to a brother who was killed in the Trade Towers. I've told him that I'm an American citizen just like him. But he says I'm from Saudi Arabia, and Saudis brought down the Towers and an Arab's an Arab as far as he's concerned."

"Start at the beginning," Jack said. "Any hint that this was coming?"

"Nothing. Everything has been going normally."

"How about someone from the old country."

"I have no 'old country.' I've spent more of my life in America than in Saudi Arabia. My father was on long-term assignment here with Saud Petroleum. I grew up in New York. I was in college here when he was transferred back. I spent two months in the land of my birth and realized that my homeland was here. I made my *Hajj*, then returned to New York. I finished school and became a citizen."

"Still could be someone from over there behind it. I mean, your wife doesn't look like she's from that part of the world."

"Barbara was born and raised in Westchester."

"Couldn't marrying someone like that drive one of these fundamentalists–"

"No. Absolutely not." Munir's face hardened. Absolute conviction steeled his voice. "An Arab would never do what this man has done to me."

"Don't be so sure."

"He made me... he made me eat..." The rest of the sentence seemed to be lodged in Munir's throat. "...pork. And made me drink alcohol with it. *Pork!*"

Jack almost laughed. Munir was most assuredly a Muslim. But still, what was the big deal? Jack could think of things a whole lot worse he could have been forced to do.

"What'd you have to do – eat a ham on rye?"

"No. Ribs. He told me to go to a certain restaurant on Forty-seventh Street last Friday at noon and buy what he called 'a rack of baby back ribs.' Then he wanted me to stand outside on the sidewalk to eat them and wash them down with a bottle of beer."

"Did you?"

Munir bowed his head. "Yes."

Jack was tempted to ask if he liked the taste but stifled the question. Some folks took this stuff very seriously. He'd never been able to fathom how otherwise intelligent people allowed their dietary habits to be controlled by something written in book hundreds or thousands of years ago by someone who didn't have indoor plumbing. But then he didn't understand a lot of things about a lot of people. He freely admitted that. And what they ate or didn't eat, for whatever reasons, was the least of those mysteries.

"So you ate pork and drank a beer to save your wife and child. Nobody's going to call out the death squads for that. Or are they?"

"He made me choose between Allah and my family," Munir said. "Forgive me, but I chose my family."

"I doubt if Allah or any sane person would forgive you if you hadn't."

"But don't you see? He made me do it at noon on Friday."

"So?"

"That is when I should have been in my mosque, praying. It is one of the five duties. No follower of Islam would make a fellow believer do that. He is not an Arab, I tell you. You need only listen to the tape to know that."

"Okay. We'll get to the tape in a minute. Munir had told Jack that he'd been using his answering machine to record the nut's calls since yesterday. "Okay. So he's not an Arab. What about enemies? Got any?"

"No. We lead a quiet life. I run the auditing department at Saud Petrol. I have no enemies. Not many friends to speak of. We keep very much to ourselves."

THE WRINGER

If that was true – and Jack had learned the hard way over the years never to take what the customer said at face value – then Munir was indeed the victim of a psycho. And Jack hated dealing with psychos. They didn't follow the rules. They tended to have their own queer logic. Anything could happen. Anything.

"All right. Let's start at the beginning. When did you first realize something was wrong?"

"When I came home from work Thursday night and found our apartment empty. I checked the answering machine and heard a distorted voice telling me that he had my wife and son and that they'd be fine if I did as I was told and didn't go to the police. And if I had any thought of going to the police in spite of what he'd said, I should look on the dresser in our bedroom. The photographs were there." Munir rubbed a hand across his eyes. "I sat up all night waiting for the phone to ring. He finally called me Friday morning."

"And told you that you had to eat pork."

Munir nodded. "He would tell me nothing about Barbara and Robby except that they were alive and well and were hoping I wouldn't 'screw up.' I did as I was told, then hurried home and tried to vomit it up. He called and said I'd 'done good.' He said he'd call me again to tell me the next trick he was going to make me do. He said he was going to 'put me through the wringer but good.' "

"What was the next trick?"

"I was to steal a woman's pocketbook in broad daylight, knock her down, and run with it. And I was *not* to get caught. He said the photos I had were 'Before.' If I was caught, he would send me 'After.' "

"So you became a purse-snatcher for a day. A successful one, I gather."

Munir lowered his head. "I'm so ashamed... that poor woman." His features hardened. "And then he sent the other photo."

"Yeah? Let's see it."

Munir suddenly seemed flustered. "It's – it's at home."

He was lying. Why?

"Bull. Let me see it."

"No. I'd rather you didn't–"

"I need to know everything if I'm going to help you." Jack thrust out his hand. "Give."

With obvious reluctance, Munir reached into his coat and passed across another still. Jack immediately understood his reluctance.

He saw the same blond woman from the first photo, only this time she was nude, tied spread-eagle on a mattress, her dark pubic triangle toward the camera, her eyes bright with tears of humiliation; an equally naked dark-haired boy crouched in terror next to her.

And I thought she was a natural blonde was written across the bottom.

Jack's jaw began to ache from clenching it closed. He handed back the photo.

"And what about yesterday?"

"I had to urinate in the street before the Imperial Theater at a quarter to three in the afternoon."

"Swell," Jack said, shaking his head. "Sunday matinee time."

"Correct. But I would do it all again if it would free Barbara and Robby."

"You might have to do worse. In fact, I'm sure you're going to have to do worse. I think this guy's looking for your limit. He wants to see how far he can push you, wants to see how far you'll go."

"But where will it end?"

"Maybe with you killing somebody."

"Him? Gladly! I–"

"No. Somebody else. A stranger. Or worse – somebody you know."

Munir blanched. "No. Surely you can't be..." His voice trailed off.

"Why not? He's got you by the balls. That sort of power can make a well man sick and a sick man sicker." He watched Munir's face, the dismay tugging at his features as he stared at the tabletop. "What'll you do?"

A pause while Munir returned from somewhere far away. "What?"

"When the time comes. When he says you've got to choose between the lives of your wife and son, and the life of someone else. What'll you do?"

Munir didn't flinch. "Do the killing, of course."

"And the next innocent victim? And the one after that, and the one after that? When do you say enough, no more, *finis*?"

Munir flinched. "I... I don't know."

Tough question. Jack wondered how he'd answer if Gia and Vicky were captives. How many innocent people would die before he stopped? What was the magic number? Jack hoped he never had to find out. The Son of Sam might end up looking like a piker.

"Let's hear that tape."

Munir pulled a cassette out of side pocket and slid it across. Jack slipped it into the Walkman. Maybe listening to this creep would help him get a read on him.

He handed Munir one headset and slipped the other over his ears. He hit PLAY.

The voice on the tape was electronically distorted. Two possible reasons for that. One obviously to prevent voice-print analysis. But he also could be worried that Munir would recognize his voice. Jack listened to the snarling Southern accent. He couldn't tell through the electronic buzz if it was authentic or not, but no question about the sincerity of the raw hate snaking through the phone line. He closed his eyes and concentrated on the voice.

Something there... something about this guy... a picture was forming...

5

Munir found it difficult to focus on the tape. After all, he had listened to that hated voice over and over until he knew by heart every filthy word, every nuance of expression. Besides, he was uneasy here. He never frequented places where liquor was served. The drinking and laughter at the bar – they were alien to his way of life. So he studied this stranger across the table from him instead.

This man called Repairman Jack was most unimpressive. True, he was taller than Munir, perhaps five-eleven, but with a slim, wiry physique. Nothing at all special about his appearance.

Brown hair with a low hairline, and such mild brown eyes; had he not been seated alone back here, he would have been almost invisible. Munir had expected a heroic figure – if not physically prepossessing, at least sharp, swift, and viper deadly. This man had none of those qualities. How was he going to wrest Barbara and Robby from their tormentor's grasp? It hardly seemed possible.

And yet, as he watched him listening to the tape with his eyes closed, stopping it here and there to rewind and hear again a sentence or phrase, he became aware of the man's quiet confidence, of a hint of furnace-hot intensity roaring beneath his ordinary surface. And Munir began to see that perhaps there was a purpose behind Jack's manner of dress, his whole demeanor being slanted toward unobtrusiveness. He realized that this man could dog your steps all day and you would never notice him.

When the tape was done, the stranger took off his headphones, removed the cassette from the player, and stared at it.

"Something screwy here," he said finally.

"What do you mean?"

"He hates you."

"Yes, I know. He hates all Arabs. He's said so, many times."

"No. He hates *you*."

"Of course. I'm an Arab."

What was he getting at?

"Wake up, Munir. I'm telling you this guy knows you and he hates your guts. This whole deal has nothing to do with nine-eleven or Arabs or any of the bullshit he's been handing you. This is personal, Munir. Very personal."

No. It wasn't possible. He had never met anyone, had never been even remotely acquainted with a person who would do this to him and his family.

"I do not believe it." His voice sounded hoarse. "It cannot be."

Jack leaned forward, his voice low. "Think about it. In the space of three days this guy has made you offend your God, offend other people, humiliate yourself, and who knows what next? There's real nastiness here, Munir. Cold, calculated malice. Especially this business of making you eat pork and drink beer at noon on Friday when you're supposed to be at the mosque. I didn't know you had to pray on Fridays at noon, but he did. That tells me he knows more than a little about your religion – studying up on it, most likely. He's not playing this by ear. He's got a plan. He's not putting you through this 'wringer' of his just for the hell of it."

"What can he possibly gain from tormenting me?"

"Torment, hell. This guy's out to *destroy* you. And as for gain, I'm guessing on revenge."

"For what?" This was so maddening. "I fear you are getting off course with this idea that somehow I know this insane man."

"Maybe. But something he said during your last conversation doesn't sit right. He said he was being 'a lot more generous than you'd ever be.' That's not a remark a stranger would make. And then he said 'faux pas' a little while after. He's trying to sound like a redneck but I don't know too many rednecks with *faux pas* in their vocabulary."

"But that doesn't necessarily mean he knows me personally."

"You said you run a department in this oil company."

"Yes. Saud Petrol. I'm head of Stateside operations division."

"Which means you've got to hire and fire, I imagine."

"Of course."

"Look there. That's where you'll find this kook – in your personnel records. He's the proverbial Disgruntled Employee. Or Former Employee. Or Almost Employee. Someone you fired, someone you didn't hire, or someone you passed over for promotion. I'd go with the first – some people get very personal about being fired."

Munir searched his past for any confrontations with members of his department. He could think of only one and that was so minor –

Jack was pushing the tape cassette across the table.

"Call the cops," he said.

Fear wrapped thick fingers around Munir's throat and squeezed. "No! He'll find out! He'll–"

"I can't help you, pal. This isn't my thing. You need more than I can give you. You need officialdom. You need a squad of paper-shufflers doing background checks on the people past and present in your department. I'm small potatoes. No staff, no access to fingerprint files. You need all of that and more if you're going to get your family through this. The FBI's good at this stuff. They can stay out of sight, work in the background while you deal with this guy up front."

"But–"

He rose and clapped a hand on Munir's shoulder as he passed. "Good luck."

And then he was walking away... blending into the crowd around the bar... gone.

6

Charlie popped out his door down the hall just as Munir was unlocking his own.

"Thought that was you." He held up a Federal Express envelope. "This came while you were out. I signed for it."

Munir snatched it from him. His heart began to thud when he saw the name Trade Towers in the sender section of the address label.

"Thanks, Charlie," he gasped and practically fell into his apartment.

"Hey, wait. Did you–?"

The door slammed on Charlie's question as Munir's fingers fumbled with the tab of the opening strip. Finally he got a grip on it and ripped it across the top. He looked inside. Empty except for shadows. No. It couldn't be. He'd felt a bulge, a thickness within. He up-ended it.

A photograph slipped out and fluttered to the floor.

Munir dropped to a squat and snatched it up. He groaned as he saw Barbara – naked, gagged, bound spread-eagle on the bed as before, but alone this time. Something white was draped across her midsection. Munir looked closer.

A newspaper. A tabloid. The Post. The headline was the same he'd seen on the newsstands this morning. And Barbara was staring at the camera. No tears this time. Alert. Angry. *Alive.*

THE WRINGER

Munir wanted to cry. He pressed the photo against his chest and sobbed once, then looked at it again to make sure there was no trickery. No, it was real.

At the bottom was another one of the madman's hateful inscriptions: *She watched.*

Barbara watched? Watched what? What did that mean?

Just then the phone rang. Munir leaped for it. He pressed the RECORD button on the answerphone as soon as he recognized the distorted voice.

"Finished barfing yet, Mooo-neeer?"

"I – I don't know what you mean. But I thank you for this photo. I'm terribly relieved to know my wife is still alive. Thank you."

He wanted to scream that he ached for the day when he could meet him face to face and flay him alive, but said nothing. Barbara and Robby could only be hurt by angering this madman.

"*'Thank you'?*" The voice on the phone sounded baffled. "*Whatta you mean, 'thank you'? Didn't you see the rest?*"

Munir went cold all over. He tried to speak but words would not come. It felt as if something was stuck in his throat. Finally, he managed a few words.

"Rest? What rest?"

"*I think you'd better take another look in that envelope, Mooo-neeer. Take a real good look before you think about thankin' me. I'll call you back later.*"

"No–!"

The line went dead.

Panic exploded within Munir as he hung up and rushed backed to the foyer.

Didn't you see the rest?

What rest? Please, Allah, what did he mean? What was he saying?

He snatched up the stiff envelope. Yes, something still in it. A bulge at the bottom, wedged into the corner. He smacked the open end of the envelope against the floor.

Once. Twice.

141

Something tumbled out. Something in a small zip-loc bag.

Short. Cylindrical. A pale, dusky pink. Bloody red at the ragged end.

Munir jammed the back of his wrist against his mouth. To hold back the screams. To hold back the vomit.

And the inscription on Barbara's photograph came back to him.

She watched.

The phone began to ring.

7

"Take it easy, guy," Jack said to the sobbing man slumped before him. "It's going to be all right."

Jack didn't believe that, and he doubted Munir did either, but he didn't know what else to say. Hard enough to deal with a sobbing woman. What do you say to a blubbering man?

He'd been on his way home from Gia's over on Sutton Square when he stopped off at the St. Moritz to make one last call to his voice mail. He never used his apartment phone for that and did his best to randomize the times and locations of his calls. When he was on Central Park South he rarely passed up a chance to call in from the lobby of the Plaza or one of its high-priced neighbors.

He heard Munir's grief-choked voice: *"Please... I have no one else to call. He's hurt Robby! He's hurt my boy! Please help me, I beg you!"*

Jack couldn't say what was behind the impulse. He didn't want to, but a moment later he found himself calling Munir back, coaxing an address out of the near-hysterical man, and coming over here. He'd pulled on a pair of thin leather gloves before entering the Turtle Bay high-rise where Munir's apartment was located. He was sure this mess was going to end up in the hands of officialdom and he wished to leave behind nothing that belonged to him, especially his fingerprints.

Munir had been so glad to see him, so grateful to him for coming that Jack practically had to peel the man off of him.

He helped him to the kitchen and found a heavy meat cleaver lying on the table there. Several deep gouges, fresh ones, marred the tabletop. Jack finally got him calmed down.

THE WRINGER

"Where is it?"

"There." He pointed to the upper section of the refrigerator. "I thought if maybe I kept it cold…"

Munir slumped forward on the table, face-down, his forehead resting on the arms crossed before him. Jack opened the freezer compartment and pulled out the plastic bag.

It was a finger. A kid's. The left pinkie. Cleanly chopped off. Probably with the cleaver in the photo of a more delicate portion of the kid's anatomy he'd seen earlier this evening.

The son of a bitch.

And then the photograph of the boy's mother. And the inscription.

Jack felt a surge of blackness from the abyss within him. He willed it back. He couldn't get involved in this, couldn't let it get personal. He turned to look back at the kitchen table and found Munir staring at him.

"Do you see?" Munir said, wiping the tears from his cheeks. "Do you see what he has done to my boy?"

Jack quickly stuffed the finger back into the freezer.

"Look, I'm really sorry about this but nothing's changed. You still need more help than one guy can offer. You need the cops."

Munir shook his head violently. "No! You haven't heard his latest demand! The police can *not* help me with this! Only you can! Please, come listen."

Jack followed him down a hall. He passed a room with an inflatable fighter jet hanging from the ceiling and a New York Giants banner tacked to the wall. In another room at the end of the hall he waited while Munir's trembling fingers fumbled with the rewind controls. Finally he got it playing. Jack barely recognized Munir's voice as he spewed his grief and rage at the caller. Then the other voice laughed.

VOICE: *Well, well. I guess you got my little present.*

MUNIR: You vile, filthy, perverted –

VOICE: *Hey-hey, Mooo-neeer. Let's not get too personal here. This ain't between you'n me. This here's a matter of international diplomacy.*

MUNIR: How… (a choking sound) how could you?

QUICK FIXES

VOICE: *Easy, Mooo-neeer. I just think about how your people blew my brother to bits and it becomes real easy. Might be a real good idea for you to keep that in mind from here on in.*

MUNIR: Let them go and take me. I'll be your prisoner. You can... you can cut me to pieces if you wish. But let them go, I beg you!

VOICE: (laughs) *Cut you to pieces! Mooo-neeer, you must be psychic or something. That's what I've been thinking too! Ain't that amazing?*

MUNIR: You mean you'll let them go?

VOICE: *Someday — when you're all the way through the wringer. But let's not change the subject here. You in pieces — now that's a thought. Only I'm not going to do it. You are.*

MUNIR: What do you mean?

VOICE: *Just what I said, Mooo-neeer. I want a piece of you. One of your fingers. I'll leave it to you to decide which one. But I want you to chop it off and have it ready to send to me by tomorrow morning.*

MUNIR: Surely you can't be serious!

VOICE: *Oh, I'm serious, all right.* Deadly *serious. You can count on that.*

MUNIR: But how? I can't!

VOICE: *You'd better find a way, Mooo-neeer. Or the next package you get will be a bit bigger. It'll be a whole hand. (laughs) Well, maybe not a* whole *hand. One of the fingers will already be missing.*

MUNIR: No! Please! There must be —

VOICE: *I'll call in the mornin' t'tell you how to deliver it. And don't even think about goin' to the cops. You do and the next package you get'll be a* lot *bigger. Like a head. Chop-chop, Mooo-neeer.*

He switched off the machine and turned to Jack.

"You see now why I need your help?"

"No. I'm telling you the police can do a better job of tracking this guy down."

"But will the police help me cut off my finger?"

"Forget it!" Jack said, swallowing hard. "No way."

"But I can't do it myself. I've tried but I can't make my hand hold still. I want to but I just can't do it myself." Munir looked him in the eyes. "Please. You're my only hope. You must."

THE WRINGER

"Don't pull that on me." Jack wanted out of here. Now. "Get this: Just because you need me doesn't mean you own me. Just because I *can* doesn't mean I *must*. And in this case I honestly doubt than I can. So keep all of your fingers and dial 9-1-1 to get some help."

"No!" Anger overcame the fear and anguish in Munir's face. "I will not risk their lives!"

He strode back to the kitchen and picked up the cleaver. Jack was suddenly on guard. The guy was nearing the end of his rope. No telling what he'd do.

"I wasn't man enough to do it before," he said, hefting the cleaver. "But I can see I'll be getting no help from you or anyone else. So I'll have to take care of this all by myself!"

Jack stood back and watched as Munir slammed his left palm down on the table top, splayed the fingers, and angled the hand around so the thumb was pointing somewhere past his left flank. Jack didn't move to stop him. Munir was doing what he thought he had to do. He raised the cleaver above his head. It poised there a moment, wavering, like a cliff diver with second thoughts, then with a whimper of fear and dismay, Munir drove the cleaver into his hand.

Or rather into the table top where his hand had been.

Weeping, he collapsed into the chair then, and his sobs of anguish and self-loathing were terrible to hear.

"All right, goddammit," Jack said. He knew this was going to be nothing but trouble, but he'd seen and heard all he could stand. He kicked the nearest wall. "I'll do it."

8

"Ready?"

Munir's left hand was lashed to the tabletop. Munir himself was loaded up with every painkiller he'd had in the medicine cabinet – Tylenol, Advil, Bufferin, Anacin 3, Nuprin. Some of them were duplicates. Jack didn't care. He wanted Munir's pain center deadened as much as possible. He wished the guy drank. He'd have much preferred doing this to someone who was dead drunk. Or doped up. Jack could have scored a bunch of Dilaudids for him. But Munir had said no to both. No booze. No dope.

Tight-ass.

Jack had never cut off anybody's finger before. He wanted to do this right. The first time. No misses. Half an inch too far to the right and Munir would lose only a piece of his pinkie; half an inch too far to the left and he'd be missing the ring finger as well. So Jack had made himself a guide. He'd found a plastic cutting board, a quarter-inch thick, and had notched one of its edges. Now he was holding the board upright with the notch clamped over the base of Munir's pinkie; the rest of his hand was safe behind the board. All Jack had to do to sever the finger cleanly was chop down as hard as he could along the vertical surface.

That was all.

Easy.

Right.

"I am ready," Munir said.

He was dripping with sweat. His dark eyes looked up at Jack, then he nodded, stuffed a dish rag in his mouth, and turned his head away.

Swell, Jack thought. I'm glad you're ready. But am I?

Now or never.

He steadied the cutting board, raised the cleaver. He couldn't do this.

Got to.

He took a deep breath, tightened his grip –

– and drove the cleaver into the wall.

Munir jumped, turned, pulled the dishrag from his mouth. "What? Why–?"

"This isn't going to work." Jack let the plastic cutting board drop and began to pace the kitchen. "Got to be another way. He's got us on the run. We're playing this whole thing by his rules."

"There aren't any others."

"Yeah, there are."

Jack continued pacing. One thing he'd learned over the years was not to let the other guy deal all the cards. Let him *think* he had control of the deck while you changed the order.

Munir wriggled his fingers. "Please. I cannot risk angering this madman."

THE WRINGER

Jack swung to face him. An idea was taking shape.

"You want me in on this?"

"Yes, of course."

"Then we do it my way. All of it." He began working at the knots that bound Munir's arm to the table. "And the first thing we do is untie you. Then we make some phone calls."

9

Munir understood none of this. He sat in a daze, sipping milk to ease a stomach that quaked from fear and burned from too many pills. Jack was on the phone, but his words made no sense.

"Yeah, Ron. It's me. Jack... Right. That Jack. Look, I need a piece of your wares... small piece. Easy thing... Right. I'll get that to you in an hour or two. Thing is, I need it by morning. Can you deliver?... Great. Be by later. By the way – how much?... Make that two and you got a deal... All right. See you."

Then he hung up, consulted a small address book, and dialed another number.

"Hey, Teddy. It's me. Jack... Yeah, I know, but this can't wait till morning. How about opening up your store for me? I need about ten minutes inside... That's no help to me, Teddy. I need to get in now. *Now...* Okay. Meet you there in twenty."

Jack hung up and took the glass from Munir's hands. Munir found himself taken by the upper arm and pulled toward the door.

"Can you get us into your office?"

Munir nodded. "I'll need my ID card and keys, but yes, they'll let me in."

"Get them. There a back way out of here?"

Munir took him down the elevator to the parking garage and out the rear door. From there they caught a late-cruising gypsy cab down to a hardware store on Bleecker Street. The lights inside were on but the sign in the window said CLOSED. Jack told the cabby to wait and knocked on the door. A painfully thin man with no hair whatsoever, not even eyebrows, opened the door.

"You coulda broke in, Jack," he said. "I wouldna minded. I need my rest, y'know."

"I know, Teddy," Jack said. "But I need the lights on for this and I couldn't risk attracting that kind of attention."

Munir followed Jack to the paint department at the rear of the store. They stopped at the display of color cards. Jack pulled a group from the brown section and turned to him.

"Give me your hand."

Baffled, he watched as Jack placed one of the color cards against the back of Munir's hand, then tossed it away. And again. One after another until –

"Here we go. Perfect match."

"We're buying *paint?*"

"No. We're buying flesh – specifically, flesh with Golden Mocha number 169 skin. Let's go."

And then they were moving again, waving good bye to Teddy, and getting back into the cab.

To the East Side now, up First Avenue to Thirty-first Street. Jack ran inside with the color card, then came out and jumped back into the cab empty-handed.

"Okay. Next stop is your office."

"My office? Why?"

"Because we've got a few hours to kill and we might as well use them to look up everyone you fired in the past year."

Munir thought this was futile but he had given himself into Jack's hands. He had to trust him. And as exhausted as he was, sleep was out of the question.

He gave the driver the address of the Saud Petrol offices.

10

"This guy looks promising," Jack said, handing him a file. "Remember him?"

Until tonight, Munir never had realized how many people he hired and fired – "down-sized" was the current euphemism – in the course of a year. He was amazed.

He opened the file. Richard Hollander. The name didn't catch until he read the man's performance report.

"Not him. Anyone but him."

"Yeah? Why not?"

THE WRINGER

"Because he was so..." As Munir searched for the right word, he pulled out all he remembered about Hollander, and it wasn't much. The man hadn't been with the company long, and had been pretty much a nonentity during his stay. Then he found the word he was looking for. "Ineffectual."

"Yeah?"

"Yes. He never got anything done. Every assignment, every report was either late or incomplete. He had a wonderful academic record – good grades from an Ivy League school, that sort of thing – but he proved incapable of putting any of his learning into practice. That was why he was let go."

"Any reaction? You know, shouting, yelling, threats?"

"No." Munir remembered giving Hollander his notice. The man had merely nodded and begun emptying his desk. He hadn't even asked for an explanation. "He knew he'd been screwing up. I think he was expecting it. Besides, he had no southern accent. It's not him."

Munir passed the folder back but instead of putting it away, Jack opened it and glanced through it again.

"I wouldn't be too sure about that. Accents can be faked. And if I was going to pick the type who'd go nuts for revenge, this guy would be it. Look: He's unmarried, lives alone–"

"Where does it say he lives alone?"

"It doesn't. But his emergency contact is his mother in Massachusetts. If he had a lover or even a roomie he'd list them, wouldn't you think? 'No moderating influences,' as the head docs like to say. And look at his favorite sports: swimming and jogging. This guy's a loner from the git-go."

"That does not make him a psychopath. I imagine you are a loner, too, and you..."

The words dribbled away as Munir's mind followed the thought to its conclusion.

Jack grinned. "Right, Munir. Think about that."

He reached for the phone and punched in a number. After a moment he spoke in a deep, authoritative voice: "Please pick up. This is an emergency. Please pick up." A moment later he hung up and began writing on a note pad. "I'm going to take down this guy's address for future reference. It's almost four a.m. and Mr. Hollander isn't home. His answering machine is on, but even if he's screening his calls, I think he'd have responded to my little emergency message, don't you?"

Munir nodded. "Most certainly. But what if he doesn't live there anymore?"

"Always a possibility." Jack glanced at his watch. "But right now I've got to go pick up a package. You sit tight and stay by the phone here. I'll call you when I've got it."

Before Munir could protest, Jack was gone, leaving him alone in his office, staring at the gallery of family photos arrayed on his desk. He began to sob.

11

The phone startled Munir out of a light doze. Confusion jerked him upright. What was he doing in his office? He should be home…

Then he remembered.

Jack was on the line: "Meet me downstairs."

Out on the street, in the pale, predawn light, two figures awaited him. One was Jack, the other a stranger – a painfully thin man of Munir's height with shoulder-length hair and a goatee. Jack made no introductions. Instead he led them around a corner to a small deli. He stared through the open window at the lights inside.

"This looks bright enough," Jack said.

Inside he ordered two coffees and two cheese Danish and carried them to the rearmost booth in the narrow, deserted store. Jack and the stranger slid into one side of the booth, Munir the other, facing them. Still no introductions.

"Okay, Munir," Jack said. "Put your hand on the table."

Munir complied, placing his left hand palm down, wondering what this was about.

"Now let's see the merchandise," Jack said to the stranger.

The thin man pulled a small, oblong package from his pocket. It appeared to be wrapped in brown paper hand towels. He unrolled the towels and placed the object next to Munir's hand.

THE WRINGER

A finger. Not Robby's. Different. Adult size.

Munir pulled his hand back onto his lap and stared.

"Come on, Munir," Jack said. "We've got to do a color check."

Munir slipped his hand back onto the table next to the grisly object, regarding it obliquely. So real looking.

"It's too long and that's only a fair color match," Jack said.

"It's close enough," the stranger said. "Pretty damn good on such short notice, I'd say."

"I suppose you're right." Jack handed him an envelope. "Here you go."

The goateed stranger took the envelope and stuffed it inside his shirt without opening it, then left without saying good bye.

Munir stared at the finger. The dried blood on the stump end, the detail over the knuckles and around the fingernail – even down to the dirt under the nail – was incredible. It almost looked real.

"This won't work," he said. "I don't care how real this looks, when he finds out it's a fake–"

"Fake?" Jack said, stirring sugar into his coffee. "Who said it's a fake?"

Munir snatched his hand away and pushed himself back. He wanted to sink into the vinyl covering of the booth seat, wanted to pass through to the other side and run from this man and the loathsome object on the table between them. He fixed his eyes on the seat beside him and managed to force a few words past his rising gorge.

"Please... take... that... away."

He heard the soft crinkle and scrape of paper being folded and dragged across the table top, then Jack's voice:

"Okay, Cinderella. You can look now. It's gone."

Munir kept his eyes averted. What had he got himself into? In order to save his family from one ruthless madman he was forced to deal with another. What sort of world was this?

He felt a sob build in his throat. Until last week, he couldn't remember crying once since his boyhood. For the past few days it seemed he wanted to cry all the time. Or scream. Or both.

He saw Jack's hand pushing a cup of coffee into his field of vision.

"Here. Drink this. Lots of it. You're going to need to stay alert."

An insane hope rose in Munir.

"Do you think... do you think the man on the phone did the same thing? With Robby's finger? Maybe he went to a morgue and..."

Jack shook his head slowly, as if the movement pained him. For an instant he saw past the wall around Jack. Saw pity there.

"Don't torture yourself," Jack said.

Yes, Munir thought. The madman on the phone was already doing too good a job of that.

"It's not going to work," Munir said, fighting the blackness of despair. "He's going to realize he's been tricked and then he's going to take it out on my boy."

"No matter what you do, he's going to find an excuse to do something nasty to your boy. Or your wife. That's the whole idea behind this gig – make you suffer. But his latest wrinkle with the fingers gives us a chance to find out who he is and where he's holed up."

"How?"

"He wants your finger. How's he going to get it? He can't very well give us an address to mail it to. So there's going to have to be a drop – someplace where we leave it and he picks it up. And that's where we nab him and make him tell us where he's got your family stashed."

"What if he refuses to tell us?"

Jack's voice was soft, his nod almost imperceptible. Munir shuddered at what he saw flashing through Jack's eyes in that instant.

"Oh... he'll tell us."

"He thinks I won't do it," Munir said, looking at his fingers – all ten of them. "He thinks I'm a coward because he thinks all Arabs are cowards. He's said so. And he was right. I couldn't do it."

"Hell," Jack said, "I couldn't do it either, and it wasn't even my hand. But I'm sure you'd have done it eventually if I hadn't come up with an alternative."

THE WRINGER

Would I have done it? Munir thought. *Could* I have done it?

Maybe he'd have done it just to demonstrate his courage to the madman on the phone. Over the years Munir had seen the Western world's image of the Arab male distorted beyond recognition by terrorism: the Arab bombed school buses and beheaded helpless hostages; Arab manhood aimed its weapons from behind the skirts of unarmed civilian women and children.

"If something goes wrong because of this, because of my calling on you to help me, I... I will never forgive myself."

"Don't think like that," Jack said. "It gets you nothing. And you've got to face it: No matter what you do – cut off one finger, two fingers, your left leg, kill somebody, blow up Manhattan – it's never going to be enough. He's going to keep escalating until you're dead. You've got to stop him now, before it goes any further. Understand?"

Munir nodded. "But I'm so afraid. Poor Robby... his terrible pain, his fear. And Barbara..."

"Exactly. And if you don't want that to go on indefinitely, you've got to take the offensive. Now. So let's get back to your place and see how he wants to take delivery on your finger."

12

Back in the apartment, Jack bandaged Munir's hand in thick layers of gauze to make to look injured. While they waited for the phone to ring, he disappeared into the bathroom with the finger to wash it.

"We want this to be as convincing as possible," he said. "You don't strike me as the type to have dirty fingernails."

When the call finally came, Munir ground his teeth at the sound of the hated voice.

Jack was beside him, gripping his arm, steadying him as he listened through an earphone he had plugged into the answering machine. He had told Munir what to say, and had coached him on how to say it, how to sound.

"*Well, Mooo-neeer. You got that finger for me?*"

"Yes," he said in the choked voice he had rehearsed. "I have it."

The caller paused, as if the caller was surprised by the response.

"You did it? You really did it?"

"Yes. You gave me no choice."

Well, I'll be damned. Hey, how come your voice sounds so funny?"

"Codeine. For the pain."

"Yeah. I'll bet that smarts. But that's okay. Pain's good for you. And just think: Your kid got through it without codeine."

Jack's grip on his arm tightened as Munir stiffened and began to rise. Jack pulled him back to a sitting position.

"Please don't hurt Robby anymore," Munir said, and this time he did not have to feign a choking voice. "I did what you asked me. Now let them go."

"Not so fast, Mooo-neeer. How do I know you really cut that finger off? You wouldn't be bullshitting me now, would you?"

"Oh, please. I would not lie about something as important as this."

Yet I *am* lying, he thought. Forgive me, my son, if this goes wrong.

"Well, we'll just have to see about that, won't we? Here's what you do: Put your offering in a brown paper lunch bag and head downtown. Go to the mailbox on the corner where Lafayette, Astor, and Eighth come together. Leave the bag on top of the mailbox, then walk half a block down and stand in front of the Astor Place Theater. Got it?"

"Yes. Yes, I think so."

"Of course you do. Even a bonehead like you should be able to handle those instructions."

"But when should I do this?"

"Ten a.m."

"This morning?" He glanced at his watch. "But it is almost 9:30!"

"Aaaay! And he can tell time too! What an intellect! Yeah, that's right, Mooo-neeer. And don't be late or I'll have to think you're lying to me. And we know what'll happen then, don't we."

"But what if–?"

"See you soon, Mooo-neeer."

The line went dead. His heart pounding, Munir fumbled the receiver back onto its cradle and turned to Jack.

THE WRINGER

"We must hurry! We have no time to waste!"

Jack nodded. "This guy's no dummy. He's not giving us a chance to set anything up."

"I'll need the... finger," Munir said. Even now, long after the shock of learning it was real, the thought of touching it made him queasy. "Could you please put it in the brown bag for me?"

Jack nodded. Munir led him to the kitchen and gave him a brown lunch bag. Jack dropped the finger inside and handed the sack back to him.

"You've got to arrive alone, so you go first," Jack said. "I'll follow a few minutes from now. If you don't see me around, don't worry. I'll be there. And whatever you do, follow his instructions – nothing else. Understand? *Nothing else.* I'll do the ad-libbing. Now get moving."

Munir fairly ran for the street, praying to Allah that it wouldn't take too long to find a taxi.

13

Somehow Jack's cab made it down to the East Village before Munir's. He had a bad moment when he couldn't find him. Then a cab screeched to a halt and Munir jumped out. Jack watched as he hurried to the mailbox and placed the brown paper bag atop it. Jack retreated to a phone booth on the uptown corner and pretended to make a call while Munir strode down to the Astor Place Theater and stopped before a Blue Man Group poster.

As Jack began an animated conversation with the dial tone, he scanned the area. Midmorning in the East Village. Members of the neighborhood's homeless brigade seemed to be the only people about, either shuffling aimlessly along, as if dazed by the bright morning sun, or huddled on the sidewalks like discarded rag piles. The nut could be among them. Easy to hide within layers of grime and ratty clothes. But not so easy to hide a purpose in life. Jack hunted for someone who looked like he had somewhere to go.

Hollander... he wished there'd been a photo in his personnel file. Jack was sure he was the bad guy here. If only he'd been able to get over to his apartment before now. Maybe he'd have found –

And then Jack spotted him. A tall bearded guy traveling westward along Eighth Street, weaving his way through the loitering horde. He was squeezed into a filthy, undersized Army fatigue jacket, the cuffs of at least three of the multiple shirts he wore under the coat protruding from the too-short sleeves; the neck of a pint bottle of Mad Dog stuck up like a periscope from the frayed edge of one of the pockets; the torn knees of his green work pants revealed threadbare jeans beneath. Piercing blue eyes peered out from under a Navy watch cap.

The sicko? Maybe. Maybe not. One thing was sure: This guy wasn't wandering; he had someplace to go.

And he was heading directly for the mailbox.

When he reached it he stopped and looked over his shoulder, back along the way he had come on Eighth, then grabbed the brown paper bag Munir had left there. He reached inside, pulled out the paper-towel-wrapped contents, and began to unwrap it.

Suddenly he let out a strangled cry and tossed the finger into the street. It rolled in an arc and came to rest in the debris matted against the curb. He glanced over his shoulder again and began a stumbling run in the other direction, across Eighth, toward Jack and away from Munir.

"*Shit!*" Jack said aloud, working the word into his one-way conversation, making it an argument, all the while pretending not to notice the doings at the mailbox.

Something tricky was going down. But what? Had the sicko sent a patsy? Jack had known the guy was sly, but he'd thought the sicko would have wanted to see the finger up close and personal, just to be sure it was real.

Unless of course the sicko was the wino and he'd done just that a few seconds ago.

He was almost up to Jack's phone booth now. The only option Jack saw was to follow him. Give him a good lead and –

He heard pounding footsteps. Munir was coming this way – *running* this way, sprinting across the pavement, teeth bared, eyes wild, reaching for the tall guy. Jack repressed an alarmed impulse to get between the two of them. It wouldn't do any good.

THE WRINGER

Munir was out of control and had built up too much momentum. Besides, no use in tipping off his own part in this.

Munir grabbed the taller man by the elbow and spun him around.

"Where are they?" he screeched. His face was flushed; tiny bubbles of saliva collected at the corners of his mouth. "Tell me, you swine!"

Swine? Maybe that was a heavy-duty insult from a Muslim but it was pabulum around here.

The tall guy jerked back, trying to shake Munir off. His open mouth revealed gapped rows of rotting teeth.

"Hey, man–!"

"Tell me or I'll kill you!" Munir shouted, grabbing the man's upper arms and shaking his lanky frame.

"Lemme go, man," he said as his head snapped back and forth like a guy in a car that had just been rear-ended. Munir was going to give him whiplash in a few seconds. "Don't know whatcher talking about!"

"You do! You went right to the package. You've seen the finger – now tell me where they are!"

"Hey, look, man, I don't know nothin' 'bout whatcher sayin'. Dude stopped me down the street and told me to go check out the bag on top the mailbox. Gave me five to do it. Told me to hold up whatever was inside it."

"Who?" Munir said, releasing the guy and turning to look back down Eighth. "Where is he?"

"Gone now."

Munir grabbed the guy again, this time by the front of his fatigue jacket.

"What did he look like?"

"I dunno. Just a guy. Whatta you want from me anyway, man? I didn't do nothin'. And I don't want nothin' to do with no dead fingers. Now getcher hands offa me!"

Jack had heard enough.

"Let him go," he told Munir, still pretending to talk into the phone.

Munir gave him a baffled look. "No. He can tell us–"

"He can't tell us anything we need to know. Let him go and get back to your apartment. You've done enough damage already."

Munir blanched and loosened his grip. The guy stumbled back a couple of steps, then turned and ran down Lafayette. Munir looked around and saw that every rheumy eye in the area was on him. He stared down at his hands – the free right and the bandaged left – as if they were traitors.

"You don't think–?"

"Get home. He'll be calling you. And so will I."

Jack watched Munir move away toward the Bowery like a sleepwalker. He hung up the phone and leaned against the booth.

What a mess. The nut had pulled a fast one. Got some wino to make the pick up. But how could a guy that kinked be satisfied with seeing Munir's finger from afar? He seemed the type to want to hold it in his grubby little hand.

But maybe he didn't care. Because maybe it didn't matter.

Jack pulled out the slip of paper on which he'd written Richard Hollander's address. Time to pay Saud Petrol's ex-employee a little visit.

14

Munir paced his apartment, going from room to room, cursing himself. Such a fool! Such an idiot! But he couldn't help it. He'd lost control. When he'd seen that man walk up to the paper bag and reach inside it, all rationality had fled. The only thing left in his mind had been the sight of Robby's little finger tumbling out of that envelope last night.

After that, everything was a blur.

The phone began to ring.

Oh, no! he thought. It's him. Please, Allah, let him be satisfied. Grant him mercifulness.

He lifted the receiver and heard the voice.

"Quite a show you put on there, Mooo-neeer."

"Please. I was upset. You've seen my severed finger. Now will you let my family go?"

"Now just hold on there a minute, Mooo-neeer. I saw a finger go flying through the air, but I don't know for sure if it was your finger."

THE WRINGER

Munir froze with the receiver jammed against his ear.

"Wh-what do you mean?"

"*I mean, how do I know that was a real finger? How do I know it wasn't one of those fake rubber things you buy in the five-and-dime?*"

"It was real! I swear it! You saw how your man reacted!"

"*He was just a wino, Mooo-neeer. Scared of his own shadow. What's he know?*"

"Oh, please! You must believe me!"

"*Well, I would, Mooo-neeer. Really, I would. Except for the way you grabbed him afterward. Now it's bad enough you went after him, but I'm willing to overlook that. I'm far more generous about forgiving mistakes than you are, Mooo-neeer. But what bothers me is the* way *you grabbed him. You used both your hands the same.*"

Munir felt his blood congealing, sludging though his arteries and veins.

"What do you mean?"

"*Well, I got trouble seeing a man who just chopped off one of his fingers doing that, Mooo-neeer. I mean, you grabbed him like you had two good hands. And that bothers me, Mooo-neeer.* Sorely *bothers me.*"

"Please. I swear–"

"*Swearing ain't good enough, I'm afraid. Seeing is believing. And I believe I saw a man with two good hands out there this morning.*"

"No. Really…"

"*So I'm gonna have to send you another package, Mooo-neeer.*"

"Oh, no! Don't–"

"*Yep. A little memento from your wife.*"

"Please, no."

He told Munir what that memento would be, then he clicked off.

"No!"

Munir jammed his knuckles into his mouth and screamed into his fist.

"NOOOOO!"

15

Jack stood outside Richard Hollander's door.

No sweat getting into the building. The address in the personnel file had led Jack to a rundown walk-up in the West Eighties.

QUICK FIXES

He'd checked the mailboxes in the dingy vestibule and found *R. Hollander* still listed for 3B. A few quick strokes with the notched flexible plastic ruler Jack kept handy, and he was in.

He knocked – not quite pounding, but with enough urgency to bring even the most cautious resident to the peephole.

Three tries, no answer. Jack put his picks to work on the deadbolt. A Quickset. He was rusty. Took him almost a minute, and a minute was a long time when you were standing in an open hallway fiddling with someone's lock – the closest a fully-clothed man could come to feeling naked in public.

Finally the bolt snapped back. He drew his 9mm backup and entered in a crouch.

Quiet. Didn't take long to check out the one-bedroom apartment. Empty. He turned on the lights and did a thorough search.

Neat. The bed was made, the furniture dusted, clothes folded in the bureau drawers, no dirty dishes in the sink. Hollander either had a maid or he was a neatnik. People who could afford maids didn't live in this building; that made him a neatnik. Not what Jack had expected from a guy who got fired because he couldn't get the job done.

He checked the bookshelves. A few novels and short story collections – literary stuff, mostly – salted in among the business texts. And in the far right corner, three books on Islam with titles like *Understanding Islam* and *An Introduction To Islam*.

Not an indictment by itself. Hollander might have bought them for reference when he'd been hired by Saud Petrol.

And he might have bought them *after* he was fired.

Jack was willing to bet on the latter. He had a gut feeling about this guy.

On the desk was a picture of a thin, pale, blond man with an older woman. Hollander and his mother maybe?

He went through the drawers and found a black ledger, a checkbook, and a pile of bills. Looked like he'd been dipping into his savings. He'd been paying only the minimum on his Master Card. A lot of late payment notices, and a couple of bad-news letters from employment agencies. Luck wasn't running his way, and maybe Mr. Richard Hollander was looking for someone to blame.

THE WRINGER

Folded between the back cover and the last page of the ledger was a receipt from the Brickell Real Estate Agency for a cash security deposit and first month's rental on Loft #629. Dated last month. Made out to Sean McCabe.

Loft #629. Where the hell was that? And why did Richard Hollander have someone else's cash receipt? Unless it wasn't someone else's. Had he rented loft #629 under a phony name? That would explain using cash. But why would a guy who was almost broke rent a loft?

Unless he was looking for a place to do something too risky to do in his own apartment.

Like holding hostages.

Jack copied down the Brickell Agency's phone number. He might need that later. Then he called Munir.

Hysteria on the phone. Sobbing, moaning, the guy was almost incoherent.

"Calm down, dammit! What exactly did he tell you?"

"He's going to cut her... he's going to cut her... he's going to cut her..."

He sounded like a stuck record player. If Munir had been within reach Jack would have whacked him alongside the head to unstick him.

"Cut her what?"

"Cut her nipple off!"

"Oh, Jeez! Stay right there. I'll call you right back."

Jack retrieved the receipt for the loft and dialed the number of the realtor. As the phone began to ring, he realized he hadn't figured out an angle to pry out the address. They wouldn't give it to just anybody. But maybe a cop...

He hoped he was right as a pleasant female voice answered on the third ring. "Brickell Agency."

Jack put a harsh, Brooklynese edge on his voice.

"Yeah. This is Lieutenant Adams of the Twelfth Precinct. Who's in charge there?"

"I am." Her voice had cooled. "Esther Brickell. This is my agency."

"Good. Here's the story. We've got a suspect in a mutilation murder but we don't know his whereabouts. However, we did find a cash receipt among his effects. Your name was on it."

"The Brickell Agency?"

"Big as life. Down payment of some sort on loft number six-two-nine. Sound familiar?"

"Not offhand. We're computerized. We access all our rental accounts by number."

"Fine. Then it'll only take you a coupla seconds to get me the address of this place."

"I'm afraid I can't do that. I have a strict policy of never giving out information about my clients. Especially over the phone. All my dealings with them are strictly confidential. I'm sure you can understand."

Swell, Jack thought. She thinks she's a priest or a reporter.

"What I understand," he said, "is that I've got a crazy perp out there and you think you've got privileged information. Well, listen, sweetie, the First Amendment don't include realtors. I need the address of your six-two-nine loft rented to" – he glanced at the name on the receipt – "Sean McCabe. Not later. Now. *Capsice?*"

"Sorry," she said. "I can't do that. Good-day, lieutenant – if indeed you are a lieutenant."

Shit! But Jack wasn't giving up. He *had* to get this address.

"Oh, I'm a lieutenant, all right. And believe me, sweetie, you don't come across with that address here and now, you've got trouble. You make me waste my time tracking down a judge to swear out a search warrant, make me come out to your dinky little office to get this one crummy address, I'm gonna do it up big. I'm gonna bring uniforms and blue-and-white units and we're gonna do a thorough search. And I do mean *thorough.* We'll be there all day. And we'll go through *all* your files. And while we're at it you can explain to any prospective clients who walk in exactly what we're doing and why – and hope they'll believe you. And if we can't find what we want in your computer we'll confiscate it. And keep it for a while. And maybe you'll get it back next Christmas. Maybe."

"Just a minute," she said.

THE WRINGER

Jack waited, hoping she hadn't gone to another phone to call her lawyer and check on his empty threats, or call the Twelfth to check on a particularly obnoxious lieutenant named Adams.

"It's on White Street," she said suddenly in cold, clipped tones. "Eighteen-twenty-two. Two-D."

"Thank–"

She hung up on him. Fine. He had what he needed.

White Street. That was in TriBeCa – the trendy triangle below Canal Street. Lots of lofts down there. Straight down Lafayette from where he and Munir had played the mailbox game. He'd been on top of the guy an hour ago.

He punched in Munir's number.

"Eighteen-twenty-two White," he said without preamble. "Get down there now."

No time for explanations. He hung up and ran for the door.

16

The building looked like a deserted factory. Probably was. Four stories with no windows on the first floor. Maybe an old sweat shop. A "NOW RENTING" sign next to the front door. The place looked empty. Had the Brickell lady stiffed him with the wrong address?

With his trusty plastic ruler ready in his gloved hand, Jack hopped out of the cab and ran for the door. It was steel, a leftover from the building's factory days. An anti-jimmy plate had been welded over the latch area. Jack pocketed the plastic and inspected the lock: a heavy-duty Schlage. A tough pick on a good day. Here on the sidewalk, with the clock ticking, in full view of the cars passing on the street, a *very* tough pick.

He ran along the front of the building and took the alley around to the back. Another door there, this one with a big red alarm warning posted front and center.

Two-D... that meant the second floor had been subdivided into at least four mini lofts. If Hollander was here at all, he'd be renting the cheapest. Usually the lower letters meant up front with a view of the street; further down the alphabet you got relegated to the rear with an alley view.

Jack stepped back and looked up. The second-floor windows to his left were bare and empty. The ones on the right were completely draped with what looked like bedsheets.

And running right smack past the middle of those windows was a downspout. Jack tested the pipe. This wasn't some flimsy aluminum tube that collapsed like a beer can; this was good old-fashioned galvanized pipe. He pulled on the fittings. They wiggled in their sockets.

Not good, but he'd have to risk it.

He began to climb, shimmying up the pipe, vising it with his knees and elbows as he sought toeholds and fingerholds on the fittings. It shuddered, it groaned, and halfway up it settled a couple of inches with a jolt, but it held. Moments later he was perched outside the shrouded second-floor windows.

Now what?

Sometimes the direct approach was the best. He knocked on the nearest pane. It was two foot high, three foot wide, and filthy. After a few seconds, he knocked again. Finally a corner of one of the sheets lifted hesitantly and a man stared out at him. Blond hair, wide blue eyes, pale face in need of a shave. The eyes got wider and the face faded a few shades paler when he saw Jack. He didn't look exactly like the guy in the photo in Hollander's apartment, but he could be. Easily.

Jack smiled and gave him a friendly wave. He raised his voice to be heard through the glass.

"Good morning. I'd like to have a word with Mrs. Habib, if you don't mind."

The corner of the sheet dropped and the guy disappeared. Which confirmed that he'd found Richard Hollander. Anybody else would have asked him what the hell he was doing out there and who the hell was Mrs. Habib?

So now Jack had to move quickly. If he had Hollander pegged right, he'd be tripping full tilt down the stairs for the street. Which was fine with Jack. But there was a small chance he'd take a second or two to do something gruesome or even fatal to the woman and the boy before he fled. Jack didn't anticipate any physical

THE WRINGER

resistance – a gutless creep who struck at another man through his wife and child was hardly the type for *mano a mano* confrontation.

Bracing his hands on the pipe, Jack planted one foot on the three-inch window sill and aimed a kick at the bottom pane.

Suddenly the glass three panes above it exploded outward as a rusty steel L-bar smashed through, narrowly missing Jack's face and showering him with glass.

On the other hand, he thought, even the lowliest rat had been known to fight when cornered.

Jack swung back onto the pipe and around to the windows on the other side. The bar retreated through the holes it had punched in the sheet and the window. As Jack shifted his weight to the opposite sill, he realized that from inside he was silhouetted on the sheet. Too late. The bar came crashing through the pane level with Jack's groin, catching him in the leg. He grunted with pain as the corner of the bar tore through his jeans and gouged the flesh across the front of his thigh. In a sudden burst of rage, he grabbed the bar and pulled.

The sheet came down and draped over Hollander. He fought it off with panicky swipes, letting go of the bar in the process. Jack pulled it the rest of the way through the window and dropped it into the alley below. Then he kicked the remaining glass out of the pane and swung inside.

Hollander was dashing for the door, something in his right hand.

Jack started after him, his mind registering strobe-flash images as he moved: a big empty space, a card table, two chairs, three mattresses on the floor, the first empty, a boy tied to the second, a naked woman tied to the third, blood on her right breast.

Jack picked up speed and caught him as he reached the door. He ducked as Hollander spun and swung a meat cleaver at his head. Jack grabbed his wrist with his left hand and smashed his right fist into the pale face. The cleaver fell from his fingers as he dropped to his knees.

"I give up," Hollander said, coughing and spitting blood. "It's over."

"No," Jack said, hauling him to his feet. The darkness was welling up in him now, whispering, taking control. "It's not."

The wide blue eyes darted about in confusion. "What? Not what?"

"Over."

Jack drove a left into his gut, then caught him with an uppercut as he doubled over, slamming him back against the door.

Hollander retched and groaned as he sank to the floor again.

"You can't do this," he moaned. "I've surrendered."

"And you think that does it? You've played dirty for days and now that things aren't going your way anymore, that's it? Finsies? Uncle? Tilt? Game over? I don't think so. I *don't* think so."

"No. You've got to read me my rights and take me in."

"Oh, I get it," Jack said. "You think I'm a cop."

Hollander looked up at him in dazed confusion. He pursed his lips, beginning a question that died before it was asked.

"I'm not." Jack grinned. "Mooo-neeer sent me."

He waited a few heartbeats as Hollander glanced over to where Munir's naked wife and mutilated child were trussed up, watched the sick horror grow in his eyes. When it filled them, when Jack was sure he was tasting a crumb of what he'd been putting Munir through for days, he rammed the heel of his hand against the creep's nose, slamming the back of his head against the door. He wanted to do it again, and again, keep on doing it until the gutless wonder's skull was bone confetti, but he fought the urge, pulled back as Hollander's eyes rolled up in his head and he collapsed the rest of the way to the floor.

He went first to the woman. She looked up at him with terrified eyes.

"Don't worry," he said. "Munir's on his way. It's all over."

She closed her eyes and began to sob through her gag.

As Jack fumbled with the knots on her wrists, he checked out the fresh blood on her left breast. The nipple was still there. An inch-long cut ran along its outer margin. A bloody straight razor lay on the mattress beside her.

If he'd tapped on that window a few minutes later...

THE WRINGER

As soon as her hands were free she sat up and tore the gag from her mouth. She looked at him with tear-flooded eyes but seemed unable to speak. Sobbing, she went to work on her ankle bonds. Jack stepped over to where the fallen sheet lay crumpled on the floor and draped it over her.

"That man, that... beast," she said. "He told us Munir didn't care about us, that he wouldn't cooperate, wouldn't do anything he was told."

Jack glanced over at Hollander's unconscious form. Was there no limit?

"He lied to you. Munir's been going crazy doing everything the guy told him."

"Did he really cut off his...?"

"No. But he would have if I hadn't stopped him."

"Who are you?"

"Nobody."

He went to the boy. The kid's eyes were bleary. He looked flushed and his skin was hot. Fever. A wad of bloody gauze encased his left hand. Jack pulled the gag from his mouth.

"Where's my dad?" he said hoarsely. Not *Who are you?* or *What's going on?* Just worried about his dad. Jack wished for a son like that someday.

"On his way."

He began untying the boy's wrists. Soon he had help from Barbara. A moment later, mother and son were crying in each other's arms. He found their clothing and handed it to them.

While they were dressing, Jack dragged Hollander over to Barbara's mattress and stuffed her gag in his mouth. As he finished tying him down with her ropes, he heard someone pounding on the downstairs door. He ushered the woman and the boy out to the landing, then went down and found Munir frantic on the sidewalk.

"Where–?"

"Upstairs," Jack said.

"Are they–?"

Jack nodded.

He stepped aside to allow Munir past, then waited outside awhile to give them all a chance to be alone together. Five minutes, then he limped back upstairs. It wasn't over yet. The kid was sick, needed medical attention. But there wasn't an ER in the city that wouldn't be phoning in a child abuse complaint as soon as they saw Robby's left hand. And that would start officialdom down a road that might lead them to Jack.

But Jack knew a doc who wouldn't call anyone. Couldn't. His license had been on permanent suspension for years.

17

Jack was sitting and waiting with Barbara and Munir. Doc Hargus had stitched up Barbara's breast first because it was a fresh wound and fairly easy to repair. Robby, he'd said, was going to be another story.

"I still cannot understand it," Munir said for what seemed like the hundredth time but was probably only the twentieth. "Richard Hollander... how could he do this to me? To anybody? I never hurt him."

"You fired him," Jack said. "He's probably been loony tunes for years, on the verge of a breakdown, walking the line. Losing his job just pushed him over the edge."

"But people lose their jobs every day. They don't kidnap and torture–"

"He was ready to blow. You just happened to be the unlucky one. It was his first job. He had to blame somebody – anybody but himself – and get even for it. He chose you. Don't look for logic. The guy's crazy."

"But the depth of his cruelty..."

"Maybe you could have been gentler with him when you fired him," Barbara said. The words sent a chill through Jack, bringing back Munir's plea from his first telephone call last night.

Please save my family!

Jack wondered if that was possible, if anyone could save Munir's family now. It had begun to unravel as soon as Barbara and Robby were kidnapped. It still had been salvageable then, up to the point when the cleaver had cut through Robby's

THE WRINGER

finger. That was probably the deathblow. Even if nothing worse had happened from there on in, that missing finger would be a permanent reminder of the nightmare, and somehow it would be Munir's fault. If he'd already gone to the police, it would be because of that; since he hadn't, it would be his fault for *not* going to the police. Munir would always blame himself; deep in her heart Barbara also would blame him. And later on, maybe years from now, Robby would blame him too.

Because there'd always be one too few fingers on Robby's left hand, always be that scar along the margin of Barbara's nipple, always the vagrant thought, sneaking through the night, that Munir hadn't done all he could, that if he'd only been a little more cooperative, Robby still would have ten fingers.

Sure, they were together now, and they'd been hugging and crying and kissing, but later on Barbara would start asking questions: Couldn't you have done more? Why *didn't* you cut your finger off when he told you to?

Even now, Barbara was suggesting that Munir could have been gentler when he'd fired Hollander. The natural progression from that was to: Maybe if you had, none of this would have happened.

The individual members might still be alive, but Munir's family was already dead. He just didn't know it yet.

And that saddened Jack. It mean that Hollander had won.

Doc Hargus shuffled out of the back room. He had an aggressively wrinkled face and a Wilford Brimley mustache.

"He's sleeping," Doc said. "Probably sleep through the night."

"But his hand," Barbara said. "You couldn't–?"

"No way that finger could be reattached, not even at the Mayo Clinic. Not after spending a night in a Federal Express envelope. I sewed up the stump good and tight. You may want to get a more cosmetic repair in a few years, but it'll do for now. He's loaded up with antibiotics and painkillers at the moment."

"Thank you, doctor," Munir said.

"And how about you?" Doc said to Barbara. "How're you feeling?"

She cupped a hand over her breast. "Fine... I think."

"Good. Your sutures can come out in five days. We'll leave Robby's in for about ten."

"How can we ever repay you?" Munir said.

"In cash," Doc said. "You'll get my bill."

As he shuffled back to where Robby was sleeping, Barbara pressed her head against her husband's shoulder.

"Oh, Munir. I can't believe it's over."

Jack watched them and knew he hadn't completely earned his fee.

Save my family...

Not yet. Hollander hadn't won yet.

"It's not over," Jack said.

They both turned to look at him.

"We've still got Richard Hollander tied up in that loft. What do we do with him?"

"I never want to see him again!" Barbara said.

"So we let him go?"

"No!" Munir spoke through his teeth. "I want him to hang! I want him to fry! He has to pay for what he did to Robby! To Barbara!"

"You really think he'll pay if we turn him in? I mean, how much faith do you have in the courts?"

They looked at him. Their bleak stares told him they felt like everybody else: No faith. No faith at all.

"So your only other option is to go back there and deal with him yourself."

Munir was nodding slowly, his mouth a tight line, his eyes angry slits. "Yes... I would like that." He rose to his feet. "I will go back there. He has... things to answer for. I must be sure this will never happen again."

Barbara was on her feet too, a feral glint in her eyes.

"I'm coming with you."

"But Robby—"

"I'll stay here," Jack said. "He knows me now. If he wakes up, I'll be here."

They hesitated.

Save my family...

THE WRINGER

If the Habibs were going to make it they were going to have to face Hollander together and resolve all those as-yet-unasked questions by settling their scores with him. All their scores.

"Get going," he said. "I never made it past Tenderfoot in the Boy Scouts. Who knows how long my knots will last?"

Jack watched them hurry out, hand-in-hand. Maybe this would fix their marriage, maybe it wouldn't. All he knew for sure was that he was glad he wasn't Richard Hollander tonight.

He got up and went looking for Doc Hargus. The doc was never without a stock of good beer in his fridge.

Introduction to "Interlude at Duane's"

In January 2005, David Morrell and I were instructors at the Borderlands Bootcamp for Writers. David had helped start the International Thriller Writers organization the previous year and induced me to join. ITW in turn induced me to donate a Repairman Jack story to their anthology (*Thriller*) to raise funds for the organization.

Thus was "Interlude at Duane's" born. The *Thriller* table of contents is a Who's Who of thriller writers. All contributors were limited to a 5K word count. I could have used more. Toward the end I was on fire, burning up the keyboard. I wish I could write with that speed and intensity all the time.

As you'll see, this one was *fun*.

Thriller went on to become one of the best if not *the* best selling anthology of all time. And I didn't get a dime royalty. But I did gain a ton of new readers. Many of the zillion or so people who bought the anthology had never heard of Jack. Since then I regularly run into devoted Jack fans who say their first contact with the character was in *Thriller*. (I'll bet a fair number of you are reading this collection because of that story.) Doing well while doing good...nothing wrong with that.

Ed Gorman chose it for his anthology *The Deadly Bride and Other Great Mystery and Crime Stories of 2005*.

Interlude at Duane's

"Lemme tell you, Jack," Loretta said, blotting perspiration from her fudgsicle skin, "these changes gots me in a baaaad mood."

They'd just finished playing some real-life Frogger jaywalking 57th and were now chugging west.

"Real bad. My feets killin me too. Nobody better hassle me afore I'm home and on the outside of a big ol glass of Jimmy."

Jack nodded, paying just enough attention to be polite. He was more interested in the passersby and was thinking how a day without your carry was like a day without clothes.

He felt naked. Had to leave his trusty Glock and backup home today because of his annual trip to the Empire State Building. He'd designated April 19th King Kong Day. Every year he made a pilgrimage to the observation deck to leave a little wreath in memory of the Big Guy. The major drawback to the outing was the metal detector everyone had to pass through before heading upstairs. That meant no heat.

He didn't think he was being paranoid. Okay, maybe a little, but he'd pissed off his share of people in this city and didn't care to run into them naked.

After the wreath-laying ceremony, he ran into Loretta and walked her back toward Hell's Kitchen. Oh, wait. It was Clinton now.

They went back a dozen or so years to when both waited tables at a now-extinct trattoria on West Fourth. She'd been fresh up from Mississippi then, and he only a few years out of Jersey. Agewise, Loretta had a good decade on Jack, maybe more – might even be knocking on the door to fifty. Had a good hundred pounds on him too. Her Rubenesque days were just a fond, slim memory, but she was solid – no jiggle. She'd dyed her Chia Pet hair orange and sheathed herself in some shapeless, green-and-yellow thing that made her look like a brown manatee in a muumuu.

She stopped and stared at a black cocktail dress in a boutique window.

"Ain't that pretty. Course I'll have to wait till I'm cremated afore I fits into it."

They continued to Seventh Avenue. As they stopped on the corner and waited for the walking green, two Asian women came up to her.

The taller one said, "You know where Saks Fifth Avenue?"

Loretta scowled. "On Fifth Avenue, fool." Then she took a breath and jerked a thumb over her shoulder. "That way."

Jack looked at her. "You weren't kidding about the bad mood."

"You ever know me to kid, Jack?" She glanced around. "Sweet Jesus, I need me some comfort food. Like some chocolate-peanut-butter-swirl ice cream." She pointed to the Duane Reade on the opposite corner. "There."

"That's a drugstore."

"Honey, you know better'n that. Duane's got everything. Shoot, if mine had a butcher section I wouldn't have to shop nowheres else. Come on."

Before he could opt out, she grabbed his arm and started hauling him across the street.

"I specially like their makeup. Some places just carry Cover Girl, y'know, which is fine if you a Wonder Bread blonde. Don't know if you noticed, but white ain't zackly a big color in these parts. Everybody darker. Cept you, a course. I know you don't like attention, Jack, but if you had a smidge of coffee in your cream you'd be *really* invisible."

Jack expended a lot of effort on being invisible. He'd inherited a good start with his average height, average build, average brown hair, and nondescript face. Today he'd accessorized with a Mets cap, flannel shirt, worn Levi's, and battered work boots.

INTERLUDE AT DUANE'S

Just another guy, maybe a construction worker, ambling along the streets of Zoo York.

Jack slowed as they approached the door.

"Think I'll take a raincheck, Lo."

She tightened her grip on his arm. "Hell you will. I need some company. I'll even buy you a Dew. Caffeine still your drug of choice?"

"Guess…till it's time for a beer." He eased his arm free. "Okay, I'll spring for five minutes, but after that, I'm gone. Things to do."

"Five minutes ain't nuthin, but okay."

"You go ahead. I'll be right with you."

He slowed in her wake so he could check out the entrance. He spotted a camera just inside the door, trained on the comers and goers.

He tugged down the brim of his hat and lowered his head. He was catching up to Loretta when he heard a loud, heavily accented voice.

"*Mira! Mira! Mira!* Look at the fine ass on you!"

Jack hoped that wasn't meant for him. He raised his head far enough to see a grinning, mustachioed Latino leaning against the wall next to the doorway. A maroon gym bag sat at his feet. He had glossy, slicked-back hair and prison tats on the backs of his hands.

Loretta stopped and stared at him. "You better not be talkin a me!"

His grin widened. "But señorita, in my country it is a privilege for a woman to be praised by someone like me."

"And just where is this country of yours?"

"Ecuador."

"Well, you in New York now, honey, and I'm a bitch from the Bronx. Talk to me like that again and I'm gonna Bruce Lee yo ass."

"But I know you would like to sit on my face."

"Why? Yo nose bigger'n yo dick?"

This cracked up a couple of teenage girls leaving the store. Mr. Ecuador's face darkened. He didn't seem to appreciate the joke.

Head down, Jack crowded close behind Loretta as she entered the store.

She said, "Told you I was in a bad mood."

"That you did, that you did. Five minutes, Loretta, okay?"

"I hear you."

He glanced over his shoulder and saw Mr. Ecuador pick up his gym bag and follow them inside.

Jack paused as Loretta veered off toward one of the cosmetic aisles. He watched to see if Ecuador was going to hassle her, but he kept on going, heading toward the rear.

Duane Reade drugstores are a staple of New York life. The city has hundreds of them. Only the hoity-toitiest Upper East Siders hadn't visited one. Their most consistent feature was their lack of consistency. No two were the same size or laid out alike. Okay, they all kept the cosmetics near the front, but after that it became anyone's guess where something might be hiding. Jack could see the method to that madness: The more time people had to spend looking for what they had come for, the greater their chances of picking up things they hadn't.

This one seemed fairly empty and Jack assigned himself the task of finding the ice cream to speed their departure. He set off through the aisles and quickly became disoriented. The overall space was L-shaped, but instead of running in parallel paths to the rear, the aisles zigged and zagged. Whoever laid out this place was either a devotee of chaos theory or a crop circle designer.

He was wandering among the six-foot-high shelves and passing the hemorrhoid treatments when he heard a harsh voice behind him.

"Keep movin, yo. Alla way to the back."

Jack looked and saw a big, steroidal black guy in a red tank top. The overhead fluorescents gleamed off his shaven scalp. He had a fat scar running through his left eyebrow, glassy eyes, and held a snub-nose .38 caliber revolver – the classic Saturday night special.

Jack kept his cool and held his ground. "What's up?"

The guy raised the gun, holding it sideways like in movies, the way no one who knew squat about pistols would be caught dead holding one.

INTERLUDE AT DUANE'S

"Ay yo, get yo ass in gear fore I bust one in yo face."

Jack waited a couple more seconds to see if the guy would move closer and put the pistol within reach. But he didn't.

Not good. On the way to the rear, the big question was whether this was personal or not. When he saw the gaggle of frightened-looking people – the white-coated ones obviously pharmacists – kneeling before the rear counter with their hands behind their necks, he figured it wasn't.

A relief... sort of.

He spotted Mr. Ecuador standing over them with a gleaming nickel-plated .357 revolver.

Robbery.

The black guy pushed him from behind.

"Assume the position, asshole."

Jack spotted two cameras trained on the pharmacy area. He knelt at the end of the line, intertwined his fingers behind his neck, and kept his eyes on the floor.

Okay, just keep your head down to stay off the cameras and off these bozos' radar, and you'll walk away with the rest of them.

He glanced up when he heard a commotion to his left. A scrawny little Sammy Davis-size Rasta man with his hair packed into a red, yellow, and green striped knit cap appeared. He was packing a sawed-off pump-action twelve and driving another half dozen people before him. A frightened-looking Loretta was among them.

And then a fourth – Christ, how many were there? This one had dirty, sloppy, light-brown dreads, piercings up the wazoo, and was humping the whole hip-hop catalog: peak-askew trucker cap, wide, baggy, ass-crack-riding jeans, huge New York Giants jersey.

He pointed another special as he propelled a dark-skinned, middle-age Indian or Pakistani by the neck.

Both the Rasta and the new guy had glazed eyes. Stoned. Maybe it would make them mellow.

What a crew. Probably met in Rikers. Or maybe the Tombs.

"Got Mister Maaaanagerrrr," the white guy singsonged.

Ecuador looked at him. "You lock the front door?"

Whitey jangled a crowded key chain and tossed it on the counter.

"Yep. All locked in safe and sound."

"*Bueno.* Get back up there and watch in case we missed somebody. Don't wan nobody gettin out."

"Yeah, in a minute. Somethin I gotta do first."

He shoved the manager forward, then slipped behind the counter and disappeared into the pharmacy area.

"Wilkins! I tol you get up front!"

Wilkins reappeared carrying three large plastic stock bottles. He plopped them down on the counter. Jack spotted "Percocet" and "Oxy-Contin" on the labels.

"These babies are mine. Don't nobody touch em."

Ecuador spoke through his teeth. "*Up front!*"

"Dude, I'm gone," Wilkins said and headed away.

Scarbrow grabbed the manager by the jacket and shook him "The combination, mofo – give it up."

Jack noticed the guy's name tag: *J. Patel.* His dark skin went a couple of shades lighter. The poor guy looked ready to faint.

"I do not know it!"

Rasta man raised his shotgun and pressed the muzzle against Patel's quaking throat.

"You tell de mon what he want to know. You tell him *now!*"

Jack saw a wet stain spreading from Patel's crotch.

"The manager's ou-out. I d-don't know the combination."

Ecuador stepped forward. "Then you not much use to us, eh?"

Patel sagged to his knees and held up his hands. "Please! I have a wife, children!"

"You wan see them again, you tell me. I know you got armored car pickup every Tuesday. I been watchin. Today is Tuesday, so give."

"But I do not–!"

Ecuador slammed his pistol barrel against the side of Patel's head, knocking him down.

"You wan die to save you boss's money? You wan see what happen when you get shot inna head? Here. I show you." He turned and looked at his prisoners. "Where that big bitch with the big mouth?" He smiled as he spotted Loretta. "There you are."

INTERLUDE AT DUANE'S

Shit.

Ecuador grabbed her by the front of her dress and pulled, making her knee-walk out from the rest. When she'd moved half a dozen feet he released her.

"Turn roun, bitch."

Without getting off her knees, she swiveled to face her fellow captives. Her lower lip quivered with terror. She made eye contact with Jack, silently pleading for him to do something, anything, *please!*

Couldn't let this happen.

His mind raced through scenarios, moves he might make to save her, but none of them worked.

As Ecuador raised the .357 and pointed it at the back of Loretta's head, Jack remembered the security cameras.

He raised his voice. "You really want to do that on TV?"

Ecuador swung the pistol toward Jack.

"What the fuck?"

Without looking around, Jack pointed toward the pharmacy security cameras.

"You're on Candid Camera."

"The fuck you care?"

Jack put on a sheepish grin. "Nothing. Just thought I'd share. Done some boosting in my day and caught a jolt in Riker's for not noticing one of them things. Now I notice – believe me, I *notice*."

Ecuador looked up at the cameras and said, "Fuck."

He turned to Rasta man and pointed. Rasta smiled, revealing a row of gold-framed teeth, and raised his shotgun.

Jack started moving with the first booming report, when all eyes were on the exploding camera. With the second boom he reached cover and streaked down an aisle.

Behind him he heard Ecuador shout, "Ay! The fuck he go? Wilkins! Somebody comin you way!"

The white guy's voice called back, "I'm ready, dog!"

Jack had hoped to surprise Wilkins and grab his pistol, but that wasn't going to happen now. Christ! On any other day he'd have a couple dozen 9mm hollowpoints loaded and ready.

He'd have to improvise.

QUICK FIXES

As he zigged and zagged along the aisles, he sent out a silent thank-you to the maniac who'd laid out these shelves. If they'd run straight, front to back, he wouldn't last a minute. He felt like a mouse hunting for cheese, but this weird, maze-like configuration gave him a chance.

He hurried along, looking for something, anything to use against them. Didn't even have his knife, damn it.

Batteries... notebooks... markers... pens... gum... greeting cards...

No help.

He saw a comb with a pointed handle and grabbed it. Without stopping, he ripped it from its package and stuck it in his back pocket.

He heard Ecuador yelling about how he was going this way and Jamal should go that way, and Demont should stay with the people.

Band-Aids... ice cream... curling iron – could he use that? Nah.

Hair color... humidifiers... Cheetos... beef jerky –

Come *on*!

He turned a corner and came to a summer cookout section. Chairs – no help. Umbrella – no help. Heavy-duty spatula – grabbed it and hefted it. Nice weight, stainless steel blade, serrated on one edge. Might be able to do a little damage with this. Spotted a grouping of butane matches. Grabbed one. Never hurt to have fire.

Fire... he looked up and saw the sprinkler system. Every store in New York had to have one. A fire would set off the sprinklers, sending an alert to the NYFD.

Do it.

He grabbed a can of lighter fluid and began spraying the shelves. When he'd emptied half of it and the fluid was puddling on the floor, he reached for the butane match –

A shot. A *whizzz!* past his head. A quick glance down the aisle to where Scarbrow – who had to be the Jamal Ecuador had called to – stood ten yards away, leveling his .38 for another go.

"Ay yo I found him! Over here!"

INTERLUDE AT DUANE'S

Jack ducked and ran around a corner as the second bullet sailed past, way wide. Typical of this sort of oxygen waster, he couldn't shoot. Junk guns like his were good for close-up damage and little else.

With footsteps behind him, Jack paused at the shelf's endcap and took a quick peek at the neighboring aisle. No one in sight. He dashed across to the next aisle and found himself facing a wall. Ten feet down to his right – a door.

EMPLOYEES ONLY

He pulled it open and stuck his head inside. Empty except for a table and some sandwich wrappers. And no goddamn exit.

Feet pounded his way from behind to the left. He slammed the door hard and ran right. He stopped at the first endcap and dared a peek.

Jamal rounded the bend and slid to a halt before the door, a big grin on his face.

"Gotcha now, asshole."

In a crouch, gun ready, he yanked open the door. After a few heartbeats he stepped into the room.

Here was Jack's chance. He squeezed his wrist through the leather thong in the barbecue spatula's handle, raised it into a two-handed kendo grip, serrated edge forward.

Then he moved, gliding in behind Jamal and swinging at his head. Maybe the guy heard something, maybe he saw a shadow, maybe he had a sixth sense. Whatever the reason, he ducked to the side and the chop landed wide. Jamal howled as the edge bit into his meaty shoulder. Jack raised the spatula for a backhand strike, but the big guy proved more agile than he looked. He rolled and raised his pistol.

Jack swung the spatula at it, made contact, but the blade bounced off without knocking the gun free.

Time to go.

He was in motion before Jamal could aim. The first shot splintered the doorframe a couple of inches to the left of his head as he dove for the opening. He hit the floor and rolled as the second went high.

Four shots. That left two – unless Jamal had brought extras. Jack couldn't imagine a guy like Jamal thinking that far ahead.

On his way toward the rear, switching aisles at every opportunity, he heard Ecuador shouting from the far side of the store.

"Jamal! You get him? You get him?"

"No. Fucker almost got me! I catch him I'm gonna skin him alive."

"Ain't got time for that! Truck be here soon! Gotta get inna the safe! Wilkins! Get back here and start lookin!"

"Who's gonna watch the front, dog?"

"Fuck the front! We're locked in, ain't we?"

"Yeah, but–"

"*Find him!*"

"A'ight. Guess I'll have to show you boys how it's done."

Jack now had a pretty good idea where Ecuador and Jamal were – too near the barbecue section to risk going back. So he moved ahead. Toward Wilkins. He sensed that if this chain had a weak link, Wilkins was it.

Along the way he scanned the shelves. He still had the spatula, the comb, and the butane match but needed something flammable.

Antibiotic ointments... laxatives... marshmallows...

Shit.

He zigged and zagged until he found the hair-care aisle. Possibilities here. Needed a spray can.

What the–?

Every goddamn bottle was pump action. He wanted fluorocarbons. Where were fluorocarbons when you needed them?

He ran down to the deodorant section. Everything here was either a roll-on or a smear-on. Whatever happened to Right Guard?

He spotted a green can on a bottom shelf, half hidden behind a Mitchum's floor display. Brut. He grabbed it and scanned the label.

DANGER: Contents under pressure... flammable...

Yes!

Then he heard Wilkins singsonging along the neighboring aisle, high as the space station.

INTERLUDE AT DUANE'S

"Hello, Mister Silly Man. Where aaaare youuu? Jimmy's got a present for you." He giggled. "No, wait. Jimmy's got six – count em – six presents for you. Come and get em."

High as the space station.

Jack decided to take him up on his offer.

He removed the Brut cap as he edged to the end of the aisle and flattened against the shelf section separating him from Wilkins. He raised the can and held the tip of the match next to it. The instant Wilkins's face came into view, Jack reached forward, pressing the nozzle and triggering the match. A ten-inch jet of flame engulfed Wilkins's eyes and nose.

He howled and dropped the gun, lurched away, kicking and screaming. His dreads had caught fire.

Jack followed him. He used the spatula to knock off the can's nozzle. Deodorant sprayed a couple of feet into the air. He shoved the can down the back of Wilkins's oversized jeans and struck the match. His seat exploded in flame. Jack grabbed the pistol and trotted into an aisle. Screams followed him toward the back.

One down, three to go.

He checked the pistol as he moved. An old .38 revolver with most of its bluing rubbed off. He opened the cylinder. Six hardball rounds. A piece of crap, but at least it was his piece of crap.

The odds had just become a little better.

A couple of pairs of feet started pounding toward the front. As he'd hoped, the screams were drawing a crowd.

He heard cries of "Oh, shit" and "Oh, fuck!" and "What he *do* to you, bro?"

Wilkins wailed in a glass-breaking pitch. "Pepe! Help me, man! I'm dyin'!"

Pepe... now Ecuador had a name.

"*Si*," Pepe said. "You are."

Wilkins screamed, "No!"

A booming gunshot – had to come from the .357.

"Fuck!" Jamal cried. "I don't believe you *did* that!"

A voice called from the back. "What goin on dere, mon? What hoppening?"

"'S'okay, Demont!" Pepe called back. "Jus stay where you are!" Then, in a lower voice to Jamal: "Wilkins jus slow us down. Now find that fuck fore he find a phone!"

Jack looked back and saw a plume of white smoke rising toward the ceiling. He waited for the alarm, the sprinklers.

Nothing.

What did he have to do – set a bonfire?

He slowed as he came upon the employee lounge again. Nah. That wasn't going to work twice. He kept going. He was passing the ice cream freezer when something boomed to his right and a glass door shattered to his left. Ice cream sandwiches and cones flew, gallons rolled.

Jack spotted Demont three aisles away, saw him pumping another shell into the chamber of his shotgun. He ducked back as the top of the nearest shelf exploded in a cloud of shredded tampons.

"Back here, mon! Back here!"

Jack hung at the opposite endcap until he heard Demont's feet crunch on broken glass in the aisle he'd just left. He eased down the neighboring lane, listening, stopping at the feminine hygiene area as he waited for Demont to come even.

As he raised his pistol and held it two inches from the flimsy metal of the shelving unit's rear wall, he noticed a "personal" douche bag box sitting at eye level. *Personal?* Was there a community model?

When he heard Demont arrive opposite him, he fired two shots. He wanted to fire four but the crappy pistol jammed. On the far side Demont grunted. His shotgun went off, punching a hole in the dropped ceiling.

Jack tossed the pistol. Demont would be down but not out. Needed something else. Douche bags had hoses didn't they? He opened the box. Yep – red and ribbed. He pulled it out.

Footsteps pounded his way from the far side of the store as he peeked around and spotted Demont clutching his right shoulder. He'd dropped the shotgun but was making for it again.

Jack ran up and kicked it away, then looped the douche hose twice around his scrawny neck and dragged him back to the ruined ice cream door. He strung the hose over the top of

INTERLUDE AT DUANE'S

the metal frame and pulled Demont off his feet. As the little man kicked and gagged, Jack slammed the door, trapping the hose. He tied two quick knots to make sure it didn't slip, then dove through the empty frame for the shotgun. He pumped out the spent shell, chambered a new one, and pulled the trigger just as Jamal and Pepe rounded the corner.

Pepe caught a few pellets, but Jamal, leading the charge, took the brunt of the blast. His shirtfront dissolved as the double-ought did a pulled-pork thing on his overdeveloped pecs. Pepe was gone by the time Jack chambered another shell. Looked back: Demont's face had gone pruney, his kicks feeble. Ahead: Jamal lay spread eagled, staring at the ceiling with unblinking eyes.

Now what? Go after Pepe or start that fire?

Fire. Start a big one. Get those red trucks rolling.

But which way to the barbecue section? He remembered it being somewhere near the middle.

Three aisles later he found it – and Pepe too, who was looking back over his shoulder as he passed it. Jack raised the shotgun and fired, but Pepe went down just before the double ought arrived. Not on purpose. He'd slipped in the spilled lighter fluid. The shot went over his head and hit the barbecue supplies. Bags of briquettes and tins of lighter fluid exploded. Punctured cans of Raid whirly-gigged in all directions, fogging the air with bug killer.

Pepe slipped and slid as he tried to regain his feet – would have been funny if he hadn't been holding a .357. Jack pumped again, aimed, and pulled the trigger.

Clink.

The hammer fell on an empty chamber.

Pepe was on his knees. He smiled as he raised his pistol. Jack ducked back and dove for the floor as one bullet after another slammed through the shelving of the cough and cold products, smashing bottles, drenching him with Robitussin and Nyquil and who knew what else.

Counted six shots. Didn't know if Pepe had a speed loader and didn't want to find out. Yanked the butane match from his back pocket and lit her up. Jammed a Sucrets pack into the trigger guard, locking the flame on, then tossed it over the shelf. He

QUICK FIXES

heard no *whoomp!* like gasoline going up, but he did hear Pepe cry out in alarm. The cry turned to screams of pain and terror as the spewing Raid cans caught.

Jack crept back and peeked around the corner.

Pepe was aflame. He had his arms over his eyes, covering them against the flying, flaming pinwheels of Raid as he rolled in the burning puddle, making matters worse. Black smoke roiled toward the ceiling.

And then it happened. Clanging bells and a deluge of cold water. Yes.

Jack saw the .357 on the floor. He sprinted by, kicking it ahead of him as he raced through the downpour to the pharmacy section. After dancing through an obstacle course of popsicles and gallons of ice cream, he found Loretta and the others cowering behind the counter. He picked up the key ring and tossed it to Patel.

"Out! Get everybody out!"

As the stampede began, he heard Loretta yelling.

"Hey, y'all! This man just saved our lives. You wanna pay him back, you say you never seen him. He don't exist. You say these gangstas got inna fight and killed each other. Y'hear me? Y'hear?"

She blew Jack a kiss and joined the exodus. Jack was about to follow when a bullet smashed a bottle of mouthwash near his head. He ducked back as a second shot narrowly missed. He dove behind the pharmacy counter and peeked over the top.

A scorched, steaming, sodden Pepe shuffled Jack's way through the rain with a small semi-auto clutched in his outstretched hand. Jack hadn't counted on him having a backup. Hell, he hadn't counted on him doing anything but burn. The sprinkler system had saved him.

Pepe said nothing as he approached. Didn't have to. He had murder in his eyes. And he had Jack cornered.

He fired again. The bullet hit the counter six inches to Jack's right, showering him with splinters as he ducked.

Nowhere to hide. Had to find a way to run out Pepe's magazine. How? A lot of those baby semis held ten shots.

Another peek. Pepe's slow progress had brought him within six feet. Jack was about to duck again when he saw a flash of bright green and yellow.

INTERLUDE AT DUANE'S

Loretta.

Moving faster than Jack ever would have thought possible, she charged with a gallon container of ice cream held high over her head in a two-handed grip. Pepe might have heard her without the hiss and splatter of the sprinklers. But he remained oblivious until she streaked up behind him and smashed the container against the back of his head.

Jack saw his eyes bulge with shock and pain as he pitched toward the floor. Probably felt like he'd been hit with a cinder block. As he landed face first, Loretta stayed on him – really on him. She jumped, landing knees first on the middle of his back... like Gamera on Barugon. The air rushed out of him with an agonized groan as his ribs shattered like glass.

But Loretta wasn't finished. Shouting, she started slamming the rock-hard container against his head and neck, matching the rhythm of her words to the blows.

"NOW you ain't NEVER pointin NO gun to MY head EVER aGAIN!"

Jack moved up beside her and touched her arm.

"Hey, Lo? Lo! *Loretta barada nikto.*"

She looked up at him. "Huh?"

"I think he's got the message."

She looked back down at Pepe. His face was flattened against the floor, his head canted at an unnatural angle. He wasn't breathing.

She nodded. "I do believe you right."

Jack pulled her to her feet and pushed her toward the front. "Go!"

But Loretta wasn't finished. She turned and kicked Pepe in the ribs.

"Told you I was a bitch!"

"Loretta – come on!"

As they hustled toward the front she said, "We even, Jack?"

"Even Steven."

"Did I happen to mention my bad mood?"

"Yes, you did, Loretta. But sometimes a bad mood can be a good thing."

Introduction to "Do-Gooder"

This was originally printed as a broadside in an edition of 200 copies in 2006. Since it's a one-sheet, I was limited to around 700 words. It's more a vignette than a full story, but it's here for the completists.

Do-Gooder

Pure luck, that's what it was. A minute earlier or ten seconds later and he woulda missed him. As it was, Perry reached the corner just as the guy opened his door and stepped inside. Yeah, it was dark, but no mistaking him.

He'd called himself Jack when he'd set Perry up, but who knew if that was his real name. Perry had had a sweet scam going on the old lady circuit, relieving old bitches of their excess cash. This Jack had come along and said he had some flush marks but wanted a cut for the info. Fair enough. But turned out the first one he delivered had an NYPD sergeant for a son. Perry'd been busted and busted up, but good. And Jack? Jack was gone like he'd never been.

Perry beat it back to his apartment for the sawed-off twelve he kept around for protection. When he returned to the block he peeked in the townhouse window and spotted the guy with a good-looking blonde and a kid. Thought about busting in but that was stupid. Be patient.

The block dead-ended at a little park hanging over the FDR. He hid in the shadows there, took the sawed-off from under his coat, and listened to the traffic below as he waited.

Sutton Square. Ritzy block. What was this guy, some rich do-gooder getting his jollies by screwing up things for working men like Perry? Well, his do-gooder days was over. When he came out Perry would get close, cut him in half with both barrels, and keep walking like nothing happened. And then –

"Hello, Perry."

Perry jumped and started to spin at the sound of the soft voice so close behind but stopped when the muzzle of a pistol pressed against his cheek. He recognized the voice and his bladder clenched.

"Jesus, Jack. Hey, what're you doing here?"

"That's my question." He took the shotgun from Perry's hands.

"I'm hidin. Got on the wrong side of a shy and he's got some boys lookin for me."

"You're watching that townhouse, Perry."

"No, I–"

"I saw you peek in the window."

Shit!

"No, I swear I was just–"

"Shhhhhh. You've got a sawed off. Isn't that against parole?"

He'd just finished his jolt in the joint. Last thing he wanted was go back inside. But that would be the do-gooder thing to do: drop a dime on him.

"You ain't gonna turn me in, are you?"

"No, Perry. Nothing like that."

"Really?" Thank God. "Hey, Jack, that's really–"

He started to turn again but the muzzle jabbed his cheek. Hard.

"The shotgun's for me, isn't it."

That soft voice, so calm, so cold . . . giving him the creeps.

"No way. Look, you can take it."

"Already have it. But seems we have a problem, Perry. You've got a hard-on for me and now you know where people I care about live. That can't be."

Can't be? He didn't like the sound of that. But wait . . .

He forced a laugh. "You tryin t'scare me, Jack?"

"Nope."

"Yeah, y'are. But it won't work. Y'know why? Because you see yourself as a do-gooder. Better'n me. Helpin old ladies. *The Equalizer.* Batman without no cape."

"Wrong, Perry. The daughter of one of your marks hired me to get you."

DO-GOODER

"Hired? Bullshit." He steeled his guts and grinned as he rose to face him. "You're a do-gooder and you ain't gonna do nothin."

Perry saw a blur of motion and then pain exploded on the left side of his head as Jack's pistol smashed against his skull. His knees went Jell-O. A second blow left him face first in the dirt, the world tilting.

Then he felt himself lifted, carried toward the barrier overhanging the highway.

On, no! Oh-no-oh-no-oh-no!

"But . . ." His lips wouldn't move right. "But you're a do-gooder."

"Wrong, Perry. I'm more into doing the right thing. And when I see myself and my two ladies threatened, the right thing to do is eliminate the threat."

Perry felt himself hoisted atop the railing. When a break in the traffic came, Jack pushed him over.

All the way down his mind screamed that this couldn't be happening. This self-styled, bullshit do-gooder had –

Introduction to "Recalled"

In the summer of 2006, Christopher Conlon emailed me, wondering if I'd be interested in writing a story for a Richard Matheson tribute anthology. Of course I would, but only if I could do a sequel to one of my all-time favorite stories, "The Distributor."

About "The Distributor"…it's rare that a story won't go away. Most stories are forgotten as soon as you turn the page; some linger for a while, then join their brethren in the void. But every so often you encounter one with a special, mysterious quality that encodes it into your synapses, making it a part of you. We all have our own set of special stories. "The Distributor" is one of mine.

But first, a little background. I was thirteen when I decided to write horror fiction. That was in 1959 – a banner year for me. I discovered Lovecraft in Donald A. Wolheim's *The Macabre Reader*, and then went out and bought everything good ol' H.P. had in print. When I exhausted him, I started in on the rest of the old masters: Bloch, Howard, Derleth, Long, Hodgson, Leiber, and whoever else I could find. The reading exacerbated a lifelong writing itch, one I'd started scratching in second grade. Now I began to believe I could write this stuff. Not at age thirteen, but later on. I could do it. I *would* do it. But for now, I'd keep reading.

Here's the point to all this me-focused stuff: All along I wanted to write horror fiction; all along I was convinced I could do it. No question about it: "Someday I'll do this."

Then I picked up a paperback called *Shock* by Richard Matheson. I'd read Matheson's work before, had been deeply touched by "Born of Man and Woman," and suitably impressed by many of his other stories. Here was a guy who delivered. And *Shock* was okay. Lots of interesting stories – sf, social commentary, suspense – but not much horror.

Then I came to the last story. "The Distributor" stopped me dead. All along I'd been telling myself, "I can do this."

Now I was muttering and mumbling, "No way I can do *that*."

I don't know how it is with other writers, but most of the time when I finish a story or novel, I may be pleased, I may even be impressed, but somewhere in the back of my mind I'm thinking, *I could have done that*.

Every so often, though, you come across a piece of fiction that blows you away, not just because you've been hanging onto every word, but because when you're done you have to admit, *I couldn't have done that*.

That's what makes certain stories special to me; those are the ones I admire most: the ones I lack the talent or insight or command of the language to write myself.

"The Distributor" was first published in *Playboy* in 1957 and look what's happened to the country since. "Mr. Gordon" (or whatever his real name is) and his fellow distributors have been busy, busy, busy.

Maybe it's a little dated. What used to be scandalous is now daily fodder for today's talk shows (more evidence of Mr. Gordon's handiwork?), but change maybe fifty words, substituting incest and pedophilia – not too many people anxious to wave those flags yet – for a couple of passé taboos, and the story is right up to date.

Why did I say *I can't do that* after reading "The Distributor"? Not because I couldn't sit down and imitate it – I couldn't have *originated* it.

Notice the utterly flat affect. "The Distributor" is an epiphany in that sense. All horror fiction I'd read until then pulsed with vibrant emotion – rage, hate, fear, lust for revenge. "The Distributor" has none of that. And that's what makes it so horrifying.

The story is a parade of simple declarative sentences (hell, he uses fewer adverbs than Elmore Leonard) with only an occasional off-the-wall adjective to let us know "Mr. Gordon" is well educated.

INTRODUCTION TO "RECALLED"

We spend the entire story in Mr. Gordon's point of view but experience no emotion; we witness only the surfaces of events. This is one of the most effective uses of minimalist technique you will ever see.

Mr. Gordon doesn't hate the residents of Sylmar Street. Nothing personal here. They're just people and this is just another town along his distribution route. It's just a job, folks.

Just a job.

But who does he work for?

That's Matheson's final coup. If he'd revealed that Mr. Gordon worked for the CIA or the KGB, or even some invented secret organization or cult, "The Distributor" would have migrated to short story limbo long ago. But he didn't. Who is behind this? Where is their home office? What is their agenda? *Why are they doing this?*

I wanted to know in 1961.

I still want to know.

So as a tribute to Matheson and his story, I wrote "Recalled." I took the same story as "The Distributor," but flipped it on its head and made it my own.

Its simple presence here gives away the twist, but I think you'll enjoy it anyway.

Recalled

Time to move.
Monday, April 26
Another town, another rental in another peaceful, unsuspecting neighborhood.

That was the easy part. As for the rest . . . it used to be so much simpler.

Listen to me, he thought. I sound like an old fart.

Well, he *was* an old fart. He'd been at this for decades, but instead of becoming routine, it had grown increasingly difficult. And he knew the problem wasn't with him.

The world had changed.

Used to be reputations could be ruined with a mere hint of impropriety – adultery, drunkenness, wantonness, porn peeping. Now it was anything goes. Only incest and pedophilia seemed to lack champions in the mass media, and it was anyone's guess as to how long before their paladins appeared and hoisted their flags.

People daily bragged on TV about what in the good old days would have had them afraid to show their faces in public. And nowadays the love that once dared not speak its name would not shut up.

But other, newer taboos had arisen from what used to be a matter of course.

And the ability to improvise was the greatest asset of an effective distributor.

———

QUICK FIXES

The last town had been a quiet little place in central Jersey known as Veni Woods. He'd called himself Clay Evanson there, a name he'd used before, way back when. Just last week, before arriving here in Wolverton, a quaint little town on Long Island's south shore, he decided to use another alias from the past: Theodore Gordon.

Every night before his arrival he'd closed his eyes and made the name his own. He was Theodore Gordon. All other names faded. He was Theodore Gordon and no one else.

After a little research, he found a furnished rental in the racially mixed Pine View Estates development on the eastern end of town. It had come down to a choice between that and another area half a mile west, but when he saw a woman wearing a striped hijab get out of a Dodge SUV on Fannen Street in Pine View and let herself into one of the houses, his decision was made.

He'd spent last Thursday night introducing himself around. As usual, he was a widower – not quite two years since his poor, dear Denise passed – and a financial consultant who worked from home, renting with intent to buy. Seven other houses made up this block of Fannen Street. He met the McCuins and their sullen fifteen-year-old son, Colin; the very Catholic Fabrinis and Robinsons; the waspish Woolbrights; the irreligious Hispanic Garcias with their noisy dog; the Muslim Rashids; and the very black Longwells. He made a point of inquiring at each stop about the best Internet access in the area. This induced Mr. Robinson and Mr. Woolbright to brag about the wi-fi networks they'd installed in their homes. Theodore had been hoping for one; two was a blessing.

Over the weekend he'd used his digital Nikon with the telephoto lens to snap photos of as many of his neighbors as possible as they worked in the garden or mowed the lawn, washed the car, or collected the mail. Between shoots he'd wandered Fannen Street, saying hello, helping unload a van, or transplant a bush. In the process he'd managed to see most of the backyards.

Since the Catholics held the majority, he'd attended mass at St. Bartholomew's yesterday morning, making sure he introduced himself to Father Bain in sight of the Fabrinis and Robinsons.

RECALLED

Tonight he'd be ready to go. He'd made starting on Monday a tradition.

The Pine View houses all sat on well-wooded half-acre lots. Four of the homes on this block – the Longwell, Woolbright, Rashid, and Fabrini places across the street – backed up to the woods that lent the development its name. His place sat directly across from the Rashids; the Robinsons were stage left on the corner, the Garcias next door to the right, and the McCuins next door to them on the far corner.

He spent the daylight hours observing the comings and goings and refining his notes. Mr. Robinson and Mr. Rashid carpooled. This was Mr. Rashid's week to drive. Theodore watched Mr. Robinson open the rear door to Mr. Rashid's car, place his briefcase on the seat, then take the passenger seat in front. Mrs. Rashid, a secretary at the grammar school, drove Robinson's girl, Chelsea, to school along with her own daughter, Farah, both ten.

Theodore noted the times of the comings and goings of everyone on the block. Today's were all consistent with last week's.

He admired consistency.

During the course of the day he used his laptop to access Mr. Robinson's wi-fi network next door, but could not enter the system due to a firewall. He would work on breaching that during the week. Firewalls were handy in that they gave people a false sense of security. He'd try the Woolbrights tonight.

Shortly before midnight he wound his way among the pines behind the houses across the street until he came to the rear extreme of the Woolbright's property. There he turned on his laptop and slowly made his way closer to the darkened house, stopping every dozen feet or so to see if he could access the wi-fi signal from their home network.

He could, and when it was good and strong, he tapped in and discovered that Mr. Woolbright had accommodatingly left his computer on and his webmail program open. Theodore had found this increasingly common over the years. Folks liked to hop out of bed and check their email before running off to work, and didn't want to fuss with all that log-in nonsense.

QUICK FIXES

Theodore found that Mrs. Woolbright's password was also stored and so he switched over to her account and logged in to the *Village Voice*'s online classified site. There he used her email address to apply for membership. He waited for the verification email, then followed the instructions. As soon as he was officially registered, he placed an ad as Mr. Woolbright in the *men-seeking-men* category. He described himself as "rich and horny and into young stuff. Send a picture or no go."

That done, he turned off his computer and crept to the tool shed by the fence between the Woolbright and Robinson properties. Easing open the door, he slipped a couple of gay porn magazines inside, then reclosed it.

When he returned home he removed a tray of ice cubes from his freezer and carried it to the extra bedroom on the second floor. He raised the window and the screen about twelve inches, then pulled his Firestorm High Performance slingshot from the night table drawer. He popped an ice cube out of the tray, loaded it into the sling, then winged it toward the wooden doghouse where Daisy, the Garcias' short-furred bitch mutt, spent her nights. Theodore had become expert with the slingshot over the years, and rarely missed, even at this distance.

The cube shattered against the doghouse, startling Daisy to full-throated wakefulness. She rushed out with a howl that progressed to frenzied barking. Finally, after inspecting the six-foot picket fence that defined the perimeter of her domain, she quieted down. With some satisfied gruffs, growls, and grumbles, she returned to her abode.

Theodore gave her time to settle down, then let fly another cube.

As Daisy repeated her howls and barks, he heard Mr. McCuin shout from a window on the Garcias' far side, "For Christ sake, Garcia, shut up that goddamn mutt or bring her inside!"

Theodore closed the screen and the window.

He made an entry in his ledger and went to bed.

A good start.

RECALLED

Tuesday, April 27

He waited until 9:30 A.M., watching the various carpool and solitary departures, before knocking on the Woolbrights' door. He'd learned last Thursday that Mrs. Woolbright was a stay-at-home wife.

She looked pale and uncertain when she answered. Perhaps she had received some disturbing emails. He gave her his brightest smile.

"Good morning, Mrs. Woolbright. My lawnmower seems to be on the fritz and I was wondering if I might borrow your husband's."

"My husband's?" She blinked and paused, as if she were translating the words. "Oh, yes. I suppose so. It's around back in the shed."

"Could you show me?" To underscore his probity, he added, "I'll walk around the side and meet you there."

They converged at the shed in the backyard.

"It's in here." She pulled open the doors.

"Thank you."

He waited for her to notice the magazines, then realized they weren't there. He poked his head in and looked around, but they were gone.

He took hold of the lawn mover handle and pulled it out, wondering if they had slipped beneath. But no . . . no magazines.

"Did your husband come out to the shed this morning?"

"What? No. He was running late. Skipped breakfast and ran. In a big hurry to get to . . . the city."

"Yes. I'm sure. I'll be sure to have it back by tonight."

She only nodded, looking distracted.

Theodore wheeled the mower across the street. Where were those magazines? He'd ponder that while he mowed the grass – something he hadn't counted on. He always hired a lawn service whenever he moved into a new town, but he'd put it off because of the Woolbrights. Today he'd planned to be so upset by the sight of those magazines that he'd forget about the mower. But now that he had it, he was obliged to use it.

QUICK FIXES

He turned off the mower. Finally. He'd forgotten what a noisy, monotonous chore it was. Plus he was no spring chicken. He was puffing a little and had wet rings in his armpits. He'd clean off the mower – always be a good neighbor – and wait for Mr. Woolbright's return before wheeling it back across the street. Might catch an earful of domestic strife along the way – though not as much as there could have been had she found those magazines. Someone had taken them. But who?

He saw the mail truck pull up to his box. Even though he'd never receive anything but flyers and contest come-ons at this address, he'd introduced himself to the mailman, whose name was Phil. He waved and Phil waved back.

After the mail truck moved on, Theodore slipped into the backyard and stood behind the big rhododendron next to the post-and-rail fence that divided his property from the Robinsons'. The bush shielded him from the street. Once he was sure no one was in line of sight, he climbed over the fence. In the old days he would have hopped it, but he wasn't as spry or as flexible as he used to be.

He hurried to their back door. When helping Mr. Robinson transplant a spirea on Saturday, he'd noted that the back door lock was a Schlage. He inserted a Schlage bump key, gave it a twist as he tapped it with a little rubber hammer, and he was in. He'd seen no evidence of an alarm system on his introductory visit, so no worry about disarming that.

He hurried upstairs and had no problem locating Chelsea Robinson's room – pink wallpaper, posters of the latest boy group. He went to her dresser and found her underwear drawer. He removed a pair of panties – pink, of course – and stuffed them into his pocket.

Then he was on his way down the stairs, out the way he'd come in – making sure to lock the door behind him – and back over the fence.

Five minutes from leaving his yard to returning. And no one the wiser.

Now that he had the panties, he could pick which photos of Chelsea to print out.

RECALLED

He watched the Rashid house until all was dark except for the glow of a TV from the master bedroom. He'd printed out half a dozen photos of Chelsea – close ups of her face, and crops centered on her flat chest and her little rump. With these trapped under his shirt, and the panties in his pocket, he stole across the street and into the Rashids' backyard. On Sunday he'd helped carry bags of wood-chip mulch from the van to the rear, and had made note that the backdoor to their garage was secured by another Schlage. No surprise. Development builders invariably used the same hardware on their houses.

A tap and a twist of the bump key and he was in. He opened the rear passenger door of Mr. Rashid's Volvo sedan and placed the photos and the panties on the floor where the pink could not fail to catch Mr. Robinson's eye. Then he would see the photos beneath.

Theodore pulled out a penlight and snooped around until he came upon an expensive-looking socket wrench set. He tucked that under his arm and slipped back outside, locking the door behind him.

Before heading for the Longwell house, he detoured to the Fabrinis' front yard where he pulled up every geranium Mr. Fabrini had planted over the weekend and scattered them across the front lawn.

He strolled the starlit street to the other end of the block where he slipped into the back of the Longwells' corner lot and hid the wrench set under the deck.

Back home, he slung ice cubes at Daisy's doghouse until Mr. McCuin screamed again from his window.

After making his daily entry in the ledger, he went to bed.

Wednesday, April 28

Theodore had set his alarm to be sure he'd be awake to see Mr. Rashid pick up Mr. Robinson. He'd given himself enough time to make coffee first.

So now, steaming cup in hand, he sat by his front picture window to wait and watch.

QUICK FIXES

Right on time, Mr. Rashid pulled out of his garage and backed into the street. Equally punctual, Mr. Robinson strode from his front door to the Rashid sedan. He opened the rear door...

...now the good part...

...and placed his briefcase in the rear...

...here we go...

...then slammed the door and slipped into the passenger seat. Mr. Rashid gunned the car and off they went.

Theodore found himself on his feet, staring through the window. How could Robinson have missed the panties and the pictures? Impossible. Unless...

Unless they weren't there.

He focused on the yard next to the Rashids where he'd pulled all the geraniums last night... where the lawn should have been littered with dead or dying plants.

But wasn't. At least it didn't appear so from here.

He threw on some clothes and hurried outside, slowing as he reached the sidewalk. Had to be calm. Had to appear to be going for a morning stroll, a constitutional, as they used to say back in the day.

But his inner pace was anything but leisurely as he passed the Fabrini yard and saw that each and every geranium he'd torn out last night had been replanted. He might have convinced himself that he'd dreamed what he'd done but for the orange petals and scattered clumps of potting dirt here and there on the lawn.

He heard a garage door rolling and saw Mr. Fabrini smiling and waving as he backed out of his driveway.

"Good morning!" he called. "Beautiful day, isn't it."

Theodore nodded. "Yes. Beautiful."

Another wave, another smile – "Have a good one!" – and Mr. Fabrini was on his way, acting nothing at all like a man who'd been forced to spend his first waking hours repairing mindless vandalism. Theodore had been all set to tell him that he'd glanced out his window last night and thought he'd seen the McCuin boy in the front yard, but no point now.

Someone was on to him.

Hard to see how that was possible. He knew no one in town, especially on this block, and no one knew him.

Or was he wrong about that?

He supposed it was possible. In fact, statistically it might even be inevitable that after all these years he would run into someone from a previous distribution point.

But he was always so careful, so circumspect. How could someone connect him with the unfortunate incidents that occurred during his brief stays?

He couldn't avoid the possibility that someone had. Judging from the missing porn magazines, the replanted geraniums, and what he had to assume were the missing panties and photos, the possibility looked more like a certainty.

Someone was undoing his work. And that meant someone was following him around, watching his every move.

But who?

He was sure he would have noticed.

It had to be someone with good tracking skills – and other skills as well. Theodore had locked the Rashids' garage door behind him. To remove the panties and photos, the one shadowing him would have to be adept at lock picking.

Who, damn it?

He took a deep breath and told himself to be calm. He prided himself on never becoming upset, never emotionally involved. This was a job, and he a professional.

And a professional could always out think an amateur.

He spent the rest of the day planning and making a few purchases. Mid afternoon he placed one call using his untraceable AT&T Go Phone.

"Mrs. Woolbright?" he said when she answered, dropping his voice an octave. "Sorry to bother you. This is Harold Mapleton with the Suffolk County parole board."

"Parole board? I have nothing to do with the parole board."

"Of course you don't, Mrs. Woolbright. But your neighbor, Cletus Longwell, does. I'm his parole officer."

"What? He's on parole? For what?"

"Grand theft. But he won't be on parole much longer. His three years will be up next month and I'm just calling to see what kind of neighbor he's been. Any reported thefts around the neighborhood? Anything missing from your premises?"

"No . . . not that I know of."

"Well, good. But ask around will you? Just in case. Sorry to bother you. Have a nice day."

Shortly before midnight he took his laptop into his yard and tried again to access the Robinsons' wi-fi network but couldn't find the signal.

Frustrated, he took up his position in the extra bedroom and set the Garcia dog to barking until Mr. McCuin screamed from his window.

After that he made a ledger entry but did not go to bed.

Thursday, April 29

Around 1:30 Theodore slipped outside and into the overcast night. He paused in the deeper shadows of the arbor vitae flanking his front door and scanned the neighborhood.

Was someone out there now, watching, waiting to undo his work?

Thursday was garbage pickup day in Pine View Estates. Everyone on the block except Theodore had their cans waiting at curbside. Fannen Street lay empty before him. Still, he had a feeling of being watched. Real? Or paranoia?

He had to assume someone was watching, but could not let that disrupt his schedule. He'd made adjustments to prevent that.

He crossed the street to the Fabrini house and emptied a can of Speed Weed, a fast-acting herbicide, on the geraniums. Nobody was going to save them now. Then he walked to the other end of the block, took the lid off the McCuin garbage can, and left the Speed Weed container on top in plain sight.

Before leaving, he dropped the lid on the grass, pulled a baggy from his pocket, and emptied a dog turd onto it.

Next he stopped back at his place and picked up a ten-quart plastic container and a wrench. Mrs. Robinson always left her car parked in the driveway. Theodore wriggled beneath it and felt around for the drain plug on the crankcase. When he found it he loosened it and let the oil empty into the container. When it

RECALLED

was completely drained, he took the container and the plug and carried them across the street, making sure to spill a little oil every six-to-eight feet or so along the way to the Fabrinis' driveway. He left everything in their backyard.

He wondered how far Mrs. Robinson would get before her engine seized up and self-destructed.

Though tired when he returned to his house, sleep was not in tonight's equation. He set himself up in his front window – where he had a pair of Rigel 3250 compact night vision goggles and a carafe of hot coffee waiting – and settled in to watch. He had no view of the McCuin house; he could see the Fabrinis' front yard but not their back where he'd left the oil and drain plug.

But he could see the Robinson car, right next door, not a hundred feet away. If anyone tried to undo Theodore's work there, he'd spot them and identify them with the help of his binocs. Then he'd start some countermeasures of his own.

―――

Theodore yawned in the dark and checked his watch. Four A.M. Did his quarry suspect that the car was under surveillance? If so –

He felt a cool breeze around his ankles. Where was that coming from?

His chest tightened. He kept all the windows closed. Had someone opened one?

He rose and walked to the stairs. No flow from the second floor. He moved through the dark dining room to the even darker kitchen –

And froze when he saw the back door standing open. He'd locked that, he was sure of it.

His heart pounded as he pushed it closed and scanned the backyard. It hadn't opened itself. What had the intruder wanted? Had he taken anything? What if he was still out there?

Theodore's heart rate doubled as a terrifying possibility struck: What if he was still in the house?

He flipped on the kitchen lights. Nothing out of place, nothing obvious missing.

He turned on all the lights on the first floor. No sign of anyone. But what about the second floor? Had he sneaked past while he'd been on sentry duty?

Was he after the ledger? It catalogued all his work. If it fell into the wrong hands –

He dashed upstairs, flipping every light switch within reach as he moved. He fairly leaped into his bedroom, turned on the lights, then dropped to his knees and jammed his hand between the mattress and box spring.

There. The ledger. He pulled it out. Safe.

But why–?

Diversion!

He ran back to the living room and peered at the Robinson car. It stood alone, just as he'd left it.

Relieved but still unsettled, he turned out all the lights and resumed his watch until dawn.

As the neighborhood came alive, Theodore wheeled his garbage can to the curb. There he made a show of stretching and yawning as he glanced down the block toward the McCuin place. He was pleased to see the lid still off their container. He couldn't see the herbicide can but didn't expect to at this distance.

Across the street he saw Mr. Fabrini scratching his head as he looked at one of his gardens. Theodore wandered over.

"Beautiful morning, isn't it," he said in a most neighborly way.

Mr. Farbini turned but didn't smile. "What? Oh, hi, Mister Gordon."

"Theodore, please."

"Right. Yeah, beautiful for us maybe." He pointed to the bed of wilted, shriveling geraniums. "But not for these things. Yesterday they were perfect. Today . . ."

Theodore knelt and touched a browning leaf. He rubbed it between his fingers, then sniffed.

"Hmm."

"What?"

Theodore tore off the leaf and handed it to Fabrini.

"Smell."

RECALLED

Mr. Fabrini did and made a face. "It smells . . . chemical."

"Right. Like Round Up or some other weed killer."

Mr. Fabrini looked dumbfounded. "Weed killer? But who . . . ?" He voice trailed off.

Theodore leaned closer. "I saw someone in your yard last night. At the time I thought it was you. Now I'm not so sure."

"It wasn't me, I can tell you that. Did you see his face?"

"No, but he looked young . . . like a teenager." He let his gaze drift toward the McCuin house.

Mr. Fabrini followed and said, "You don't think it was Colin, do you?"

Theodore backed away a step, as if the conversation had just entered taboo territory. "I'm not pointing any fingers. Like I said, I didn't see a face." He clapped Mr. Fabrini on the upper arm. "Don't take it personally. Some kids have a lot of anger to work out of their systems." With that he turned and waved. "Have a nice day."

Mr. Fabrini's drive to work would take him past the McCuin house. He'd be looking at it. He'd see the Speed Weed can – if it was still there. If someone had interfered and removed it, no matter. A seed had been planted.

As he crossed the street he glanced at the blacktop, searching for the trail of oil he'd left. Where–?

He stopped and stared at a discolored spot on the pavement. It might have been an oil splotch at one time, but now it was . . . something else. It looked like someone had sprayed it with a detergent solution, emulsifying the oil . . . erasing the trail.

When? When had this happened?

He jumped at the sound of a toot. When he looked around he saw Mr. Rashid smiling and waving from his car. Theodore realized he was standing in the middle of the street.

He managed a smile and stepped toward the curb. As he did he glanced at the Robinson car and almost tripped when he saw the puddle of oil spreading out from beneath it. Where had that come from?

Unless . . . while Theodore had been searching the house for an intruder, perhaps his nemesis had tried to replace the drained oil. But that wouldn't have worked because of the missing drain plug. Whatever he added would have ended on the driveway.

Standing next to the vehicle was a very angry looking Mr. Robinson.

"What the hell?" he was saying. "What the fucking hell?"

"My goodness," Theodore said, walking over to him. "It looks like you've sprung a leak."

He was looking at the oil. It didn't look fresh at all. In fact it looked well used, ready for a change.

"Leak, hell. The plug's missing. Somebody *did* this."

Theodore put on a shocked expression. "Someone from around *here*?"

"Who knows? But why me?" He looked past Theodore and waved to Mr. Rashid. "Be right there, Munaf."

Theodore made a point of looking up and down the block. "Maybe it was simply opportunity. After all, you are the only one who leaves a car out overnight. Has anyone ever complained about that?"

Robinson made a face. "No. And as for–" He broke off and stepped around to the front of the car, pointing at the driveway. "I'll be damned. Look at this – footprints."

Theodore did look, and hid his shock as he saw clear imprints of treaded footprints – sneakers, most likely – leading from the oil slick, across the driveway, and into the grass between Theodore's house and the Robinsons'.

"They head toward your place."

He started across the grass. Theodore, hiding his alarm, followed to his front walk where Robinson stopped, pointing. "They go right to your front door."

He was right. They were fainter here, but no mistaking them.

He wheeled on Theodore. "What the hell's going on, Gordon?"

Theodore didn't have to feign shock. "You can't think *I* had anything to do with this!"

Robinson pointed to the prints. "What else am I supposed to think?"

"I barely know you. Why would I do this? And I don't own any shoes with soles like that. And have a little respect for my intelligence. Would I be dumb enough to leave a trail right to my front door?"

"Maybe you're a dumbass, what do I know? But I do know there's been some strange shit going on lately."

"Like . . . like what?"

"Like someone hacking into Herb Woolbright's computer system and signing him up for a gay website or classified or some such shit. Herb's about as gay as I am. That convinced me to shut mine down. Yesterday Munaf found his socket wrench set gone, and now my car." He fixed Theodore with a narrow-eyed glare. "Nothing like this ever happened around here before you moved in."

Nothing like this had happened to Theodore so early. Later in a job, when a neighborhood was falling apart, suspicion naturally drifted to the newcomer, but by then he was packing up to leave. This was only day four.

But he held his ground.

"I won't stand here and be spoken to like this. And I warn you, if you slander me with these lies, you'll be hearing from my lawyer."

He turned and stomped to his front door. But once inside, he slumped against the door, mind racing, thoughts whirling.

He went to the window and watched Mr. Fabrini pull out of his driveway and coast down the block. He slowed as he passed the McCuin house – within a few feet of their open garbage can – but he didn't stop to inspect it, merely drove on.

Theodore ground his teeth. His nemesis had most likely removed the herbicide can. Blocked at every turn. Nothing like this had ever happened before.

An unfamiliar sensation began to burn in his gut: uncertainty. What to do? Abort?

―――

Theodore spent the rest of the day debating it, finally deciding on no – he'd never aborted a job and wasn't about to blemish his record now.

He went to his front window and looked out. The commuters were all home by now, eating dinner or having a drink with their spouses. Well, not everyone. Look at this . . .

Across the street, at the far end of the block, he saw Mr. Rashid and Mr. Longwell in what looked like animated conversation – perhaps even an argument.

He decided a stroll might be in order.

As he neared, he saw Mr. Longwell's usually placid black face contorted in anger.

"So, you're missing something from your garage, and what's the first thing you do? You think of the neighborhood nigger? Is that it?"

Mr. Rashid looked offended. "I have never used the N-word in my life!"

The N-word . . . really, the world had become pathetic.

"You came to me looking for stolen property. Why me? Why not your buddy, Robinson?"

"Because he isn't on parole for robbery!"

Mr. Rashid looked instantly regretful for saying that, while Mr. Longwell gaped in shock.

"What? What did you say? Me? On parole? Where'd you hear that bullshit?"

"Your parole officer called Jean Woolbright yesterday and–"

"My *parole* officer?" He stared at the Woolbright house. "I know she never liked us living next door, but I never thought she'd stoop to this. Is she insane?" He glanced at Theodore. "What are you looking at?"

Theodore had hoped his bold stare would trigger just that remark.

"Sorry. I couldn't help overhearing."

"This doesn't concern you."

"Well, I am a member of this community now. Perhaps, as a disinterested third party, I might help mediate this disagreement." Before either could object he turned to Mr. Rashid. "You are apparently missing something, and you think Mister Longwell might have it." He turned to Mr. Longwell. "Since I'm sure you don't, why not let Mister Rashid check your grounds and, say, your garage and–?"

"Nobody's snooping through my property without a search warrant, so you both can go to hell!"

RECALLED

So saying, he turned and stomped back into his house.

"My, my," Theodore said. "You'd think if he had nothing to hide he'd want to clear this up."

Mr. Rashid nodded. "Yes. You'd think he would."

He shook his head and walked away toward his home.

Thinking that this job could yet be salvaged, Theodore continued his walk. Even if his nemesis had removed the wrench set from the Longwell yard, Mr. Longwell's refusal to let Mr. Rashid look would be perceived as a sign of guilt.

He began to whistle.

———

Around 11:30 he began his nightly task of inciting Daisy. Finally, just shy of midnight, he heard Mr. McCuin shout, "I'm gonna kill that dog if you don't shut it up!"

Just what Theodore had been waiting for.

He waited until Daisy calmed down, then whacked her dog house with another ice cube. As she renewed her frenzied barking, Theodore shut the window and went down to the kitchen refrigerator. He pulled out the nice piece of sirloin he'd been saving. He removed a box of mole poison from under the sink. The label said each tablet contained 1.0 mg. of strychnine. He estimated Daisy's weight at thirty pounds. A dozen tablets would be plenty.

Just to be sure, he cut fifteen angled slits into the meat and pressed a pellet into each.

Friday, April 30

At exactly 3 A.M. he tossed the meat over the fence so that it landed near Daisy's house. She came out with a howl but stopped when she caught the scent of the meat. She was on it in an instant, wolfing it down in a single gulp.

Good dog.

Next he pulled out another can of Speed Weed and used it to write on Mr. Longwell's lawn. He'd thought of using gasoline to burn the word into the grass, but decided this would be more discrete.

Under normal circumstances he would hide the box of poison in the McCuin garage and the empty herbicide can in the Rashids' bushes, but his nemesis would undoubtedly remove them.

He returned home and stood on his front steps where he surveyed dark and slumbering Fannen Street. He sent out a challenge:

Let's see you undo these.

———

He was up early the next morning, waiting. At 7:10 he heard Mr. Garcia's distraught wail.

"Daisy? Oh, my God, Daisy!"

Theodore immediately stepped out onto his rear deck and called over the fence.

"Mister Garcia? Is anything wrong?"

"It's Daisy! She's not breathing!"

"Oh, dear. Quick! Bring her around front and I'll get my car and take you to the vet."

Never pass up an opportunity to be a good neighbor.

———

Theodore comforted the sobbing Mr. Garcia on the way home. Daisy's corpse lay draped across his legs.

"Was the vet sure she was poisoned? Who would do such an awful thing?"

Mr. Garcia's tear-stained face contorted into a mask of rage. "I have a pretty goddamn good idea."

Theodore glanced at Daisy. He'd had nothing against the dog. He had nothing against anyone. Collateral damage.

"Oh, dear," he said as he turned onto Fannen Street and saw the police car. "What's happened here?"

He slowed and watched Mr. Longwell pointing to the browned letters spelling *NIGGER* on his lawn, then down the street toward the Rashid house.

A hate crime was such a terrible thing.

———

He'd intended to spend the rest of the day making notes in his ledger and quietly planning his next moves – a productive way to while away the time before Mr. McCuin and Mr. Rashid came home to the inevitable confrontations with, respectively, Mr. Garcia and Mr. Longwell.

A knock on the door interrupted him. He found Phil the postman glaring at him. He thrust something into Theodore's hands.

"What do you think you're doing, Gordon?"

Theodore looked down and started when he saw the two gay porn magazines he'd left in Mr. Woolbright's shed. They'd been wrapped in clear plastic and addressed to someone he'd never heard of. The return address was his.

"I don't care what you're into, but you oughta know you can't mail something like that so it's out there for everyone to see."

He turned and strode back to his truck before Theodore could answer. He stared at the magazines. They must have been in his mailbox. He closed the door and dropped them on the dining room table. He stood there thinking.

What was happening now? Had the contest moved to another level, with his nemesis switching from defense to offense?

He went to the window where he saw Phil, the postman, across the street talking to Mrs. Woolbright. Theodore saw him pointing his way.

Perhaps it was indeed time to abort. He'd make that decision tonight after seeing how things went with the McCuin-Garcia and Longwell-Rashid bouts.

Shortly after six, Theodore positioned a chair at his front window, hoping for some fireworks. He was about to seat himself when he heard a sound. He whirled and saw a man standing behind him, but had only a glimpse before a fist smashed into his gut. He doubled over and turned away. Two more blows followed, one to each kidney, driving him to his knees and then onto his side, writhing in agony.

"That was for the dog," said a voice.

When Theodore's pain-blurred vision cleared, he saw a man sitting in a chair, looking down at him. He was average height, average build, average features, with brown hair and eyes. Theodore thought he was the most nondescript man he had ever seen.

A silenced, small-caliber pistol rested on his thigh, pointed in Theodore's direction.

"I'm really pissed about the dog," he said in a flat tone. "That was the last straw. I'm seriously thinking of kneecapping you for that."

Kneecapping? A vision of that almost made him forget the agony in his kidneys.

"No, wait. Who are you? Do I know you? Why are you doing this?"

"You don't know me, and I'm here because someone's paying me to be."

"Paying? Who–?"

"Remember Nelson Pershall, former resident of Veni Woods, New Jersey?"

Mr. Pershall . . . was that what this was about?

"I've never heard of Veni Woods. I don't even like New Jersey."

"You did a good job of pretending to when you were living there and calling yourself Clay Evanson."

How did he know all this?

"Ridiculous!"

Slowly, painfully, he started to push himself off the floor but the intruder kicked him back down.

"I prefer you on your belly. Anyway, Nelson Pershall hung himself after being caught in a kiddie-porn sting. His computer was loaded with graphic photos."

"If you're looking for sympathy for a pedophile, you're in the wrong house."

"His daughter swears he wasn't. He lived alone and ran a website that published poetry by codgers like himself."

"What does a daughter know about a parent's hidden life?"

"That's what I thought at first. But she said he was something of a techie and had set up a wi-fi network in his house. Someone could have been using his computer without him knowing it. Sound familiar?"

Theodore said nothing. That was exactly what had happened. He'd even triggered the police sting through Mr. Pershall's computer. But he certainly wasn't admitting it to this thug.

RECALLED

"She said she suspected a man named Clay Evanson. Told me her father's neighborhood had been friendly and peaceful until shortly after this clown arrived. Before he moved on, two people were dead – her father and a woman killed by her husband for cheating – a house had burned to the ground, one man had been arrested for assaulting his next-door neighbor, and another arrested for a hate crime. Are we seeing a pattern here?"

Theodore felt ice sludging through his gut.

"I haven't the faintest idea what this has to do with me. I've never heard of this Clay Evanson. And this woman is obviously paranoid."

"Yeah, that's pretty much what I thought, but she wanted me to fix it and she had the fee. Since I had the time, I took the job. Funny thing was, the day I started, you moved out. So I followed you here. And all of a sudden you're Theodore Gordon. I decided to stick around." He shook his head. "Whoever you really are, you're one sick bastard."

"You're mistaken, I tell you. I–"

"Shut up." He cocked his head. "Listen. Sounds like your neighbors. Let's take a look."

He grabbed Theodore by the back of his neck and hauled him into the chair he'd set up by the window. He was stronger than he looked. Theodore felt the muzzle of the pistol press against the base of his neck.

"Ever wonder what it's like being a quadriplegic? Do anything stupid and you'll find out."

Through the picture window he saw Mr. Robinson between Mr. Rashid and Mr. Longwell. The side window was open so he could hear their angry words. Normally it would be music to his ears. Mr. Fabrini and Mr. Woolbright came out of their houses to try to calm things down. Mr. McCuin joined them.

Suddenly, seemingly from nowhere, Mr. Garcia was racing across the street. He took Mr. McCuin down with a flying tackle. It took three men to pull him off.

"Hold it, guys," Mr. Robinson shouted. "Hold it for just one goddamn minute!" When the men calmed, he said, "Look at us. We were never like this. What's going on here?"

QUICK FIXES

"I can tell you what's going on," Mr. Longwell said, pointing a finger at Mr. Rashid. "He calls me a thief and writes 'nigger' on my lawn!"

Mr. Robinson said, "Hold it! Hold it! Do you know what kind of abuse Munaf gets? He gets called a 'towel head' or a 'terrorist' or – you'll like this one, Cletus – a 'sand nigger.' You really think he's gonna write 'nigger' on your lawn? And by the way, I heard the story about Cletus's parole and asked a friend in the DA's office to do a little checking. The call was a lie."

"Who'd do something like that?"

"Look around," Mr. Robinson said. "Who's not here?"

Theodore held his breath as all heads swiveled his way.

"All this started after Gordon moved in. And I'm pretty damn sure he drained my crankcase."

"And that homo classified I got signed up for," Mr. Woolbright said. "Phil told Jean he had gay porn in his mailbox today."

"But why?" Mr. Garcia said.

"Why don't we go ask him?"

The muzzle pressed harder against his spine.

"That's what *I* want to know. Why? That ledger of yours – looks like you're writing reports. Who are they going to?"

He had the ledger! How–?

How didn't matter. Everything was falling apart. And he was asking the question Theodore never would answer. Never.

"I don't know what you're talking about."

The muzzle pressed deeper into his flesh, then was removed.

"If we had time, you'd tell. But things are moving faster than I'd planned. Robinson is sharp, and you're about to have some very angry people on your doorstep."

"I'll talk to them, reason with them."

"No amount of talk will calm them after they see what's in your garage."

"My garage?"

"Yeah. I raised the door halfway. Front and center is Rashid's wrench set. But there's also an empty can of Speed Weed, some strychnine-containing rat poison, and Robinson's drain plug along with pink panties and photos of his daughter."

Theodore felt as if his bones were dissolving.

"What do you think Robinson is going do when he sees all that?" the intruder continued. "Oh, and I called the vet. I said I was from poison control and he told me it looked like the Garcia dog died from strychnine. So I called Garcia – again as poison control – and told him to make sure he didn't have any strychnine-containing pest control around. How do you think he'll react when he sees that box of rat poison?"

Theodore closed his eyes and trembled.

"You're busted, pal. I'd love to have more time with you, but I don't want to be here when company comes calling. Have a nice day."

Rising on wobbly legs, Theodore turned and faced him. He found his voice. "You'd make a good distributor."

"Is that your game?"

Game? It wasn't a game. It was serious business.

"Who would I be working for?"

Theodore shook his head.

A gloved hand shot out and smashed against his jaw, rocking his head back and sending him to the floor.

"Just in case you thought I'd forgotten about the dog."

Theodore lay there, groaning. After a moment he heard the back door open and close. And then he heard the voices in his front yard.

"What if he's not home?"

"He's always home – haven't you noticed?"

"Maybe he – hey! That's my wrench set! What's it doing–?"

The voices moved toward the garage.

"Speed Weed! That kills grass doesn't?"

"And geraniums too."

"What's this? Pictures of Chelsea and – oh shit!"

"Rat poison! The motherfucker!"

An angry babble rose as someone began pounding on the door.

Theodore struggled to his feet and stumbled upstairs.

Exposed . . . bad enough, but losing the ledger was the final humiliation

QUICK FIXES

He was finished. Nothing to do now but bow out and avoid further embarrassment.

He jumped at the sound of smashing glass. Something had crashed through the front window.

His shaking fingers removed the cyanide capsule from its container. He put it between his teeth and bit hard.

Time to move.

Introduction to "Piney Power"

In mid-2008 I agreed to donate a short young-adult thriller to another ITW-sponsored anthology. Once again, I'd be limited to 5k words. At the time I was deep into the young-adult Repairman Jack novels I'd contracted to write and had introduced some piney kids into the trilogy. (If you're not familiar with what a piney is, it's explained in the story.) I thought maybe I'd take them out for a spin in their own story (with young Jack along, of course) and see what they could do.

Piney Power

1

Old Man Foster had the signs posted all over his land.
**NO FISHING
NO HUNTING
NO TRAPPING
NO TRESPASSING**

No kidding. And no big deal.

Jack never paid them much attention. He figured since he wasn't involved in the first three, he deserved a pass on the last. No, what caught Jack's eye was the bright red object tacked to the bark just below the sign.

"Hey, check it out," he said, hitting the brakes. His tires skidded in the sandy soil as his BMX came to a stop. "Who'd put a reflector way out here?"

Weezy stopped her bike beside his. "Doesn't make sense."

Her birth certificate said "Louise" but no one had called her that since she turned two. She was older than Jack – hit fifteen last week, while Jack still had a few months to go. As usual, she was all in black – sneaks, jeans, Bauhaus T-shirt. She'd wound her dark hair into two braids today, giving her a Wednesday Addams look.

"Never noticed it before."

"Because it wasn't there," she said.

Jack accepted that as fact. They used this firebreak trail a lot when they were cruising the Barrens, and if the reflector had been here before, she'd remember. Weezy never forgot anything. Ever.

He touched the clear sap coating on the head of the nail that fixed it to the tree. His fingertip came away wet. He showed her.

"This is fresh – really fresh."

Weezy touched the goop and nodded. "Like maybe this morning."

Jack checked the ground and saw tire tracks. It had rained last night and these weren't washed out in the slightest.

"Looks like a truck," he said, pointing.

Weezy nodded. "Two sets – coming and going. And one's deeper than the other." She looked at Jack. "Hauled something in or took something out."

"Maybe it was Old Man Foster himself."

"Could be."

Foster had supposedly owned this chunk of the Jersey Pine Barrens forever, but no one had ever seen him. No one had ever seen anyone posting the land, either, but the signs were everywhere.

"Want to follow?"

She glanced at her watch and shook her head. "Got to go to Medford with my mom."

"Again? What's this – an every Wednesday thing?"

She looked away. "No. Just works out that way." When she looked back, disappointment shone in her eyes. "You going without me?"

Jack sensed she wanted them to go together, but he didn't think he could hold off.

"Yeah. Probably nothing to see. If I find anything, we can come back together."

She nodded and offered half a smile. "Sure you won't get lost without me?"

He glanced at the sun sliding down the western sky. Every year, people – mostly hunters – entered the Barrens and were never seen again. Folks assumed they got lost and starved. No big surprise in a million-plus acres of mostly uninhabited pine forest. If a vanilla sky moved in, you could lose all sense of direction and wander in circles for days. But with the sun visible, Jack knew all he had to do was keep heading west and he'd hit civilization.

"I'll manage somehow. See you later."

He watched her turn her Schwinn, straddle the banana seat, and ride off with a wave. After the trees had swallowed her,

PINEY POWER

Jack turned off the fire trail and began following the tire tracks along the narrow passage – little more than two ruts separated by a grassy ridge and flanked by the forty-foot scrub pines that dominated the Barrens. They formed a thick wall, crowding the edges of the path, reaching over him with their crooked, scraggly branches.

The passage forked and the tracks bore to the right. A half dozen feet into the fork he spotted another reflector. At the next fork the tracks bore left, and sure enough, another reflector.

Odd. He'd figured the first had been a marker for the starting point of the trail. Grass and trees could thicken over a growing season and obscure what had once been an obvious opening. But whoever had come along here this morning was marking every turn, placing reflectors where headlights would pick them up as they approached. That meant he was planning to come back in the dark. Maybe tonight. Maybe many nights.

Why?

Jack found the answer a half mile farther on where the tire tracks ended in a clearing with a large, solitary oak in its center. Near its base someone had dumped a dozen or more 55-gallon oil drums – old ones, rusted, banged up, and leaky.

He jumped at the sound of a car engine roaring his way. A few seconds later a weird-looking contraption bounced into the clearing on the far side. It had the frame of a small Jeep, maybe a Wrangler, with no roof, sides, or hood. The engine was exposed, though the firewall was still in place, and instead of a steering wheel, someone had fixed a long-handled wrench to the column. The front and rear seats had been replaced by a pair of ratty-looking sofas occupied by three kids in their mid teens. Jack recognized the driver: Elvin Neolin from his civics class. He'd seen the other boy around school as well, but the white-haired girl was new.

Pineys.

They lived out here in the woods. Some had jobs in the towns around the Pines, and some lived off the land – hunting, fishing, gardening. All were poor and a few were a little scary looking in their mismatched, ill-fitting clothes and odd features. Hard to say why they seemed odd. Not like they had bug eyes and snaggle teeth; more like looking at a reflection in one of those old-time mirrors where the glass wasn't even.

Some folks called them inbreds, talking about brothers and sisters getting together and having kids. Jack didn't know if any of that was true. People liked to talk, and some people just naturally exaggerated as they went along. But no one could deny that some Pineys didn't look quite right.

The kid riding shotgun was Levi Coffin, a sophomore at SRB High. Coffin was an old Quaker name that Jack envied. Jack Coffin... how cool to have a name like that.

Levi jumped out and strode toward Jack. He was tall and lanky, and his clothes were too short in the arms and legs. His mismatched eyes – one blue and one brown – blazed.

"This your doin'?"

Jack tensed. Levi looked a little scary.

"No way. I just got here." He jerked a thumb over his shoulder, north. "Followed tire tracks from back there. They ended here."

Levi glanced over his shoulder at Elvin who was staring his way. Elvin was on the short side with piercing dark eyes, stiff black hair, and high cheekbones. Looked like he might have some Lenape Indian in him.

Their eyes locked, then Levi turned away, muttering, "All right, all right."

What's *that* all about? Jack wondered.

Levi inspected the tire tracks while Elvin hopped out and walked over to the drums. Jack sensed the white-haired girl staring at him from the buggy. He realized with a start that she had pink irises. White hair... milk-white skin... what was that called...?

Albino... she was an albino.

"I can't see him, Levi," she said in a high-pitched voice.

Was she blind?

"What?" Levi swiveled to stare at Jack.

Elvin was struggling with the top to one of the drums. He looked toward Levi who turned back, then gave his head a sideways jerk toward Jack.

Elvin nodded, saying, "Hey, Levi. Gimme a hand."

PINEY POWER

Levi walked over and touched the lid – barely touched it – and it popped loose.

Jack felt a funny sensation ripple down his spine as he remembered an incident in school with Levi. Something way strange here. He hesitated, then started toward the drums as the two boys lifted the lid. They dropped it when they saw what was inside.

"Damn!" Levi said. "Damn them to hell!"

Jack might have quipped about where else you could damn someone to, but the rage in Levi's voice warned him off. He stepped up and saw the thick, cloudy green liquid; his nose stung from the sharp chemical odor.

"What is it?"

"Some sort of toxic crap," Levi said. "They're using this spot as a dumping ground."

"Who?"

"Crooks from upstate. We've found stuff like this before."

Jack said, "Better than dumping it in some river, I guess."

Levi glared at him and pointed to a barrel on its side. The sand near its top was wet with gunk.

"That one's leaking. It sinks into the ground water. And guess who gets their water from wells out here. *We* do. But who cares about Pineys."

Jack understood some of the reaction. Kids at school tended to rag on the Pineys, make fun of their clothes, joke about the brother-sister connections. But Jack wasn't one of those and didn't like being lumped in with them.

"No fair."

Another look passed between Levi and Elvin, and then Levi shrugged. "Forget it. El says you're okay."

Fine, but Jack hadn't heard El say anything.

"We should tell the cops," Jack said. "My sister used to date a deputy and–"

Levi and Elvin and the girl were shaking their heads... same direction, same speed, moving as one. Jack was getting creeped.

"Uh-uh," Levi said. "Cops ain't gonna go patrolling the Pines looking for someone they don't know, who might or might not come back."

"Oh, they'll be back."

Levi's eyes narrowed. "How do you know?"

"Because they marked the path with reflectors."

"Yeah? Show us."

As Jack reached for his bike, Elvin pointed to the weird buggy. "With us."

"You're old enough to drive?"

The two boys laughed.

"Plenty old enough to drive," Levi said. Elvin never said much at school and didn't seem to have much more to say out here. "Just not old enough for a license."

"Aren't you af–?" Jack began, then cut himself off. Afraid of being caught? Out here? By what – the Jersey Devil in a sheriff's Stetson? Stupid question.

He spotted a "Piney Power" sticker on the rusted rear bumper. "What's that mean?"

Levi shrugged. "Some folks hereabouts think Pineys should get organized and vote and all that." He glanced at Elvin. "We just like the sound of it."

Elvin laughed. "Yeah. Sounds cool."

The girl said nothing, simply stared at him.

Jack gave the buggy another once-over. Without sides, a top, or even a roll bar, it had to be the most dangerous car he'd ever seen. He'd be risking his life in that thing.

"Well," Levi said, "you ridin' or not?"

Jack couldn't wait.

"Wouldn't miss it for the world."

As he seated himself on the rear sofa, the albino girl scooched away and squeezed against the far end. Her pink gaze never wavered from his face.

"I can't see him."

"Yeah?" Levi turned in the front sofa and looked at Jack. "El says he's okay."

"But I can't *see* him!"

Jack waved his hand between them and she flinched.

"You can see me."

"That's Saree," Levi said. "She's talking about a different kind of seeing."

PINEY POWER

Jack was going to ask what he meant but then Elvin started the engine with a roar.

Trying to ignore Saree's unwavering stare, he directed Elvin down the path, following his own bike tracks, till they came to the firebreak trail. Elvin turned around and drove back.

Levi was right. The Burlington County sheriff's department didn't have the manpower to stake out Old Man Foster's land or even this one path. Could be weeks before the dumpers made a return trip. Had to be a way to make them give themselves away. Or better yet...

An idea began to form.

"What's down that way?" Jack said, pointing left as they approached the first fork.

"More of the same," Levi said. "Why?"

"Wondering if there's a spong nearby... the deeper and wetter the better."

"I know a cripple," Saree said, still staring.

Elvin followed her directions through a few more forks that left Jack totally disoriented.

"You know where we are, right?"

Saree rolled her eyes.

Okay, dumb question to ask a Piney. But at least she seemed to be relaxing a little.

A few minutes later, she said, "Right up here."

Elvin rolled to a stop before a thirty-foot-wide cripple – a water-filled depression half-surrounded by white cedars. Without the cedars it would have been called a spong.

Jack couldn't help smiling when he saw it.

"Yeah, this'll do."

"Do what?"

When he told them their eyes lit. Saree even smiled.

"I still can't see you," she said. "But I think you're okay."

Weird. Too weird.

2

"What's wrong with inbreeding?" Jack said as he spooned some niblets into the well he'd made in his mashed potatoes.

His mother gasped. "Not at the dinner table."

"No, really. I want to know."

His father cleared his throat and adjusted his steel-rimmed glasses. "Thinking of marrying Kate?"

Kate laughed as Jack said, "No!"

His folks sat at opposite ends while Jack and his older sister Kate sat across from each other. Only his missing brother Tom kept it from being a full family meal. Jack didn't miss him. Tom was a pain.

"Then where's this coming from?"

Jack shrugged. "Kids at school talk about Pineys..."

He couldn't get those weird kids out of his mind. They seemed so different... like they had their own language... an unspoken one. And that lid on the barrel... Elvin couldn't budge it but Levi just touched it and it popped free. It reminded Jack of the time Levi and Jake Shuett faced off in the caf a couple of weeks ago over some remark Jake had made about Pineys. Suddenly a catsup pack Jake was holding squirted all over him and his lunch plate dumped in his lap. Jack had written it off to a spaz attack. He hadn't given it much thought, but now...

He wasn't expecting much information from his folks, but Kate was home on a laundry run from medical school – it was only in Stratford, barely thirty miles away – and maybe she'd know.

He glanced at her. "Why's it bad?"

Kate was slim with pale blue eyes and faint freckles. After starting med school she'd cut her long blond hair back to a short, almost boyish length. Jack still wasn't used to it.

She paused, then said, "It's bad because we all have defective 'recessive genes' hidden in our DNA that are passed on from parent to child. Now, as long as that defective recessive gene is matched up with a working gene, all is well. But if a mother and a father both have the same recessive gene, and each gives it to a child, that child could have problems."

"I saw an albino girl today–"

She nodded. "Perfect example: Two normal-skinned parents, each carrying an albino gene, have a one-in-four chance of having an albino child. Family members tend to share a lot of the same recessives, and so inbreeding – when close relatives have children – increases the risk of genetic diseases, because the closer you're related, the greater the odds of matching up the same recessives in your kids."

Now the important question: "But are all recessive genes bad? Could there be ones for, like, big muscles or a good memory?"

Kate smiled. "You're thinking. That's good. Yes, plants and animals are bred for drought resistance and giving more milk and the like."

"Well, in that case, inbreeding people could have some good effects, right?"

"Theoretically, yes. But for every Einstein or Muhammad Ali, you could get a number of kids with cystic fibrosis."

Or weird powers?

Or maybe I read too much science fiction, Jack thought.

3

Jack awoke to the sound of someone whispering his name… coming from the window. He hopped out of bed and crossed his darkened room. The high moon lit the grinning face on the far side of the screen.

"Levi?"

"Would you believe they came back again tonight?"

Jack felt his heart rate kick into high gear. "They took the bait?"

"Hook, line, and sinkhole. Figured since it was your idea, you oughta come see. We got the car. Wanna?"

"Be right there."

He pulled on jeans and a rugby shirt, stepped into his Vans, then unlatched the screen and slipped into the night. Levi led him around the corner to where Elvin and Saree were waiting in the buggy, Saree behind the wheel – no, wrench. Her white hair looked silver in the moonlight. They hopped in and Saree took off without a word. At least she couldn't stare at him.

The Pines were practically in Jack's backyard, but she entered along a path he didn't know. She made seemingly random turns through the trees but seemed to know where she was going. Finally she stopped in a small clearing.

"Gotta walk from here," Levi said, "else they'll hear us."

The four of them hopped out and this time Saree led the way, single file, down a deer path.

"They fell for it, Jack," Levi said from behind him. "Just like you said. I never would've thought of that in a million years. You got a twisted mind. I like that."

Jack enjoyed the praise, but thought the solution had been obvious. Whoever had dumped those barrels didn't know the Pines, otherwise he wouldn't have needed to post reflectors. So Jack's idea had been to move the reflectors off the path to the dumping ground and onto a path that led to the cripple instead.

He heard angry voices before he saw anyone. Saree slowed her pace and gradually a glow began to grow through the trunks. They crouched as they neared the treeline. Jack peeked through the underbrush and saw a flatbed truck angled nose down into the cripple. Its headlights were still on and its motor running. A blue tarp covered whatever was stacked in its bed. Its front end sat bumper deep in the water and its rear wheels had dug ruts in the soil from trying to reverse its way out.

One man was cursing and swearing as he stood in the two-foot-deep water and pushed against the front grille while another gunned the engine and spun the tires.

"Now that we've got them," Jack said, "what do we do with them? Call the sheriff?"

Levi shook his head. "No way. We bring in some grownups. They'll take care of them."

"Take care of them how?"

"Piney justice."

Piney justice... Jack had heard about that. He was going to say something, but right then the one in the water gave up pushing and slammed a hand on the hood.

"Ain't gonna happen, Tony!"

Tony – dark, heavyset with a thick mustache – jumped out and began kicking the water in a rage.

PINEY POWER

"Save it, man," said the other guy as he splashed past him, heading toward the rim of the cripple. "We're gonna have to offload this stuff to get outa here."

"How'd this happen, Sammy? We marked the trail!"

"Must've made a wrong turn. Or..." He stopped and looked around. "Or somebody moved the markers."

Tony stared at him. "Who?"

"Wise-ass locals, my guess. Probably out there right now having a good laugh."

Uh-oh, Jack thought. Time to leave.

"Yeah?" Tony reached into the truck cab and pulled out a revolver. "Well, laugh at this!"

He began firing wildly. One of the slugs zipped through the brush between Jack and Saree, narrowly missing them. Jack froze in terrified shock while Saree let out a shrill yelp of surprise.

"There!" Sammy shouted, pointing their way.

Levi yanked on Jack's arm. "Run!"

Jack didn't need to be told twice – or even once. The next half minute became a riot of crouched running, snapping brush and branches, darkness ahead, shouting behind, and then a high-pitched scream that brought everything to an abrupt, panting halt.

"Saree?" Levi said, looking back. "I thought she was – aw, man, they got Saree!" He turned to Jack. "Go with El for help!"

"You're staying?"

He nodded. "Can't leave her."

Jack wavered. Why had he come here? He wanted to be home. Then Saree screamed again.

"I'll stay with you."

"No way. You go–"

"Elvin doesn't need help. Saree does."

Elvin was already at the car, starting it up. He wasn't waiting. That settled it.

"I don't get it," Levi said as he turned and started back toward the cripple.

"What's there to get?"

"You don't owe her. She's not kin."

Jack couldn't see what that had to do with anything. He wished he'd stayed in bed, but he was here now.

"We came together, we leave together."

Levi didn't reply. They were almost back to the cripple.

"Come out, come out wherever you are," a voice was sing-songing. "We got your ugly girlfriend."

Jack peeked through the brush. The moonlight and backwash from the headlights revealed Tony standing on the rim of the cripple by the rear of the truck. He had his gun in one hand and a fistful of Saree's hair in the other. She looked terrified.

Sammy, standing a few feet to his right, shouted, "The rest of you get out here now. We ain't gonna hurt you. Just put you to work. You got us into this mess, so you're gonna get us out."

Jack saw three options. Help was on the way, so until it arrived they either could do nothing, find ways to distract them, or show themselves and do whatever they wanted.

"Get out here or this could get ugly," Tony said, twisting Saree's hair and making her wince. "You don't wanna see *how* ugly."

Jack winced too, and crossed doing nothing off the list. He decided on distraction. He could always show himself if that didn't work.

"Stay here," he whispered. "Gonna try something."

"Wait–" Levi grabbed for his arm but Jack pulled out of reach.

He moved counterclockwise along the treeline, feeling around the ground until he found a fist-sized hunk of shale.

Perfect.

He backed up, cocked his arm, and let fly toward the truck. The rock bounced off the tarp with a gonging sound, then splashed in the water.

"Son of a bitch!" Sammy yelled, flinching.

"You guys deaf?" Tony shouted. "Remember what I said about things getting ugly?"

Oh no. Jack's gut knotted as he saw Tony yank Saree backward. She lost her balance and fell into the water. Tony stayed with her and held her head under the surface as her arms and legs thrashed and splashed. It was only a couple of feet deep, but plenty enough to drown her.

"She stays under till you come out!" Tony yelled.

Jack couldn't take it. Only option three remained.

"Okay! Okay!"

His bladder ached to empty as he jumped out of the bushes with his hands raised.

To his left Levi also stepped out, hands high, saying, "Let her up!"

As Sammy started toward them, Tony pointed the gun their way and grinned. "When I'm damn good and ready. You kids – *aah!*" He dropped the gun and released Saree as he grabbed his right hand with his left. "She broke my finger!"

Saree sat up, choking and gasping and crying. Jack had seen one of her thrashing arms come near Tony's hand but no way it touched him. She lurched to her feet and staggered away toward dry ground.

Tony started after her. "You little – my gun!" He turned and bent, feeling around underwater.

As Sammy turned to look at his buddy, Jack took off toward Saree. He grabbed her outstretched hand and pulled her up the bank of the cripple.

Sammy started toward them. "Hey–!"

Suddenly he tripped and fell face first into the water. But instead of rebounding to his feet, he stayed down and began kicking and thrashing as Saree had. He couldn't seem to get up.

Tony finally noticed. "What the hell are you doing?"

He started toward Sammy but tripped himself. He went down and stayed down too. Were they stuck in the mud? No, their arms and legs were free. It almost looked like they were being held down. But –

Jack saw Levi on his knees, white-faced, eyes focused on the men in the cripple. As Jack headed for him, Saree grabbed his arm.

"Leave Levi be."

Jack pulled free. As he neared he could see the boy's lips pulled back in a snarl. His face and hair dripped sweat, his shirt was soaked, and air hissed between his clenched teeth like he was bench pressing twice his own weight.

"Levi...?"

He glanced at Jack and just then the two men in the cripple got their heads back above water. But not for long. Before they could draw a full breath they plunged their faces back beneath the surface.

And then everything seemed to happen at once. Elvin roared out of the trees in the buggy followed by a pickup full of rough-clothed men with shotguns, Levi let out a breath and slumped forward onto his hands, the two men in the cripple got their heads out of water and sucked air.

When they caught their breath and looked around they found themselves staring into the headlights of the buggy and the pickup, and down the muzzles of half a dozen shotguns. One of the Piney men, tall with a gray beard and features that looked like they'd been taken apart and put back together wrong, had lifted the tarp and was looking at the barrels hidden beneath.

"Not good," he said, shaking his head. "Not good ay-tall."

"You don't wanna mess with us," Tony said, still panting. "We're connected, if you know what I mean."

"I'm right sure of that," the old Piney said. "And we'll want to know who to." He swiveled and his gaze fell on Jack. "Who's this un?"

"Friend of ours," Levi said, rising to his feet. He'd caught his breath. "He set the trap."

"Well, we're right grateful for that, but he ain't one of us. Take him back wherever he came from."

"What about them?" Jack said, pointing to Tony and Sammy.

"You forget about them. We're all gonna have us a nice chat, then we'll send 'em home."

"But–"

Levi grabbed his arm and pulled him away. "No questions. Let's go."

Elvin and Saree were already in the buggy. As soon as Jack and Levi settled on the rear couch, Elvin put it in gear and they roared off.

PINEY POWER

"What happened back there?" Jack said.

He was feeling weak and shaky. That guy had almost drowned Saree, and he'd never been shot at before – never dreamed it would ever happen and never wanted it to happen again. Ever.

Levi shook his head. "Nothing. And don't go yakking about it."

"You kidding? Tell my folks I snuck out tonight to see some toxic dumpers we trapped and wound up getting shot at? Yeah, right. Soon as I get home I'm gonna run into their bedroom and blab all about it."

Levi laughed. "Okay."

Of course he'd tell Weezy. She'd eat it up.

But Jack hadn't been talking about the dumpers.

"I meant you. What did you do to those guys?"

The smiled vanished. "Nothing."

"But I saw–"

He stared straight ahead. "You saw a couple of guys slipping around on a mucky cripple bottom and getting stuck. That's all."

He was sure it had been more than that. But what exactly?

Saree turned to face him. "Yeah, that's all it was, Jack. But what about you? What's your talent? Is it being able to hide? Is that why I can't see you?"

What was she talking about?

"I don't have any talent."

"Maybe you just don't know about it yet. You're hiding something, but that's okay. You came back for me. I never expected that. I still can't see you, but I like you."

Jack had no idea how to respond to that, so he didn't.

They dropped him off about a block from his house. As they raced off he saw their bumper sticker flash in the moonlight.

Piney Power.

He had an idea why those kids liked the sound of it.

4

"I can't believe all that happened without me," Weezy said as they entered Jack's house though the kitchen.

He'd waited till after school to tell her about it.

"Believe me, you were better off at home." He shuddered at a vision of that Tony guy holding Weezy's head underwater instead of Saree's. "While it was happening, I wanted to be *anywhere* but there."

As they stepped into the front room where his folks were watching the 6:30 news, a TV reporter said, *"The two bodies found inside those barrels of toxic waste have been identified."*

Jack stiffened as he recognized the mug shots on the screen.

"Anthony Lapomarda and Santo 'Sammy' Carlopoli have long rap sheets. Their bodies were found outside a South Philly body shop this morning along with two dozen barrels of toxic waste. More waste was found inside the body shop, along with a number of stolen cars. The suspected chop shop–"

He nudged Weezy and whispered, "That's them!"

The old Piney's parting words came back: *We're all gonna have us a nice chat, then we'll send 'em home.*

He hadn't mentioned *how* they'd be sent home. He glanced at Weezy and found her staring back with wide, dark eyes.

"Piney justice," he said, feeling a chill.

His father looked up. "What?"

"Nothing."

Dad pointed to the TV. "That's why we live out here. To get away from scum like that. You don't have to worry about running into any of their sort in these parts."

"I guess not, Dad."

At least not anymore.

www.repairmanjack.com

THE SECRET HISTORY OF THE WORLD

The preponderance of my work deals with a history of the world that remains undiscovered, unexplored, and unknown to most of humanity. Some of this secret history has been revealed in the Adversary Cycle, some in the Repairman Jack novels, and bits and pieces in other, seemingly unconnected works. Taken together, even these millions of words barely scratch the surface of what has been going on behind the scenes, hidden from the workaday world. I've listed them below in chronological order. (NB: "Year Zero" is the end of civilization as we know it; "Year Zero Minus One" is the year preceding it, etc.)

The Past:
"Demonsong" (prehistory)
"Aryans and Absinthe" (1923-1924)**
Black Wind (1926-1945)
The Keep (1941)
Reborn (February-March 1968)
"Dat Tay Vao" (March 1968)***
Jack: Secret Histories (1983)
Jack: Secret Circles (1983)
Jack: Secret Vengeance (1983)
"Faces" (1989)**

Year Zero Minus Three:
Sibs (February)
The Tomb (summer)
"The Barrens" (ends in September)*

"A Day in the Life" (October)**
"The Long Way Home"
Legacies (December)

Year Zero Minus Two:
"Interlude at Duane's" (April)**
Conspiracies (April) (includes "Home Repairs")
All The Rage (May) (includes "The Last Rakosh")
Hosts (June)
The Haunted Air (August)
Gateways (September)
Crisscross (November)
Infernal (December)

Year Zero Minus One:
Harbingers (January)
Bloodline (April)
By the Sword (May)
Ground Zero (July)
The Touch (ends in August)
"Tenants"**
The Peabody-Ozymandias Traveling Circus & Oddity Emporium

Year Zero:
"Pelts"*
Reprisal (ends in February)
Fatal Error (February) (includes "The Wringer")
The Dark at the End (March)
Nightworld (May)

Reprisal will be back in print by the end of 2011. I'm writing a total of fifteen Repairman Jack novels (not counting the young adult titles), ending the Secret History with the publication of a heavily revised *Nightworld* due in 2012

* available in *The Barrens and Others*
** available in *Aftershock and Others*
*** available in the 2009 reissue of *The Touch*

THE SECRET HISTORY OF THE WORLD

also by F. Paul Wilson

Repairman Jack
The Tomb
Legacies
Conspiracies
All the Rage
Hosts
The Haunted Air
Gateways
Crisscross
Infernal
Harbingers
Bloodline
By the Sword
Ground Zero
Fatal Error
The Dark at the End
Quick Fixes – tales of Repairman Jack

Young Adult
Jack: Secret Histories
Jack: Secret Circles
Jack: Secret Vengeance

The Adversary Cycle
The Keep
The Tomb
The Touch
Reborn
Reprisal
Nightworld

QUICK FIXES

The LaNague Federation Series
Healer
Wheels Within Wheels
An Enemy of the State
Dydeetown World
The Tery

Other Novels
Black Wind
Sibs
The Select
Virgin
Implant
Deep As the Marrow
Mirage (with Matthew J. Costello)
Nightkill (with Steven Spruill)
Masque (with Matthew J. Costello)
The Christmas Thingy
Sims
The Fifth Harmonic
Midnight Mass

Short Fiction
Soft & Others
The Barrens & Others
Aftershocks & Others
The Peabody-Ozymandias Traveling Circus & Oddity Emporium

Editor
Freak Show
Diagnosis: Terminal

Made in the USA
Lexington, KY
13 August 2012